PRAISE FOR
WHITE TRASH *Beautiful*

"An incredibly moving story . . . I felt like I was right there with Cass. You feel all her emotions to the point where you're connecting with her so much, you feel like you are her. [Mummert's] best book to date!"

—*USA Today* bestselling author Molly McAdams

"Enthralling . . . I felt a strong pull to Cass from the first line in the book . . . an emotional roller coaster that I never wanted to get off of. I couldn't put this book down."

—Amanda Bennett, author of *Time to Let Go*

"I loved it! . . . This story is filled with heartache and hope. Heartache for circumstance and life in general, but hope for a future."

—Romantic Reading Escapes

"I am beyond speechless. . . . fantastic storytelling."

—Lives and Breathes Books

"I loved this book. . . . Mummert put a lot of depth and soul into her characters."

—Contagious Reads

"Dark, edgy, emotional . . . I didn't want it to end!"

—Belle's Book Blog

"This is one of those books that will stay with you. The characters are so real that they set up residence in your heart and they will live there for the rest of your life. . . . My heart ached for more."

—Selena-Lost-in-Thought

"Wow. LOVE doesn't even begin to describe my feelings for this book. I instantly fell in love with Cass."

—KTReads

"*White Trash Beautiful* is the first book I have read by Teresa Mummert, but it is definitely not my last! I loved every minute of it even though parts of it broke my heart. . . . Just writing this review makes me want to read the book again."

—Smardy Pants Book Blog

"I absolutely love the characters Mummert creates! With a title like *White Trash Beautiful*, how could I not be intrigued . . . a fabulous read!"

—Flirty and Dirty Book Blog

"Completely engrossing."

—Ana's Attic Book Blog

WHITE TRASH

Beautiful

Teresa Mummert

G

GALLERY BOOKS

New York   London   Toronto   Sydney   New Delhi

G

Gallery Books
A Division of Simon & Schuster, Inc.
1230 Avenue of the Americas
New York, NY 10020

This book is a work of fiction. Any references to historical events, real people, or real places are used fictitiously. Other names, characters, places, and events are products of the author's imagination, and any resemblance to actual events or places or persons, living or dead, is entirely coincidental.

Copyright © 2013 by Teresa Mummert

All rights reserved, including the right to reproduce this book or portions thereof in any form whatsoever. For information address Gallery Books Subsidiary Rights Department, 1230 Avenue of the Americas, New York, NY 10020.

First Gallery Books trade paperback edition July 2013

GALLERY BOOKS and colophon are registered trademarks of Simon & Schuster, Inc.

For information about special discounts for bulk purchases, please contact Simon & Schuster Special Sales at 1-866-506-1949 or business@simonandschuster.com.

The Simon & Schuster Speakers Bureau can bring authors to your live event. For more information or to book an event contact the Simon & Schuster Speakers Bureau at 1-866-248-3049 or visit our website at www.simonspeakers.com.

Designed by Davina Mock-Maniscalco

ISBN 978-1-4767-3202-2
ISBN 978-1-4767-3201-5 (ebook)

"EMPTY SHEETS"

By Teresa Mummert

Lying crumpled and broken on empty sheets, feel the pain
settle deep within me,
I stand to fight another day, bracing for the blows on shaky
legs,
I take this pen and find my voice, fill the sheets with words
of noise,
My heart races to set the beat, as I bare my soul on empty
sheets.

They don't know how their words have cut me,
Bleeding and dying but you can never hurt me,
Again . . .
I refuse to let this break me, my soul is bruised but you can't
shake me.
If I die alone in bed, wrapped in my thoughts trapped in my head,
I will forgive all you have done wrong, with pen to paper and tell
my song
Fill these sheets with my pain, and one day I will learn to love
again.

The truth is told through blurred vision, this is the world
that I must live in,
I've lost everything to you, but these words will get me
through,
If you take this life from me, I will fly with broken wings,
Let me fill these empty sheets, with those lies of love you
told to me.

They don't know how their words have cut me,
Bleeding and dying but you can never hurt me,
Again . . .
I refuse to let this break me, my soul is bruised but you can't
*   shake me.*
If I die alone in bed, wrapped in my thoughts, trapped in my head,
I will forgive all you have done wrong, with pen to paper and tell
*   my song*
Fill these sheets with my pain, and one day I will learn to love
*   again.*

Angels have found their wings from you, battered and
    bruised when they come through,
This world was cruel and unforgiving, not fit for angels to
    live in,
As I fill these sheets with my story, I think of how you used
    to adore me,
Said I would never be alone, lying on empty sheets in a
    place that's not my home.

They don't know how their words have cut me,
Bleeding and dying but you can never hurt me,
Again . . .
I refuse to let this break me, my soul is bruised but you can't
*   shake me.*
If I die alone in bed, wrapped in my thoughts trapped in my head,
I will forgive all you have done wrong, with pen to paper and tell
*   my song*
Fill these sheets with my pain, and one day I will learn to love
*   again.*

CHAPTER

One

I'M NOT NAÏVE. I know I don't get the happily-ever-after. My knight in shining armor took the highway detour around this godforsaken shit hole. I've made peace with that. That doesn't mean I'm going to lie down like a doormat and let every cocky prick in the trailer park have his way with me.

"I'll be right there," I snarled at Larry. He is the cook here at Aggie's Diner, and he is also Aggie's husband. His hair is long and greasy, hanging in thick, gray clumps around his weathered face. He is almost always a mean and nasty old man.

I turned back to my heavyset, middle-aged customer with a quick smile as he continued to leer at my chest. I slid the milk for his coffee across the table, making sure it tipped into his lap "accidentally."

"I'm a waitress, not a whore," I warned through gritted teeth. I tucked a strand of my dirty-blond hair (which some would call dark wheat) that had fallen loose from its ponytail behind my ear and gave a loud sigh. Cass Daniels was a lot of things, but not that.

It was always the same. Some guy pulls off the main highway and decides to try out a little local joint, maybe try his chances at getting lucky with a waitress. Some even took him up on it. But I wasn't that kind of girl. Besides, I had a man of my own. My blond hair and blue eyes were nothing but a curse sometimes.

I made a beeline to the back, my empty tray held tightly between my fingers as I talked myself out of hitting Larry upside his damn head.

"I hit the bell five minutes ago, Cass," he scolded. I ignored him as he went on and on as I put the hot plates onto my tray, burning my fingers. I rolled my eyes and walked back out to the floor as he continued, getting louder as I walked away.

"Don't act like you're the only one in the trailer park who can carry a plate of food. You ain't nothin' special!"

I slapped my tray down on table four with a little more force than I intended, biting back my tears. I didn't need some low-rent cook in a run-down diner telling me I wasn't worth a damn. I forced a smile at the elderly lady in front of me.

Her hand moved on top of mine as I placed her dish in front of her. It startled me, and I had to force myself not to pull back.

"Don't let anyone tell you that you're not special," she said in a hushed tone.

I smiled as a single tear escaped my eye and trailed down my cheek. I pulled my hand free and wiped it away quickly, looking at the dingy peach-colored walls to hide my crying. "Enjoy your meal." My voice cracked with my words.

I turned quickly and made my way across the dining room and out the back entrance marked EMPLOYEES ONLY. I pulled my pack of cigarettes from my apron and stared at the box while I walked to the corner of the building. I hadn't had one for four days, but I couldn't force myself to throw the pack away.

I stared off at the trailers that were on the other side of the parking lot. A tattered fence lined the area with an array of signs that read KEEP OUT. I snorted.

No one went in there unless the person had no choice. The fence just kept us away from the people who mattered.

I held the lighter to the end of my cigarette and closed my

eyes as I inhaled deeply, filling my lungs with the delicious smoke.

"That'll kill ya, you know," a deep voice called from in front of me. My eyes shot open. A man in worn-out dark-wash jeans and a formfitting, dark-gray T-shirt that read I'M WITH THE BAND stood in front of me, motorcycle helmet in hand. His head was cocked to the side, and a half grin played across his lips. His hair was dark brown and unruly, but something told me he took time to make it look so effortlessly disheveled. His arms had elaborate tattoos to the wrists, and his blue eyes were bright in the sun. This was the guy your mama would warn you about—if your mama wasn't too high to function. He stood at least a foot taller than my own five foot three. I guessed he was near my age of twenty-three, or maybe a couple of years older.

"Not fast enough." I rolled my eyes and took another drag. He laughed as he ran his fingers over his hair from back to front and nodded, then turned to walk to the front door of the diner. He stopped for a moment, his back to me as if he had something to say, but didn't. He opened the door and disappeared inside instead without a backward glance.

At least my shitty life was entertainment for someone else. I held my cigarette sideways, glaring down at it before flicking it off into the dirt of the parking lot. I stood and straightened my apron, wiping the now-drying tears from my face, and went back to work.

Mr. Dark and Dangerous was sitting in a booth in my section and I cursed under my breath. I was a magnet for bad boys; only in my world, it meant beatings and heartbreak.

"Welcome to Aggie's Diner. My name is Cass and I'll be your waitress. Can I start you off with something to drink?" I slapped a menu down in front of him. I did my best to smile, but it didn't reach my eyes. It never did. I raked my eyes over the tattoos that crawled out from under his T-shirt sleeves in intricate, swirling patterns.

"Tucker White." He grinned. That smile must get him whatever he wanted.

My eyes snapped back to his. "Do you want something to drink, Tucker White?" I tried not to sound impatient. I didn't want to exchange witty banter with some hot guy fresh off the highway. I wanted to go home and take a hot shower, if we even had hot water. This job barely paid the bills, and with my mom's mouth to feed, we could hardly afford luxuries such as water, let alone solid meals or cable.

"I'll have a beer, sweetheart. Whatever you recommend." His smile didn't waver.

I glanced around the diner and back to him. I was sure he could read the *Are you fucking kidding me?* look on my face. This wasn't the place for exotic delicacies or fancy beers. "I'm not your sweetheart."

"Challenge accepted." He laughed.

These guys were all the same. I sighed. "I'll grab you a Bud." I turned on my heel and made my way into the back to grab him a beer out of the fridge.

"Cass, what are you doing with my beer?" Larry called from behind the cook line.

"It's for a customer," I called over my shoulder. "I'll pay you back when he settles the check." I pushed through the kitchen doors and got away from Larry before he could start screaming again.

I set the bottle down in front of Tucker and wiped the condensation on my hand onto my apron.

"Thanks." He winked and twisted the top off the bottle. He tipped it up to his lips and began to drink, his eyes still locked on me.

I grabbed my pen and order pad from my apron pocket and waited for him to finish his drink. "Have you decided on what you want?" I shifted my weight from one foot to the other. I had been on them for seven hours now and they ached.

"Oh, yeah." His eyes slowly trailed down my body as his tongue flicked out over his lips, wetting them. "Burger and fries." He set his bottle down on the table and spun it in his fingers. His cell phone rang and he rolled his eyes, picking it up to answer the call. "Tucker speaking."

"I'll get that right out to ya." I smiled politely and went to place the order. Larry was fuming. He was seconds from ripping into me when the bell above the door chimed. I turned around and caught sight of Jackson.

"Hey, Jax." I smiled and walked toward him to meet halfway across the room. He ran his hands through his dirty long, brown hair. His skin was flushed and his emerald eyes were glazed over. Drugs had really done a number on him. He was slim but not muscular, tall but always hunched over.

"I need some money." His jaw was clenched and his voice barely a whisper. He wiped his hands over his stained white T-shirt.

"Jax, I don't have any money."

Jackson grabbed my arm just above the elbow, pulling me closer. His breath reeked of liquor.

"It's fucking important, Cass. I need it now."

I knew he had no patience. He was impossible to reason with when he was using. I took a step back.

"Can I get a refill, sweetheart?" Tucker called from his table, holding up the bottle.

"Who the fuck is that?" Jackson's eyes blazed with anger.

"Just a customer," I whispered. "Just a minute!" I called back to Tucker, who was watching Jackson and me.

"I won't have any money until the end of my shift, Jax. You know that." I placed my fingertips on his chest and he knocked them away.

Tucker had moved next to me. His fingertips grazed my back, startling me. "I have to run, so won't be able to eat, but here is what I owe you, and more than enough to make up for the *trouble*." His eyes darted to Jackson, sizing him up.

I was speechless. I've never known anyone to give something without wanting something in return. The simple touch from his fingertips sent my body into a frenzy, and I struggled to slow my heart rate back to normal, worried Jax could feel it thudding in my arm.

"See you later, sweetheart." Tucker shot me a wink before popping a toothpick in his mouth and smiling at Jax, sliding in between us to get to the front door.

Jackson didn't care about this guy. All he saw was the stack of bills in my hand.

"Thanks. Have a good day," I called after Tucker as he ran a hand through his hair and left through the front door. I didn't know if he did it out of pity or kindness, but my faith in humanity was momentarily restored, even if the guy was a cocky asshole. The bell signaling the order was ready dinged, and my eyes drifted back to Jackson.

"Perfect timing." Jax smiled and grabbed the twenty from the top of the small stack of bills in my hand.

"Jax, wait," I called after him, but he had already turned to leave as quickly as possible.

I counted the money I had left. Just enough to cover the meal. Fucking perfect. A motorcycle revved angrily outside the door and took off, growing quieter as it drove away.

"Order up, Cass," Larry hissed from the kitchen. Fuck. I grabbed the burger and fries and set it on the farthest table in my section. At least I would get to eat some real food today. I picked up a hot fry and popped it in my mouth, my eyes roaming over the dingy blue curtains that didn't match anything else in the place. I wanted to be selfish and eat every last bite, but my mind wandered to my mother. I grabbed a to-go box and slipped the food inside. As soon as I could take another break, I would take her the food. She was hungry, I was sure, and didn't do much of anything for herself, let alone cook.

Another hour slipped by. I was busy, but never enough to

make this job worth it financially. Not that there were any other options.

"I'm takin' a break!" I slipped off my apron and made eye contact with Marla, the other waitress at Aggie's. She nodded and I grabbed the box of food I had saved and went out the back. I made my way across the dusty parking lot and through the fence to the trailer park.

"Mom," I called as I opened the trailer door. "Mom?" I made my way down the narrow hall, avoiding the bucket that sat on the floor to catch water when it rained. I leaned against the wood paneling as I slipped by it. I pushed open the door to the master bedroom. I stopped short. Jax and my mother sat in a cloud of cigarette smoke, dazed and disoriented. A thin rubber tube was tied around her arm and a needle jutted out of her vein.

"I told you not to bring that shit around here again, Jax," I screamed. Jax's green eyes were bright and glazed against the bloodshot white surrounding the irises.

Disgusted, I threw the food on the floor in front of me, then rushed to my mother's side, carefully pulling the needle from her arm.

"She fucking likes it. It shuts her the fuck up." Jax motioned to my mother, who was practically catatonic.

I was the spitting image of her, only with a thinner body, fewer years on my face, and more self-respect.

Was this what my future looked like?

My mother used to be a good person before her mind went. When Daddy left us, he took her sanity with him. She soon lost the sparkle in her eyes, and next went any reason or logic. She didn't bathe or feed herself. She sat in her own filth until I did something about it.

"You promised me you wouldn't do that anymore. You promised." Tears formed in my eyes, but I struggled to keep them from falling.

Jax ignored me and tightened the belt around his arm. I balled my hands into tight fists and stormed out of the trailer, slamming the flimsy door behind me. My mind flashed to all the other girls my age who were just graduating from college, stepping into a bright future full of possibility.

I wouldn't allow myself to look over my shoulder at the trailer again. I didn't need a reminder of what I was.

I WIPED MY EYES as I slipped back in the employee entrance at the diner. I grabbed my apron and tied it on quickly over my all-black uniform and then began cleaning my empty tables. I scrubbed, taking my anger out on the old, dilapidated beige Formica tops. I hated this place, my life . . . myself. I sighed finally and sank down into a booth, my head in my hands. The bell chimed above the door and I didn't have any energy left to see who it was.

"Can I get that burger now, sweetheart?"

I glanced up through my hands and stared into Tucker's dark, stormy blue eyes, which seemed even brighter than they had when I'd last seen them just two hours ago.

"You know there are much better restaurants around here, and I'm still not your sweetheart," I said drily.

"But the service here is amazing." He smiled and winked at me, revealing deep dimples in his cheeks as he slid into the booth on the bench across from me. Combined with his great hair and dark brows over those beautiful eyes, it made him butterfly-worthy eye candy. Jax used to make my stomach fill with butterflies when he smiled at me. But they fled with my dreams a long time ago.

"You okay, Cass?" Tucker asked quietly.

How did he know my name? Right, I'd told him when I took his order. I was surprised he still remembered it. Most people left this place and never looked back. It felt incredibly personal having him address me by something other than "Miss" or "Hey, you."

"I'll get you that burger." I sighed as I put my hand on the table to push myself up. His hand landed on mine and I jumped at the unexpected contact. Maybe it was the years of having to shield myself from my mother's boyfriend of the week, but I hated to be touched, even if that touch caused my heart to race the way it was now. My flinching was now commonplace with any human contact. He glanced at my hand and at me, slowly sliding his fingers back. He swallowed and nodded.

I couldn't get away from him fast enough. Did he want to watch me cry? Did he not get enough of my humiliation the first time he stopped in? That's why he'd left in such a hurry, no doubt. I put in the order as Larry eyed me curiously, but he didn't say anything.

I lingered by the waitress station, not wanting to go back over to Tucker's table. He was the only customer I had. I was sure it was obvious to him that I was avoiding him. I glanced over my shoulder at him. He stared out the dirty window, lost in thought. I let myself have a minute to eye him up and down. His jeans looked dirty and well worn, but upon closer inspection, it appeared he paid to have his clothes look as if they were falling apart. I rolled my eyes and looked back at the station. What an asshole. He actually paid money to look poor. I looked over my shoulder again, and this time my eyes landed directly on his. I blushed and grabbed a bottle of ketchup, taking it over and setting it on the table in front of him.

"You want a beer?" I tucked a long, straight strand of hair behind my ear. What was I doing? Larry was going to have a fit.

Tucker smiled and gave a quick nod. "You *do* still owe me one from earlier."

I turned on my heel and went into the kitchen. Larry raised his spatula as I opened the fridge and grabbed two beers, and I gave him an evil glare, silently warning him not to fuck with me. He wiped the spatula on his tattered apron and flipped the burger over. I owed Tucker for being so generous. That was what I told myself. I was only being nice to return the favor.

I'd had all the shit I could take for one day. With a mental shrug, I slipped out the door. I hoped Larry didn't see the beers and make good on his threat to get me fired. His wife was only half as mean as he was, and I was sure that was the only reason I still had this job. It was my only escape from the life that sat just across the dusty parking lot. This place may have looked as if it should have been condemned years ago, but it was my sanctuary.

I set the beers on the table and slipped into the booth across from Tucker. He grinned and grabbed my bottle, twisting the cap off for me before taking care of his own. I managed a genuine smile and picked up my beer.

Tucker took a long drink from his beer before sighing and tilting the bottle in his hand to read the label. "So . . . that asshole from earlier . . ." His voice trailed off and his eyes stayed glued to the label of the bottle as if it had the answers to his questions. I took a drink and eyed him suspiciously. Why did he care? Was he just making small talk? That's all this was. Clearly I was his entertainment for the night.

"Boyfriend," I sighed, and began to peel the label from my drink. The alcohol warmed my body quickly. On an empty stomach, the effects took hold much quicker.

Tucker nodded and drank his beer until the bottle was empty. "That's a shame."

"His bark is worse than his bite." That wasn't the least bit true, but I wasn't about to admit how weak I actually was to a total stranger.

"Maybe someone needs to muzzle him."

"What about you? Do you have a girlfriend?"

He laughed and spun his bottle in his hand before his eyes connected with mine.

"Depends." He leaned forward on his elbows. "You gonna leave that asshole?"

I sat back in my seat, completely shocked by his forwardness.

The bell dinged, signaling his food was ready, and I jumped. "I'll go get that." I smiled awkwardly as I rushed to the kitchen.

"Tryin' to make you some extra cash tonight?" Larry made a disgusting motion with his hips that made bile rise in my throat.

I shook my head. "Fuck off, you old perv!" I grabbed the food and stormed away angrily. I was mostly angry at myself. Why did I sit down with the guy in the first place? If Larry decided to make small talk with Jax about this, there would be hell to pay.

I set the food on the table and nodded politely at Tucker before turning to leave.

"Wait! You aren't going to keep me company?" I could hear the smile in his voice. It pushed me over the edge. I knew what guys like him wanted; it was what all guys wanted.

I turned around and took three steps, closing the gap between us. I placed my hands on the table and leaned in closer to him. He smelled of coconut. That caught me off guard. It was the beach, the scent of freedom wafting from his hair.

"I'm not some fucking whore. You can't buy my time."

He sat back in his seat, taken aback by my remark. I knew I was taking out my anger at Larry on him, but I couldn't stop myself.

"I just wanted some company, and you looked like . . ."

"I looked like what? An easy lay?" I crossed my arms over my chest.

"Nothing about you is easy, that much I can already tell." He grinned as he picked up his burger and took a big bite, then dropped it back on his plate, his eyes staring ahead of him.

My stomach growled with hunger, and I turned and stormed away, completely taken aback by his response.

I didn't approach Tucker again until I was certain he was finished eating. I dropped off his check without a word. I watched from the kitchen as he dug some cash out of his wallet and dropped it on the table. He looked around one last time and left. The sound of his motorcycle growled in the distance.

I sighed and went to his table to collect the money so I could cash out my final table of the evening. I grabbed the money and reached for his plate. Spelled out in ketchup was the word *sorry*. I sighed and wiped down the table. I needed sleep.

I cashed out quickly and yelled to Larry that I was leaving and set off across the dark dirt lot toward home. The trailer was quiet, and I knew that Mom and Jax were probably passed out. At least, I hoped they were.

I tiptoed inside and made my way down the hall. Just as I had hoped, they were both fast asleep. A drug-induced coma would be a more accurate description. I pulled off my red Chuck Taylor sneakers and tossed them into my room, then made my way back to the front door, grabbing my cigarettes on the way outside.

I didn't hesitate this time to light one. What was the point of maintaining my health? Did I really want to live any longer in this hellhole? It was a relatively quiet night. If I closed my eyes, I could almost pretend I was someone else. Almost. Off in the distance, a dog barked wildly and I could hear the Hansons a few trailers down fighting or . . . whatever it was they did that made her sound like that. Gross.

After a last drag, I threw my cigarette out into a puddle on the road and headed back inside. I waited a few minutes until my nerves could not take any more. They were asleep. No one was watching. I tiptoed into my room and slipped my old, tattered teddy bear from my dresser. My father had given it to me when I was little. That was before he forgot about me. I slipped my fingers into a hidden slit in his back and pulled out a small wad of money. I had been saving for what felt like a lifetime. I needed enough for first and last months' rent for a new place. Somewhere a few towns away. I smiled. A few more weeks, and I might be able to pull it off.

Someone stirred and I slipped the money back inside the safety of my bear.

I snuck out into the living room and flipped on the television. A few minutes later, Jax came out of the bathroom in a daze.

"Hey," he said, scrubbing his eyes with the heels of his hands.

"Hey." I didn't look at him. A nothingness was in his eyes anyway. The way he always looked when he used. He'd promised me a million times he would stop. Lies. It was always lies. I flipped between the three channels that we got, looking for something other than the news.

"You got any money?" Now he was scratching his stomach under his wifebeater.

"When do I ever have any money?" I snapped, and clicked off the television. I got up and pushed past him, hitting him hard with my shoulder.

"Fuck, Cass, you don't have to be such a bitch about it."

I slammed the door to my bedroom and dropped down on the bed, burying my face in my floral comforter. For the countless time, I cried myself to sleep.

CHAPTER

Three

"UGGHH . . ." I REACHED for the alarm and swatted it a few times until it finally stopped beeping. I didn't want to open my eyes. Dreams were always better than reality. Last night, I was four years old again, and with my mother and father. He was tall and strong with wispy blond hair. My mother still had the light in her eyes that had since burned out. She looked identical to me in my memories. She smiled and laughed while she and my father each held one of my hands. Every few steps they would raise their arms, lifting me off the ground. It felt as if I were flying and I'd loved it. The adult me remembered and missed those times.

Resigned, I stretched and sat up, looking around my room. The walls were dingy green and the carpet a stained blue. It was hideous. I kept it clean, but no amount of scrubbing could make it easy on the eyes. All of my furniture was secondhand and broken.

"Cass!" Jax screamed from the living room. I yawned and allowed myself another moment of peace before dressing for work and walking out to the living room to find him. He was sprawled on the brown couch, rubbing his temples.

"I don't feel good," he moaned, his brows drawn together.

"What's wrong?" I sat down beside him and put my hand on his forehead. He didn't feel feverish. "Headache?" He nodded and pulled me down to his chest. I wanted to fight him. I hated that he had lied to me again. But instead I rested my head on his chest and listened to the beating of his heart.

He ran a hand through my hair. "I didn't mean to, Cass. I fucked up."

I knew he didn't want to be a junkie. He was addicted and had no way out. I'd tried to get him to join a group to help him through it. I'd even brought a pamphlet home. He tore it up and threw it in my face. He said that groups were for pussies. He could quit on his own. I looked up at his face and his eyes were still squeezed shut. *He was wrong*, I thought with a sigh.

"I have to get ready for work." I sat up, but Jackson grabbed my wrists and tried to pull me back to him.

"Stay." He pulled harder until my body fell against his.

I slapped him in the chest and stood again. "I have to go to work. I don't want to be stuck here forever."

His eyes shot open and I knew I had said the wrong thing.

"What's wrong with *here*, Cass? You too good for this place? You would be living on the street right now if I hadn't got us this place." His voice was low and cold.

I took a step backward.

He sat up and slowly pushed to his feet. "You want to suck dick for a living like your mama used to?" He stepped closer. My legs were against the chair now, and I was struggling to keep from falling back into it. "I bet that's how you get your tips."

"I'm sorry." My voice was barely a whisper. My throat had dried and I could barely speak. The attitude I used to protect myself from the world disappeared around Jax. It always did. He was stronger than me physically, but that isn't what eventually broke me down. His words were what hurt the most. After being told for so long that I was worthless and no one else would want me, I began to believe it. I always put on a strong face for others. Trying to prove I wasn't the weak little girl I felt like inside, but Jax saw through my façade; it crumbled under his penetrating stare.

He wasn't always like this. It was only when he used and needed another fix. His hand shot out and grabbed my upper arm. He squeezed and I cried out in pain as my knees buckled.

His face was over mine now, his jaw clenched. "You ungrateful . . . worthless little bitch."

I flinched at his words. They hurt worse than his hands. "I'm just trying to make it better for us," I whispered.

"Oh, I am not man enough to provide for you?"

"I have to go. I have to . . ."

He leaned in closer until our noses touched. "You are nothing but white trash."

He let go of my arm, pushing me back into the chair. I fell less than gracefully. I quickly put my hands over my face to shield myself from any blows that might come my way. Nothing. I peeked between my fingers and sighed. I was alone. I grabbed my apron and left as quickly as possible.

I was working morning and evening shifts that day. While I hated my job, it was better than the alternative. I would do anything to keep from becoming homeless. Plus, I had so far been able to save $600. I could almost taste freedom. A new life. I just had to push myself a little harder and I could make things better for us. I could get Jackson some help and maybe help my mother find some friends, a network of support. I wanted a home that was all my own. I wanted to be proud of who I was and not have to worry if I would be able to afford food or hot water. For once, I wanted to take those basic necessities for granted.

"You're a half hour early," Larry called from the kitchen. I pushed into the room and began my prep work for the shift.

"I won't clock in early. I just needed to get away." I shrugged and began to fill the salt and pepper shakers. He didn't respond, didn't make any smart-ass remarks. He knew what went on at my place. The whole trailer park knew. Not that they cared. Everyone had his or her own problems and mine weren't special. In fact, a lot of people had it worse.

When the diner finally opened, it took half an hour for any customers to show up. Larry made some eggs and toast for us to eat. Every once in a while, he was kind. I appreciated those times. I knew I was rude and lashed out at almost everyone, but it was the only way to protect myself. I didn't want to be hurt by anyone else. If I opened myself up, I was inviting someone in to hurt me, to leave me.

I ate breakfast while rolling silverware into napkins and securing them with little paper strips. My table only needed the occasional coffee refill, so the morning dragged.

During the lull, I went to the bathroom and braided my hair to the side, looking over my reflection. I was a plain Jane with freckles on my nose and a heart-shaped face that made me look too much like a teenager. I hated it.

I sighed and lifted my sleeve to check the bruises underneath it. *Great.* These weren't going to fade anytime soon. My eyes, normally a sky blue, looked dull and faded. It felt as though my life were literally draining out of them. I was becoming my mother. All I needed was a drug habit and about forty extra pounds. I rolled my eyes and snorted at my private joke. Blond-haired, blue-eyed nothing. The tiny smile at my internal joke quickly faded as I looked myself over once more before switching off the light and heading back to work.

I stepped out into the dining room and my jaw nearly hit the floor. Tucker was making himself comfortable at one of my tables, menu in hand. I glanced over at Larry, who was leaning against the waitress station. He grinned and looked back at Tucker. I straightened my apron and ran my hand over my hair. Was I nervous? What the hell for? This guy was clearly trouble and a glutton for punishment if he thought hanging around this place was fun.

"Hey." I gave him my best fake smile, but I didn't have to force myself as much as usual.

"Hey, sweetheart." His smile beamed.

My heart fluttered a beat and I swallowed hard. "Can I start you off with something to drink?"

"Orange juice sounds good."

I took off for the kitchen to get him the drink.

"Who's your new friend?" Larry asked with a stupid grin on his face. I rolled my eyes and ignored him as I poured Tucker his juice.

"Jax is gonna be pissed." Larry laughed. I wanted to punch him in his stupid mouth. He had no idea what Jax did when he was pissed. I glared at Larry and walked back out to the dining area and took Tucker his glass of orange juice.

"So, you aren't from around here, are you?" I had never before seen him. I would remember a face like his. He didn't fit in here. He was covered in tattoos, which was the norm, but they all looked like works of art. Not the typical home-drawn doodles or jail tats most people sported around here. Tucker ran his hand through his messy hair. It stood up in spikes with no rhyme or reason.

"Just in town for a few days for work. Staying over in Savannah."

"Savannah? They have all sorts of places to eat. What brings you to Eddington?" I was being nosy. I didn't even know why I cared. Curiosity, I guess. No one ever made an effort or went out of his or her way to come here.

"I like the small-town feel." He shrugged.

That pissed me off. I'm not sure why, but it did. I was nearly killing myself to get out of this godforsaken place and he came here to feel cozy?

"Have you decided on anything?" I raised an eyebrow, and he stared at me for a moment as if he didn't understand me. Apparently, my frustration at his comment showed.

"Yeah, I'll have the ham steak with a couple of eggs. Over easy." He held out the menu for me to take.

"You like 'em easy, got it."

"Actually, I'm enjoying the challenge."

My cheeks burned as I flushed in embarrassment. I turned and headed for the kitchen. *Just fucking great.*

Larry took the order with a huge grin on his face. While I waited for the food, I turned on the radio in the diner. I clicked on my favorite station and began to sing along as I wiped down menus. Music was an escape for me. It took me out of my life and placed me magically in another world. I loved it. I continued to sing along as one song faded into the next.

Even Larry seemed in better spirits, humming along to the songs as he set the plate of food up for me to take. I was still lost in the song as I carried it over to Tucker.

"You like this song?" he asked as he unwrapped his silverware.

"It's beautiful."

Tucker grinned and I returned the gesture.

"Wanna sit? Doesn't look like you're that busy."

I glanced around the empty diner. He was right. Today was going to be a slow day, and after I'd bitten his head off the day before, I owed him that much.

I sighed and slid into the bench seat across from him. He ate while I tapped my fingers to the music.

He watched me as he chewed. "Damaged."

"What?"

"The band. Have you seen them in concert?" He took another bite of his ham and shoved it in his mouth. He had nice lips.

I shook my head, realizing he had said something to me. "I'm sorry, what?"

"They play in Savannah in a few days." He smiled.

"I don't go in town much."

"Why not?"

"I don't know. Cabs are too expensive I guess. What is this? Twenty Questions?"

"Well, you're not exactly an open book."

"Maybe because my life isn't your business." I raised an eyebrow at him as I grabbed his orange juice and took a sip.

He laughed and set down his silverware. "Ask me something. Anything."

"Okay." I set the glass back on the table as I tried to come up with something to ask. "What do you do for a living?"

He made a face and took another bite of food. "Ask me something else."

I sighed and rested my head on my hand. "What's your favorite color?"

"*That's* what you want to know?"

"It's all I could think of." I shrugged as I crumpled his straw paper into a ball between my fingers.

He leaned forward again, his blue eyes searching mine. "Ask me why I'm here. Ask me why I keep coming back."

The bell above the door dinged and Jackson stumbled in. His eyes narrowed in rage.

"Fuck," I whispered as I nervously tucked my hair behind my ear.

Tucker glanced over his shoulder to see what had suddenly made me so upset.

"You dirty little whore!" Jackson was seething mad.

I waved my hands in front of me, begging him to stop. He was obviously high and not thinking clearly. "Jax, it's not what you think." The smell of liquor wafted off him.

"Everything all right?" Tucker's eyes were locked on mine. He looked to be itching to fight.

"None of your fucking business, asshole." Jackson leaned in toward Tucker, arms stretched. Jax grabbed my arm to pull me from the booth. His hand wrapped around my tender bruises and I flinched, a squeal escaping my lips.

Tucker jumped from his seat and was nose to nose with Jackson in a heartbeat. "Get your fucking hands off her." Tucker's voice was low and frighteningly calm. The muscles in his jaw ticked as he waited.

Jax loosened his grip on me momentarily. I rubbed at my tender flesh, trying to make the pain subside.

Jackson's attention was now on Tucker. "Why do you care? She's *my* girl. I'll put my hands anywhere I want on her." Jax had a few inches on him, but Tucker was slim and fit. He obviously spent time keeping himself in shape, unlike Jackson.

"You want to fight someone, I'm right here, motherfucker." Tucker was shifting from foot to foot. It reminded me of how a boxer hops around the ring during a fight, only more subtle.

I pushed my way between them, putting myself face-to-face with Tucker. "Stop this! I'm fine." *God, he has nice lips. Shit. Stop staring at his lips.* "Please," I whispered.

"You're fine with some asshole manhandling you?" Tucker was fuming and looked around me to glare at Jax.

I moved so my face was in Tucker's line of vision again, just inches from his face. "It's not what you think. He's just upset." I was trying desperately to defuse the situation.

"I don't need you to defend me, Cass. I don't give a fuck what he thinks." I knew Jax was moments away from really losing his temper.

"Want to know what I think?" Tucker stepped closer and now his chest was against mine. I could feel the heat radiating off his body. "I think that you're a worthless prick who likes to beat up little girls to make his dick feel bigger."

"Jesus Christ, Tucker." I felt as if my world were imploding. I knew he could feel my heart racing in my chest as I pushed back against him, struggling to keep this fight nonphysical. I closed my eyes, bracing for a blow to come from behind me. I didn't know if Jax had the balls to fight Tucker, but I knew he wouldn't mind taking his anger out on me. "Please stop this. I appreciate your concern, but this is between me and my boyfriend." I stared into Tucker's eyes, pleading with him to let it go.

He took a step back, his expression turning sad.

"Cass? What is going on out there?" Larry was standing in the doorway to the kitchen.

I took a deep breath. *Coconut. I love that smell.* "Nothing," I called back, and turned around to grab Jax by the wrist. I pulled him toward the door, keeping my gaze fixed on Tucker, hoping he wouldn't follow. He would only make things worse for me later.

Once we were in the parking lot, I began to lose my cool. "What are you doing here, Jax?" I asked, crossing my arms over my chest.

"I needed some money, but I guess you were busy with the fuckstick." His voice grew louder with every word. "I hope he tips you well."

"Go home, Jax. I can't afford to lose this job."

"Who the fuck do you think you're talking to, Cass?" He stepped forward, our noses touching.

I refused to back down. I balled my hands into fists at my sides and begged for strength. "Please, Jax. I need this job. Please?"

"I thought you needed me."

"You know I do, Jax. I'll be home in a few hours."

He took a step back and kicked dirt at me before retreating toward the trailer. I let out the breath I had been holding and turned back to the diner.

I slipped inside the door, suddenly nervous as hell.

Tucker was pulling money from his wallet as I entered. He tossed it on the table. His eyes caught mine for a brief moment before he shook his head. "You deserve better, Cass." He walked past me and out the door.

I felt horrible. Why had Tucker defended me anyway? He didn't even know me. Why did he give a shit? I forced myself to take deep breaths and count to ten. I didn't want to cry. I would never hear the end of it from Larry. If he wanted me fired, he could make it happen.

CHAPTER

Four

THE NEXT FEW hours dragged by painfully slowly. I never had more than two tables at a time. Larry wasn't speaking to me. He would just shake his head and look away whenever I came near him. It was obnoxious. I passed the time decorating my future home in my head. I imagined an immaculate two-story home, white from floor to ceiling. I would plant a garden in my yard and learn to live off my land as much as possible. As much as I tried to picture Jax with me, I could no longer see it. No matter how many times I went through the scenario in my head, it always ended badly between him and me. It was becoming harder and harder to imagine my own mother the way she used to be when I was little. The world was nothing like the fairy tale she'd painted in my head as a child.

The sound of a motorcycle made my heart begin to race. I leaned over a table to look out the dusty window. It wasn't Tucker, so I turned away, disappointed. Why did I even care? Some random man showed me kindness for the first time in years and I wait by the window like a puppy?

The man who came in looked to be in his early twenties. He ran his hand through hair that hung in black curls to his shoulders. His clothing seemed extreme for the warm weather. He wore a leather jacket and had a motorcycle helmet topped with a red Mohawk under his arm. He pulled off his mirrored sunglasses and glanced around. His eyes landed on me and he smiled before sliding into an oversize booth. He looked exotic with light eyes and a strong, angular jawline.

Just what I needed. I grabbed a menu and made my way to his table. He was looking around the surroundings, and if it were a nicer place, I would think he wanted to rob us. Here, of course, there would be no point. No self-respecting fool would bother.

"Hello. My name is Cass. Can I start you off with something to drink?"

He peeled off his jacket, revealing a wifebeater underneath. His tattoos showed right through it as if it were made of gauze rather than cotton. He was extremely muscular and intimidating. "Beer?"

I just nodded. I could have told him no, but it didn't seem as if no was an answer he was used to hearing. I hoped Larry wouldn't mind. I slipped into the kitchen and grabbed a longneck from the fridge. As long as it was paid for, it shouldn't matter. At least, that's what I told myself as I got the damn beer.

When I stepped back into the dining room, I did a double take. He'd multiplied. What the . . . A man identical in every way sat directly across from him.

"Hi. I am . . ." I slowly set the beer down in front of the original biker.

"I'll have a beer, too, Cass. Thanks." He smiled and I stood stunned, staring at him for a moment before fetching another of Larry's beers.

What a strange fucking day. I took the doppelgänger his drink and asked them if they wanted to order any food. They declined so I left them to their own devices while I tended to my other customer.

Larry kept an eye on them and made sure I knew he thought they were up to no good, but they didn't cause any trouble. The only sound from them was the occasional outburst of laughter.

That is, until Jackson appeared about forty-five minutes later. He stumbled inside the door and scanned the room for me. It took a minute for his eyes to focus, but when he finally saw me, he yelled across the diner, slurring, "Get your ass over here, Cass."

I hustled toward him, not wanting him to make another scene.

I made it a few steps from him before a hand grabbed my shoulder and pulled me backward and the menacing-looking twins stepped in front of me. Jackson was in absolute shock, as was I.

"What the fuck, Cass?" He tried to yell around them but they blocked his view. "You better hope I'm not up when you get home." It wasn't an empty threat. I knew I would suffer for this later.

They never said a word to him, just kept their arms crossed over their chests until Jax gave up and left out the front door.

I was speechless. The bell above the door chimed as it closed, and the men slid back into their booth and continued talking as if nothing had happened. I hurried to the kitchen and slipped inside. I grabbed each twin a beer. Larry shot me an angry glare, but I ignored him and took the bottles out to the guys. One of them was on the phone, but he paused to say thank you. I nodded, not wanting to interrupt his conversation.

"Here she is," the guy said, and held out the phone for me to take.

I looked at it as if it might explode in my hand, but still, I took it and slowly raised it to my ear.

"Cass, sorry I wasn't there this time. I have some work things to take care of. My boys promised they won't let anything happen to you." It was Tucker, his voice laced with concern.

"Wait . . . what?" I ran my hand over my hair as I tried to process what the hell was going on.

"You really shouldn't let that guy treat you like that. You deserve better, sweetheart."

There was a long, pregnant pause as I listened to his breathing on the other end of the phone. I should have told him I was not his sweetheart. I should have told him I wasn't his problem.

"Thanks," I whispered, my voice barely making a sound. *Why does he care?* He didn't know me. He didn't know my situation. My free hand ran up my arm to the fresh bruises from this morning. Maybe he understood better than I realized.

"No problem. I'll drop by as soon as I can get out of here. You working until closing?"

I chewed my lip as I looked at the guys sitting in front of me. "Yeah . . . yes."

"Good. I'll see you later."

"Bye." I handed the phone back to the twin and made a beeline for the restroom.

Once inside, I leaned against the door and took a deep breath. No one had ever cared. Not for years. Not my parents. Not my boyfriend. It was overwhelming.

I floated through the next few hours in a daze. I was nervous about seeing Tucker. I didn't understand why. He was the only person . . . a stranger . . . who gave a damn about me. I should have been excited, but I found myself questioning his motives. Trust wasn't easily earned from me, not that anyone had ever before made an effort to gain it.

I washed down every empty table in the restaurant. When the place was sufficiently clean, I used my tips to buy myself an order of fries. I was starving and I didn't want to pass out in front of Tucker. He already saw me as the damsel in distress.

I ate by myself on the far side of the diner, keeping my eyes on the twins. They had to be really good friends with Tucker to waste hours out of their day keeping an eye on me. I wanted to know more about them, but I wasn't going to ask. Maybe they belonged to some weird altruistic biker gang that went out of their way to help others. I snorted and laughed to myself. I wished they would leave. I had taken care of myself all of these years, I didn't need someone to babysit me now. Still, it felt good that someone cared. I still wished that someone were Jackson.

I finished my fries and grabbed the old broom and dustpan

from the supply closet to clean the ancient tile floor. I'd never put this much effort into taking care of the diner, not that it made a difference. It didn't shine like a new penny, and all I had successfully done was wear myself down.

The bell above the door chimed and I stopped dead in my tracks, holding my breath as Tucker stepped inside. He scanned the diner, and when his eyes met mine, he smiled. I smiled back and felt heat as a blush washed over my face. This boy was nothing but trouble, but damned if I cared.

He slipped into the booth with his friends, and I headed to the kitchen to grab him a beer, leaving the broom propped against the wall. My palms were sweating and I felt excited. This was new for me. I couldn't remember the last time I'd felt excited about anything.

I grabbed a longneck from the fridge and took a deep breath before slipping back out onto the main floor.

I placed the drink in front of Tucker on the table and gave him a smile. A genuine smile.

"Thanks."

I looked down at my feet and back to him. "Anytime."

He smiled, and his cheeks dimpled. "This is Chris and Terry." He pointed to the guys with him with the neck of his bottle.

I nodded. "Nice to meet you." I felt like an idiot, standing there grinning like a fool.

Terry . . . or was it Chris? One of the twins broke the silence. "We're gonna head out, man. Got that party to hit, and Eric is probably already swinging naked from a chandelier. You sure you ain't coming?"

Tucker's eyes flickered to mine and back to his friend.

"Yeah, I didn't think so," the twin said, and gave me a small grin. The guys got up from the table and headed for the front door.

Tucker and I stared at each other awkwardly for a moment as the bell chimed, signaling their exit.

"Wanna sit?" He motioned to the seat across from him.

I had no other customers to tend to, so I slid onto the bench seat and fidgeted nervously with my fingers. "Why did you do that?"

He gave a half grin. "Well, I couldn't be here. I had a work obligation." He took a drink from his bottle.

"I don't mean why did you send someone here, I meant why did you try to protect me at all?"

He looked at me as if I were speaking a foreign language. "Why wouldn't I?" He sounded insulted. He took a long drink from his beer, his eyes trained on mine.

It made me nervous. I dug into my bottom lip with my teeth and stared down at my hands. He had to want something from me. No one goes this far out of his way to be nice to someone without wanting something in return. "And you still aren't going to tell me what you do for a living?"

He sat his beer on the table and shook his head no.

"I'm not going to judge you." I laughed. "I'm a waitress, for God's sake."

"Don't do that."

"Do what?"

"Make it sound like you're beneath everyone else."

"I don't even know why you care."

"That's because you didn't ask."

"Are we playing Twenty Questions again? I don't think it ended very well last time."

He laughed and drank the remainder of his beer.

CHAPTER

Five

O FOR A ride with me."

I glanced up at him, shocked.

"On my bike. Let's ride around the city. You can give me the tour."

The idea sent my stomach into somersaults. "I don't think so." I tucked the loose pieces of my hair behind my ear as I shook my head.

"Why not?" He grinned that wicked smile of his, and my eyes became glued to his pouty lips. He leaned over and lowered his voice. "What have you got to lose?"

Everything. I could lose everything. "I don't even know you."

"What do you want to know?"

"Why are you wasting your time here talking to me?"

"You think you're a waste of time?"

"I think a guy like you has better things to do."

"Better things to do than *you*, sweetheart?" He winked, and my skin immediately heated and for once I had no idea what to say. "You got a pen?"

"Yeah." I grabbed the pen from my apron and slid it across the table to him, confused. He slipped his napkin in front of him and began to write. "What are you doing?" My curiosity was getting the best of me.

"Making a note of this. I'd imagine it isn't often a girl like you is speechless." He laughed as I grabbed the napkin and crumpled it into a ball, throwing it at him. He playfully dodged it.

I glanced up at the clock. We would be closing in a few minutes, and all of my side work had been completed this morning before my shift. My mom and Jax would most likely be passed out cold. They wouldn't even notice I was gone. I wasn't anxious to see Jax after his threat earlier, anyway. I jumped up from the table and made my way to the kitchen.

"Where ya going? I was only playing!" Tucker called after me.

I smiled to myself. "I'm taking off, Larry." I untied my apron and tossed it on the counter. He gave me a curious look, but I ignored him and headed back into the dining area. "Let's go before I change my mind."

Tucker grinned from ear to ear. He hopped up and placed his hand on the small of my back as we made our way out into the parking lot. "You know I don't back down from a challenge."

I was exhausted from the tense day, but my adrenaline was racing now with the tingle from his fingers on my spine. We reached his bike and I took a moment to look it over. I had never been on one before, and I suddenly became afraid.

Tucker let out a small chuckle and held out his spare helmet to me. "It'll be fine, I promise. I won't let you get hurt."

I took the helmet and slid it over my head. Many people had made promises to me in the past and I knew better than to ever take them seriously, but for some reason I believed Tucker. He went out of his way to make me safe, keep me protected, even when he couldn't do it in person, and that had to count for something.

He slipped his leg over the bike and stood it upright, knocking back the kickstand with his boot. "Come on." He slipped his helmet onto his head and held out his hand for me.

Electricity shot through the tips of my fingers as they connected with his. I honestly couldn't remember ever getting this feeling with Jax, even when things weren't so bad. It was both frightening and incredibly exciting. I lifted my leg over the back of the giant black machine and settled my body against his. It was awkward being so close to someone I didn't know. "Where do I hold on?"

He reached back and grabbed my hands, wrapping them around his waist. "Hold on to me, sweetheart." He rubbed my hand, then quickly went back to the handlebars. The bike roared to life, but I hardly heard it over the sound of my heart thumping in my ears. His body was rock hard under my fingers, and I could feel the ridges of his stomach muscles as they pulled and tensed under my fingertips.

We rode a few miles into the city under the cloak of darkness. Everything was so much more beautiful at night. The stores and restaurants were lit with softly glowing signs. We traveled up Interstate 95 for about twenty minutes, but it didn't feel long enough. I wasn't ready to give up my seat on the back of Tucker's bike, even if it was only mine for the night.

I guided him down River Street. The bike jumped against the cobblestones of the road, and we had to slow to nearly walking speed to keep from rattling our brains.

River Street is a popular tourist spot during the day, but at night it comes alive with the locals out to have some fun. Music overflowed into the street along with the people who were drinking and having a good time. Vendors line up outside the shops to sell their homemade crafts and paintings.

"Let's grab a drink," he called over his shoulder as he pulled the bike to the designated parking lot along the river. I pulled off my helmet and yanked off the tie on my hair, shaking it free to cascade down my back. *What was I thinking, going out in my work clothes?* My eyes scanned the crowd of women wearing miniskirts and cutoff shorts to help fight off the heat on this balmy night.

Tucker took the helmet from my hand and secured it to the back of his bike while he watched me play with my hair.

"I'm not really dressed for this." I looked down at my black polo shirt and black slacks. I looked horrible.

Tucker's eyes scanned the storefronts. "There!" He pointed to one of the little shops along the river. A red canopy hung over the door. In thick black cursive was written SCARLETT'S. He grabbed my hand and pulled me across the street. The shop owner was just taking their dress racks inside to close for the evening.

"Wait! One second! We need a dress." He grinned his impossibly sexy smile and pulled me past her. I gave her an apologetic grin as we slipped inside the store, but she was busy drooling over Tucker. He seemed to have that effect on everyone. The store was small and crammed with racks of bohemian-style dresses and cases of jewelry. The walls were stone and painted a beautiful gold.

Tucker began leafing through the dresses on the racks, finally selecting one that he handed over to me. "Try this one."

"That's not a dress, it's a scarf." I glared at him.

He smiled and stuck it back on the rack, flipping through a few more. "How about this?"

I held the dress to my body. It was beautiful and definitely not my style. Not that I had a style. I wore hand-me-downs and thrift-store finds. This was an elegant, cream-colored garment decorated with pale purple flowers. The halter dress reminded me of Marilyn Monroe.

"I can't afford this." I made a face at him.

He rolled his eyes. "I'll buy it, just try it on."

I hesitated, suddenly bristling at his unsolicited generosity. What did he want from me? Did he think of me as a charity case? I didn't need his handouts. I was doing just fine on my own. I began to place the dress back in his hands. I didn't need or want someone to swoop in and rescue me from my life. Everything comes with a price, and he would surely want something from me I was not willing to give.

"No, it's fine . . . this really isn't my style—"

"Cass. Please just try on the dress. I'm not trying anything here, I just really think it will look beautiful on you. And you . . . you deserve to wear something as stunning as you are tonight, sweetheart."

I searched his face, trying to figure this guy out.

His fingers wrapped around my hand that was holding the dress as he sighed. "I know you don't want anyone to help you." He laughed. "You're stubborn like I am, but I'll win this argument."

I made a face at him, frustrated that he was able to read me so well. I was usually so good at guarding myself. But I wasn't willing to relent yet. I held his gaze, silently willing him to say more.

"Fine." He cleared his throat. "I know what it's like, Cass, to feel like nobody gives a shit about you. I also know that sometimes we need someone else to make us feel like we're worth something . . . to make us feel special, you know?"

"I'm not."

Tucker cocked his head to the side, a small, nervous smile playing on his lips. He paused before continuing, "When I was little, my parents were always too busy for me. They were more concerned about chasing their next high than whether or not their son had learned his alphabet or even taken his first steps." His gaze dropped to our joined hands. I gave him a reassuring squeeze so he would continue. "I was so desperate to have someone notice me, to show me I was important to them, that I spent my fourth birthday in a hospital." His eyes flicked to mine, gauging my response.

"What happened?" I held my breath as I waited to hear the rest of his story.

"You remember the cartoon *Underdog*?"

I nodded.

"Well, I was determined to teach myself to fly like him. I figured if I could fly, I could be a superhero and save my family. Only it turns out I couldn't, and the fall from a tree in our backyard broke my leg."

"Oh my God." I covered my mouth with my free hand.

"The worst part was not being found for over an hour."

"I'm so sorry, Tucker."

"Don't be. The point is, you can't always fix things on your own. Sometimes you need someone to help you. Sometimes we just need to be noticed. I couldn't fly but I don't regret trying. How would I know I couldn't if I didn't at least try? Besides, if it weren't for that, I may have spent the rest of my childhood with them. I was removed from the house and spent a few years being sent to different foster homes until I ended up with Dorris. It was worth it in the end." He smiled, his eyes still downcast. "Sometimes you have to fall before you can fly . . . and sometimes you need someone to catch you." He looked up. "Even you, Cass."

He was right. I never tried to step outside my life and make things better. I never took a chance. He was also right about winning this argument. How could I refuse to try on the dress now?

"You win." I glanced around the store and found a small area curtained off in the far right corner of the shop. I dashed for it as Tucker grabbed a pair of sandals. I slipped off my clothes and pulled the dress over my head. There was no mirror, so I looked down at myself, trying to see if it looked okay.

"Come on, Cass. I'm dying out here."

I took a deep breath, pulled back the curtain, and stepped out into the main area. Tucker's eyes lit up and he smiled, but as he looked me over, his expression soon turned dark.

I couldn't keep from pouting. Did I look that bad? Was his effort to transform this white-trash waitress into a swan that much of a failure? He stepped closer, and I self-consciously turned to go back into the changing area. He grabbed my arm gently before I could enter. I looked down at his hand and realized what had upset him. The dark purple bruises wrapped around my arm like a barbaric tattoo. My hand shot up to cover the area. Tucker clenched his jaw in anger.

He turned to a rack behind him, grabbed a light purple cardigan, and handed it to me. I gave him a small smile as I slipped it off the hanger and slid it on.

"My mother wore one of these every day." He gave me a weak smile and grabbed my discarded clothing. I tried to push the thought of a young Tucker seeing his mother covered in bruises out of my mind.

I barely recognized myself in the mirror that hung behind the register. I no longer looked like a dirty girl from the trailer park. I raised my chin and smiled at myself.

"You look beautiful." He took my hand and pulled me to the register.

I slipped out of my sneakers and slid on my new brown strappy sandals, mildly surprised he'd guessed my shoe size. No one had ever called me beautiful before, not even Jax. *Hot* maybe, but never *beautiful*. The word made me feel elegant, worldly. I wondered if he said it out of pity.

He grabbed a silver locket that hung next to the register. I gasped when I saw the price, but Tucker slid his credit card to the salesgirl, saying, "Please. I dragged you out tonight, and it's the least I can do."

He shoved my old belongings in a bag. We made our way back to the bike and he tucked my bag next to the helmets. "Turn around."

I hesitated, but slowly turned toward the water.

"Lift your hair," he whispered next to my ear, his warm, minty breath blowing against my neck.

I gathered my hair and held it up as he slipped the delicate chain around my neck and fastened it. I let my hair fall down over my shoulders and turned to face him, my fingers tracing the small piece of heart-shaped metal.

"Perfect," he said, his eyes never leaving mine.

I couldn't help but smile.

He took my hand again and pulled me across the cobblestone road. We passed Scarlett's and made our way a few doors up to one of the livelier bars. The doors were wide-open and a mechanical bull sat straight ahead. I shot him a warning look and he just shook his head and smiled.

"Wait here." His hand left mine as he snaked his way to the bar.

I stood awkwardly alone as I glanced around the bar. Three guys were looking in my direction, smiling and whispering something. I ran my hand over the front of my new dress and looked away, embarrassed. I wasn't fooling anyone. I didn't belong here.

Tucker returned with two beers. He held one out for me and I took it with an appreciative smile. He followed my gaze and glared at the men, who turned back to their table as if they didn't see us.

"Thanks." I took a long pull from the bottle, drinking half of it in one long sip. He laughed and ran his hand through his hair, following suit.

We stood together, watching the other patrons dance. The song switched and I immediately recognized it as "Loved" by Damaged, the song that had played at the diner.

Tucker smiled, taking a sip of his drink and setting it on the table behind him. He took the beer from my hand as well, set it down, and pulled me into the middle of the bar. "It's our song," he said with a laugh.

"Oh, no . . . no . . . no . . . I don't dance." I tried to pull back but he tightened his grip on my hand and winked.

"I don't have to tell you another sad story to get my way, do I, sweetheart?"

My stomach knotted with guilt as I thought of Jax waiting at home for me. I knew that even if I jumped from a tree, he wouldn't notice. My heart stopped for a moment, and the world around us seemed to fade away. All rational thought escaped me as I let myself be pulled onto the dance floor.

Once we were deep enough into the crowd, he stopped and pulled me into him. My hands landed on his hard chest as his found their way to my lower back, tugging me flush against him.

His hips began to move against mine, and I was stuck, frozen like a deer.

"Just do what I do. It's not hard." His hips continued to rock. I slowly began to move against him as my hands slid up to his neck. He pulled me closer until our cheeks touched, his warm breath blowing against my ear. Quietly he sang along to the lyrics as we moved together—"'I want to make you feel beautiful'"—sending a chill through my body even in the warmth of the room.

The place was packed, but it felt as if everyone else had disappeared. I closed my eyes and listened to his beautiful voice in my ear. My own private concert.

His hand slowly rubbed my back, relaxing me. In that moment, I forgot about everything. Forgot my life in the trailer park. About Jackson and my mother. All I saw was Tucker. All I felt was the sweet and gentle way he touched me. No one had ever held me like this before. Looking at Tucker, you wouldn't think he had such a sweet side to him. I realized I had judged him the way people judge me. He was so much more under those sexy tattoos.

One song bled into the next. The tempo picked up, and with a little more liquid courage, I was dancing right along with Tucker. I felt free.

"Where did you learn to dance like this?" I asked loudly into his ear so he could hear me over the music.

"You like that? You know what they say about how a man dances?"

"I don't want to know what they say." I laughed and shook my head as our bodies moved together.

"I'd be happy to demonstrate." He raised an eyebrow as I laughed.

"Now I know you were raised better than to talk to a lady like that."

"Let's have a shot," Tucker said over the pulsing bass of the music. I smiled and nodded. He held up two fingers to the bartender and yelled, "Cuervo." The bartender quickly poured two shots.

My eyes drifted over the crowd of carefree people letting go and having fun. I smiled as I turned back to Tucker, who was scribbling something down on a sliver of paper for a young brunette who had approached him. She looked as if it took all she had to keep from pouncing on top of him. He was giving out his phone number while he was out with me? I tried to hide the scowl from my face and the disappointment that settled in my belly like a rock. *Tucker's not your boyfriend,* I admonished myself. *You already have one of those, a fact that you seem all too willing to forget tonight.* Tucker grabbed the shots from the bar and held one out for me. I paused, then relented. Why not let the fantasy continue, at least for a little while longer? I took it, my fingers lightly brushing against his. I smiled as I tilted my head back and drank it down in one gulp.

He smiled, taking the empty glass from my hand. "Another?"

"Why not?" I yelled over the music as a huge grin spread across his face.

"You tryin' to outdrink me? Is this a challenge?"

I couldn't help but laugh. Drinking was in my blood. This was one game he couldn't win. "You scared?"

"Hell no. I'm excited. Makes getting into your panties even easier."

I smacked him on the arm with the back of my hand as hard as I could and turned to leave.

His hand shot out, catching me at the wrist. He pulled me back into his chest, causing my breath to catch in my throat. The look in his eyes was deadly serious. "I was kidding, Cass. I don't want to take advantage of you. I want to have fun with you."

"Let the fun begin."

"That's what I'm talking about!" His hand found its place on the small of my back as we pushed through the crowd to the bar. His fingers slipped lower, and I reached behind me to raise them back into place, glaring at him in warning. He shot me a wink, not the least bit fazed by my attitude.

"Two more," he called down to the bartender, who nodded in acknowledgment.

The bartender filled his other orders from the far end of the bar, then made his way to our end. I stared at the glass bottles on the wall behind him, watching the lights from the dance floor bounce off them, sending beams of colored light into the mirror behind them. I caught Tucker's reflection, his eyes locked on me.

"Cuervo?" the bartender yelled over the noise, startling me from my trance.

"Two," Tucker said, his eyes still not leaving me.

I looked down at the old wooden bar top in front of me, wishing. How did he make me feel so nervous and excited at the same time?

"You want a chaser?" The bartender filled our shot glasses, the liquid spilling over onto the bar.

"I've been chasing her all night." Tucker laughed and I shook my head at the bartender. I grabbed our glasses and turned to hold one up for Tucker. His fingers wrapped around mine, and I was completely lost in the moment. That is, until the man behind me bumped into me, spilling my shot straight down my chest, into my cleavage.

Tucker grabbed a stack of napkins and began to blot the wetness, which caused me to turn ten shades of red before I pulled them from his hand and took care of it myself.

The man behind me was laughing with a friend and didn't even think to apologize, not that I was surprised.

"Hey! You need to apologize for spilling my girl's drink."

"Just throw her an extra twenty. She won't mind."

"I mind, you asshole."

My head was spinning with how quickly things went from amazing to shit. The bartender whistled through his fingers to get the attention of a bouncer near the door. He pointed to the man behind me, who groaned and slammed his glass on the bar.

"You've got to be fucking kidding me. I'm getting kicked out over that bitch?"

The bouncer reached our side in time to catch Tucker as he lurched at the man. Tucker's fist connected with the side of the man's face, sending him spinning backward into his friend.

"I said fucking apologize!"

I grabbed Tucker's arm in an attempt to pull him away from the chaos. I didn't want to spend the night in jail over some drunken prick.

"You're out of here!" The bouncer grabbed the asshole's arm and dragged him toward the door. "You're next if you don't calm the hell down!" The bouncer pointed at Tucker but was trying to hide a smile.

I didn't find the situation quite as funny. I lived with violence every day of my life. I wanted to escape it. Not be thrown in the middle of more. "Don't worry. I'm leaving." I began to make my way to the door.

Tucker reached out and caught me by the waist. "Where are you going?"

"I'll find my own way home."

He sobered up immediately, placing his hands on my shoulders. "I was protecting you."

"No, Tucker. You were being a macho prick. I don't need someone to fight my battles. If I wanted to see someone get their ass kicked, I would have stayed home."

He didn't respond as my words sank in. He pulled me into his arms and hugged me tightly. "Fuck, Cass. I didn't mean to scare you. I'm so sorry."

I let my arms rise up to his sides, holding on to the fabric of his shirt.

"I would *never* hurt you, Cass."

I nodded into the crook of his neck. I wanted to be angry but I couldn't. As much as my mind wanted to compare all men to Jax, there was no comparison.

"It won't happen again." He pulled me back so I could look into his eyes. I believed him. His gaze didn't waver.

"I trust you."

"Not yet. But you will."

I smiled and glanced around us. No one was paying attention to our conversation, the skirmish long forgotten now that a leggy blonde had climbed up on the mechanical bull.

"Come on." He grinned, grabbing my hand and pulling me back onto the floor.

My fingers slid up his muscular arms and looped behind his neck as we danced through several more songs. I wasn't sure if I was dancing to the beat of the song or his heart. Normally I would have felt embarrassed, or at least out of place, but with his strong arms around me, I felt safe. His hands never left my body as we moved. His cheek was pressed against mine as his minty, liquor-laced breath blew across my neck. I let my eyes fall closed as he pulled back slowly, certain he was going to kiss me. Instead, his thumb traced my lower lip, tugging on it slightly before his palm slid up my cheek to cup it. I opened my eyes to Tucker's hungry gaze.

"I want nothing more than to kiss you, Cass. But I need to know you trust me first. I don't want you to ever think of me the way you think of that asshole you have back home. You deserve better, Cass, really."

My eyes closed again and I nodded, wishing in this one moment he would just take what he wanted. His lips fell on my forehead and held there as the world moved around us. The club was packed and the Southern night air was muggy and hot. Our bodies were coated with a fresh layer of sweat as we ground together. Wanting radiated from every nerve ending in my body. Tucker's forehead pushed against mine as his hands slowly traced my collarbone and trailed down my arms, pushing my sweater off with his fingers as his breathing grew more ragged. I slipped my hands under the bottom of his shirt and ran my fingers over his stomach. He groaned as I traced the edge of his boxers that stuck out above his jeans. Our eyes locked as he skimmed over my bruised arm without thinking, but the sudden twinge of pain snapped me back to reality. I pulled the sweater back over my shoulders and took a small step back from him, embarrassed. We stood only a few inches from each other, but it felt like the width of an ocean as we both struggled to calm our breathing.

"I should get back. Everyone's going to wonder where I am." I pulled my sweater tightly around my body, glancing around to see if anyone had noticed my bruises. He looked disappointed but nodded and took my hand. He led me from the bar and we walked slowly to his bike. We didn't speak as we made our way down the cobblestone street. His jaw flexed continuously and I could tell he was deep in thought. I knew he was angry with himself, but I wasn't. I was mad at Jax for giving me the bruises in the first place.

I didn't want this night to end, but I knew there would be hell to pay if anyone found out where I had been. The fantasy night had to come to an end. Tucker seemed to be on the same page. His pace slowed, prolonging the inevitable good-bye. His hand slipped around mine. I still didn't understand why he would want to spend his time with me. He was handsome and had a job that paid him well enough to afford such luxuries as designer clothes and a motorcycle. It would be easy for him to find a woman to go to bed with without all the baggage—not to mention attitude—I had.

I wished I had asked him more about himself, but it didn't really matter. He would be gone soon, off to another town, leaving me in his dust. It was better this way.

CHAPTER

Six

I SLIPPED MY LEG over the back of his bike as he revved the engine, and we took off into the night.

He drove slowly, taking in the sights of the town that never seemed to sleep. It was a far cry from Eddington, and I still couldn't understand why he would ever set foot in my tiny town if he didn't have to.

The big city faded into long stretches of empty highway. I hugged him tighter as we made our way into the outskirts of Eddington. We slowed to a snail's pace as we crossed the dirt parking lot. The bike sounded like thunder in the quiet little trailer park.

He turned off the bike and his hands went to mine, holding me in place for a few more moments. I didn't mind. I pressed my cheek against his back and closed my eyes, drinking in the scent of coconut and sweat from his body. I never wanted this to end. I hated myself for it. A few trailers away, my boyfriend was inside, probably wondering where I was. And likely fuming. But I kept my hands latched around Tucker.

I didn't want to break the silence, as if it would somehow make him disappear. He had no idea how much it meant to me that he'd confided in me the secrets of his childhood. I knew how difficult it was to reveal the uglier sides of life. It always changed people's perceptions of you; they didn't want to hear it, and who could blame them? Wouldn't everyone prefer to live in blissful ignorance?

Eventually he spoke. "Thanks for hanging out with me tonight." His fingers rubbed lightly over mine.

I didn't know how to respond. I wanted to thank him. I couldn't remember the last time I'd allowed myself to just let loose and not worry about anything—or anybody—for a night. "Thanks, I had a lot of fun. I don't remember the last time . . ." I tried to tone down the smile on my face but I couldn't. My cheeks hurt from the effort. I slipped my leg over the bike and pulled off my helmet. I ran my fingers through my hair, letting the sentence dangle.

Tucker slid off his bike and took off his helmet as well. He took mine from my hand and placed it on the bike, handing me my bag of work clothes. "I'm sorry about—"

"Don't. Please don't. Tonight was amazing. I don't want to talk about what he did."

Tucker nodded but didn't look any less upset.

"Will you be coming by again?" I couldn't help asking the question that had been on my mind since we'd left the dance floor. I didn't want to sound desperate, but my voice came out high-pitched. I braced for him to tell me that he was leaving town. I didn't expect him to stick around, and I knew it would only cause trouble if he did. Still, my heart sank as I waited for him to tell me the inevitable. I wanted to know more about him, and it seemed as if he genuinely wanted to know more about me, too. For some reason, I felt an unfamiliar urge to open the vault in which I'd stashed away years of painful memories and lay them bare before him.

He smiled and looked down at the ground, kicking the dirt with his boot. "You can't get rid of me that easily, Cass." He ran his hand through my hair and gave me a half smile.

"Great." I chewed on my lip and waved a small good-bye to him, trying to contain the happiness that suddenly washed over me as I took a few steps backward. He slipped his helmet back on and started his bike. I watched the cloud of dust whirl around him as he took off out of the parking lot.

I walked quickly to my trailer, hoping no one had seen our good-bye. I ducked behind the trailer and pulled my slacks on under my dress. After a fast look around to make sure no one was watching, I pulled my sweater off and slipped the dress over my head, replacing it with my black work polo. I tucked the small locket under my shirt. I couldn't stand to take it off. It would make this entire night seem like a figment of my imagination. I needed to have the reminder that Tucker was real, that he cared, if only for a few more minutes.

I listened for any sound coming from inside the trailer as I kicked off the new sandals and tied my sneakers on my feet. I didn't hear anything.

I opened the front door, cringing as it squeaked loudly. I snuck inside with my bag of clothes behind my back.

Jax lay on the couch, his breathing deep and steady. I let out the breath I didn't realize I had been holding. I tiptoed back down the hallway and slid my new outfit to the back of my closet. I smiled as I buried it under a few boxes. A secret memory of the perfect night. I slipped the necklace off and wrapped it inside the dress.

I quickly undressed and took a fast shower, dancing and humming the song "Loved" to myself. The water was cold, but it didn't dampen my mood in the least.

As I slipped into bed, I wondered if Tucker was thinking of me the way I was of him. Surely this night didn't even register on the list of greatest nights of his life, but for me it was at the very top.

I dreamed of dancing in that club for hours, my fingers sliding up Tucker's neck and his hands rubbing the length of my back. I pictured us with our foreheads pressed together—and suddenly pain shot through my head. In my dream, I shot Tucker an anguished look, confused, as our bodies were pulled apart.

"Get up, you fucking bitch!"

The smell of whiskey and cigarettes filled my nose, replacing the sweet smell of freedom. My hands flew to the back of my head as I struggled to pry Jackson's fingers from my hair. "Jax, let go of me!" I struggled to get my footing as he lifted me from the bed by my hair.

"Where the fuck were you?" His eyes were glazed over and bloodshot.

I knew it was no good to fight with him. My mind searched for an excuse and his hand clenched tighter. "I went out with Marla, after work." I strained to keep balanced on the balls of my feet. Jackson was a lot taller than I was.

"Marla?" He looked at me as if he didn't believe me. Why would he? Marla and I fought constantly at work. I fought with everyone. It was hard to believe anyone would put up with me more than they had to.

"Where'd you go?" He narrowed his eyes and clenched his jaw, but his grip loosened slightly.

I struggled to even out my breathing. "She took me into town. She had to go pick up her kid from his dad. I swear, Jax!"

He looked me over and seemed to believe me. His fingers slipped from my still-damp hair and I rubbed the tender spot. "I'm sorry, Cass." He pulled me into his chest. I balled my fists against him and cried silently. I wanted to run away. Where would I go? I had nowhere, nothing. Jackson had been with me since the day we'd met. I knew the way he treated me wasn't right, but at least he was always there. And he hadn't always been this way. My father had left my mom and me when I was young. Jax offered me stability and the love I so desperately craved from someone. He also protected me from the parade of boyfriends my mother had in her life. During that unstable period, it seemed that he was always there when I needed him. He was the one person who knew all of my secrets and didn't judge me for them. I cringed as I thought of how Tucker would react if I told him what my mother would do to make ends meet, or how her boyfriends would get touchy with me when she would pass out from taking drugs. Jax didn't judge me then; he never wavered. Not until he started using. How could I leave him now, when he needed me the most? The good guy that he once was, was still in there somewhere; I tried to remind myself of that every day. He just needed me to help him find his way back. Maybe he just needed me to help him fly.

I relaxed and let my arms slip around his sides. He had every right to hate me right now, even if he didn't know the truth.

We slept in my bed with his arms wrapped tightly around me. I felt as if I couldn't breathe in his embrace. What had I done? I had run off with a guy who saw me as some sort of project. Maybe it was pity I saw in his eyes, not the sense of longing that surely reflected in mine. This was where I belonged. In this trailer, in Jax's arms. My fate had already been written, and some guy on a motorcycle was not going to swoop in and rescue me. This wasn't a fairy tale. This was my life. No matter how much I fucking hated it, it was of my own creation, and it was mine.

The next morning I awoke to a steady thumping of a headache. The back of my head was sore and throbbing with a constant dull, aching reminder of how I'd lied to Jax. I couldn't tell him the truth, of course. I couldn't afford the hospital visit.

I slipped out of his grip and made my way down to the small bathroom. I tried the handle but it was locked.

"Mom!" I banged on the door with the palm of my hand. "Mom! Open the fucking door. Some of us have jobs we gotta get to." I waited, my arms crossed over my chest. Nothing. "Damn it," I screamed, and kicked the door. I slipped back into my room and grabbed a clean uniform for work. I was on my last one and would need to make a trip to the Laundromat soon.

I avoided that place as much as possible. There was nothing safe about the Laundromat. All the tweakers in the neighborhood hung out there to buy or sell dope. A few weeks back, Deb from three trailers down was jumped and nearly raped. The thought made my stomach twist in knots.

I looked over at Jax, who was still sound asleep. I slid my closet open and moved the boxes around until my fingers touched the silky-soft fabric of my new dress. I couldn't help but smile. One day my closet would be full of pretty dresses like this. I just needed to work a little harder. I carefully buried it again and stood to leave my room, stopping to rub my teddy bear, which secretly held my dreams inside it.

I made my way to the kitchen to find something, anything, to eat. The top shelf of the fridge held mustard and mayonnaise. The next two shelves were empty. I closed it. "Fuck," I whispered, rubbing my hands over my face.

My mother made her way down the hall, tripping and kicking the bucket that held the dirty water from our leaky roof.

"Jesus, Mom! Look what you did!" My tone turned sympathetic when I saw her face, so sad and defeated. "I'll get a towel." I patted her on the arm and squeezed past her to the bathroom.

A needle lay on the sink next to some yellowish rubber tubing that I recognized right away. I grabbed it in my hand and went after her.

"Damn it, Mom! Damn you! You promised you would stop! You promised!" Tears poured down my face as I threw the flimsy rubber tubing at her.

She flinched as if I were throwing a punch and rested her weight against the wood paneling behind her. "I'm sorry," she slurred.

Memories of my childhood flooded my thoughts.

"I want to look like a princess!" I was excited.

"Hold still, Cassie. Mommy can't braid your hair if you keep squirming like a worm in your seat!"

I giggled as Daddy walked in through the front door. "Daddy!" I jumped from the chair, steadying my balance before running into my father's open arms. "Mommy is my fairy godmother and she's going to make me look like a princess!"

Mom laughed from behind me as my father set me back on the floor, groaning as he stretched his aching back from a long day of work at Rich-

ardson Automotive. He rubbed my head, messing up my freshly braided hair. *"That's nice, Cassie."* He made his way to the fridge and pulled out a bottle of beer. He took a long sip and leaned back against the counter.

"You get any housework done today or you too busy playing hair-dresser?" he asked my mother coldly as he took another drink.

She smiled down at me, smoothing my hair down. "I can make a good career out of hairdressin'. Women love to feel beautiful."

"Most women love to take care of their husbands." He pushed from the counter and stepped in front of my mother, grabbing her arm in his free hand. She pulled back slightly, wincing at the pain. *"Jessie said he saw you over at the grocery store talking to Robbie. You out sluttin' around on me while I'm working hard to put food on the table?"*

"Robbie has just been wondering why he hasn't seen us at church."

"Everyone knows what you've been doin'. You have no business talking to another man. You're mine, remember? Or do I need to remind you again?"

"Why don't you go find your prettiest princess dress while Mommy cooks up a feast?" She bent down to eye level with me. I giggled nervously, sensing that something had made my father upset, and gave her a quick kiss on the cheek before running down the hallway to my bedroom to find my finest dress.

"I'm sorry," I heard her quietly sob as her words faded away, echoing in my memory.

I suddenly felt sick. That look in her eye, that defeat that I remembered so clearly, suddenly became all too familiar. It was the same look I saw in the mirror every day.

CHAPTER

Seven

I BOLTED OUT THE front door. I couldn't get to work fast enough. I rubbed the tears from my cheeks as I ran, my lungs burning. I stopped dead in my tracks as I reached the edge of the dirt lot.

Tucker sat sideways leaning against his bike. I stopped, suddenly angry and unable to form any words. I was overwhelmed by the realization that I was reliving my mother's life, following in the footsteps of her volatile relationship. I had become her without even realizing it. One thing I had learned from my mother's mistakes was that I had no business talking to Tucker. I didn't need Jax to remind me to whom I belonged. My feet began to move double time now. Tucker stood and waited for me to reach him. I pushed past his shoulder and headed for the diner.

"What's wrong?" He jogged to catch up to me.

"Just go home, Tucker." I wiped my eyes again.

"Hey." He grabbed my arm gently and I flinched as he made contact with the bruises. "Sorry. I'm sorry. Did he hurt you again? Cass, tell me if he hurt you. I will go take care of him right now. He won't ever touch you again."

I stopped and took a minute to find my voice. "You hurt me.

You do." I poked him in the chest. "Why are you here? Is this fun for you, waltzing into my train wreck of a life and playing the hero?" I threw my hands up dramatically. "You like to see girls cryin' and getting knocked around?" I didn't like the idea of being someone's guest of honor at a pity party. Looking at Tucker only reminded me of everything in the world I wasn't privileged enough to have, a reminder I didn't need.

He looked at me as if I had lost my mind. I felt as if I had.

"No . . . Why would you say that, Cass? Of course I don't want to hurt you. I want to help you." He reached for me but I put my hands up to keep him back.

"You're not a knight on a white horse who can whisk me away to fairyland and save me, Tucker. You're just some prick on a motorcycle who'll disappear as quickly as he came. My life isn't your problem." I swallowed hard as I prepared for a low blow. "I'm not your mom."

He flinched at my words. He threw up his hands in defeat, dropping a small piece of paper onto the ground.

"Have it your way, sweetheart." He walked back to his bike and turned to face me, "I'm only walking away because it's what you want. I'd never do anything you didn't want, Cass. I don't want to hurt you, and if that's what I'm doing right now, then I will gladly leave you alone." He turned away from me and straddled his motorcycle, starting it angrily. It roared to life and he took off, leaving me in a cloud of dirt, confusion, and sadness.

"Just fucking great," I mumbled as I kicked a pile of gravel and picked up the small stub of paper. The front read Damaged. It was a concert ticket for tonight in Savannah. Could this day get any worse? I shoved it in my apron and forced myself to forget Tucker ever rode into this town. He would be gone before I knew it anyway.

"Hey, Larry," I yelled as I made my way into the diner. Larry looked out the kitchen window at me and gave me a nod. I cranked the radio and began rolling the silverware. We didn't have any customers yet . . . at least none I hadn't run off.

I sang along as I rushed through my busywork. A few minutes later, Larry appeared with two hot plates full of eggs and toast.

"Thanks," I said, giving him a smile. He nodded but didn't smile back.

I devoured every bite.

"Jesus, Cass. You ain't knocked up now, are ya?" He laughed, but I knew he was seriously asking.

"Fuck, Larry. No. I'm not pregnant. You have to actually have sex to get knocked up." I rolled my eyes and popped the last bite of toast in my mouth. I couldn't remember the last time Jax and I had been together, and I was thankful for that. I no longer had a say in the matter, and the only thing that saved me was his ramped-up drug abuse.

"Why are you still with that worthless boyfriend of yours? He ain't no good."

As if Larry were telling me something I didn't know. But it wasn't any of his business. I shrugged and grabbed both of our plates and took them to the kitchen. I washed them up quickly and set them on the drying rack.

It wouldn't be long before people started rolling in for coffee. The bell above the door chimed, and I threw the old dishrag onto the sink and made my way back out onto the floor.

A woman sat in a booth with her son. I didn't recognize them. More people who took the wrong exit off the highway. I plastered on my biggest fake smile and grabbed a couple of menus. We didn't have kid menus, but I had made it a point to pick up a couple of coloring books and packs of crayons from the dollar store. It made the kids happy and less likely to make a mess.

"Good morning and welcome to Aggie's Diner. My name is Cass and I'll be your server today. Can I start you off with something to drink?" I gave the boy a wink and handed him the crayons. His face lit up. He looked to be about five years old. I remembered how great life was at that age, so full of promise. It goes downhill quickly.

"I'll have an orange juice and chocolate milk for him." She didn't even look at me. This was going to be a great day.

I rolled my eyes as I headed off to the kitchen to get their drinks. The bell above the door went off repeatedly before I could take the beverages out to my customers. I stuck my head out of the kitchen door and my jaw went slack. The diner was filling up. I glanced back at Larry, who shrugged his shoulders.

I grabbed the glasses and took them out to my table. I got their order and moved on to the next table. The diner was never this busy on a weekday. The diner was never this busy period.

We called in Marla about an hour later just to help deal with the crowd. She was the definition of white trash, and we didn't get along well. Her hair was a crispy, frizzy bleach blond with dark roots; her skin was tanned orange and looked like leather. We split the diner into sections. Most of our guests were twentysomething. I hardly had the patience to deal with this obnoxiously loud crowd. If I ever needed more proof that the universe viewed me as some sort of cosmic joke, the message was received loud and clear.

As I was clearing off a table, I overheard the girls beside me talking about the Damaged concert tonight. That explained why we had such a crazy crowd today. I slipped my hand into my apron pocket, feeling the ticket that Tucker had dropped on the ground earlier.

"I know, third row center. Tucker White will be practically right in front of us," a girl gushed.

That stopped me cold. I moved over to their table and asked if they needed any refills on their drinks.

They declined.

"I'm sorry, did I hear you say Tucker White?" I tried to keep my voice even.

"Yeah, the lead singer in Damaged. He is way fucking hot." The girl turned back to her friends as they all continued to talk about how they planned to sneak backstage after the show and sleep with Tucker.

I backed away from the table and tried my best not to run as I made my way to the bathroom. I closed the door and leaned over the sink trying to process this new information. I felt as if I had been punched in the stomach. Why hadn't he told me?

I turned on the sink and splashed some cold water on my face. It didn't matter. I was sure Tucker hated me now following my outburst this morning. And I had a boyfriend and a life that was a million miles from his, even if he was right up the road tonight.

I chewed on my lip as I stared at my reflection. No matter what I thought of myself, Tucker clearly saw something else. I leaned in closer. I didn't see it, didn't understand it, but I wanted to know what it was. I thought about the glimpse into Tucker's childhood. He hadn't needed to confide in me, to trust me, but he did. I'd avoided telling anyone about my past, afraid to be judged. But he'd laid it all on the line for me in hopes I would do the same, and instead I blew him off, doing exactly what I feared he would do to me. Suddenly I knew I needed to see him again. I needed to know why he didn't tell me who he really was—why trust me with his tortured past but keep from me this huge detail about his current life? But most important, I needed him to know he hadn't made a mistake by telling me his secret.

I suddenly felt that fate was intervening and Tucker was meant to be in my life somehow.

I did my best to keep myself busy for the rest of the afternoon. The concert was three hours away. If I worked my ass off, maybe I could convince Marla to finish out the night for me. I could give her my tips from the day. It was a great deal of money. The most I ever made in a single shift, but it felt worth it to me. After this show, Tucker would be off on another adventure. If I wanted to see him, tonight was my last chance. My only chance. Time to fly in hopes I wouldn't fall.

In between tables I did my busywork, filling salt and pepper shakers and rolling silverware. When the clock hit seven, I couldn't wait any longer.

"Marla, I know you're probably dead on your feet, but I was wondering if you could take my shift. I know I'm asking a lot. I can give you all of my tips. I made nearly one hundred dollars." I was practically begging at her feet.

She gave me a sour look and didn't answer me for a moment.

I lost all hope.

"All your tips?"

I grinned from ear to ear and wrapped my arms around her neck. "Thank you! Thank you so much!"

I dashed out of the diner as quickly as possible. Heading across the dirt lot, my head was spinning. I had no idea what I was thinking. I was sure he didn't want to see me after the way I'd treated him earlier.

As I headed to my trailer, I slipped behind it and listened for anyone inside. I could hear my mother and Jackson in the living room. My bedroom was down the hall. I could get in and out without anyone noticing if I was quiet.

I slipped open the tiny window to my bedroom. I grabbed an old crate that was lying in the yard and set it underneath the window. I wasn't sure it could support my weight, but there was no other way.

I stepped up and grabbed hold of the sill. I pulled my body halfway through the window. I suddenly realized that if anyone saw me, that person would think I was a burglar since I was dressed from head to toe in black. I wiggled through the tiny space and quietly tumbled onto my bed below. I lay perfectly still, waiting for someone to burst through the door to see what was going on. I held my breath and waited. Nothing.

I rolled off the bed and dug around in my closet until I found the bag with my new dress and sandals. I changed as quickly as I could, running my fingers through my hair. I slipped the tiny locket around my neck, letting my finger linger on the metal heart for a moment. I grabbed my work clothes and shoved them into the bag, then dropped it out the window to the ground below.

I grabbed my teddy bear off the dresser and pulled out enough money for a cab and change for the pay phone. I couldn't get the stupid grin off my face. I was excited—happy even. I slipped out the window and lowered myself onto the crate. I grabbed my bag of work clothes and tucked it under the skirting of the trailer.

CHAPTER

Eight

I REACHED THE PAY phone at the corner of the lot. I called a cab and waited, shifting my weight nervously from one foot to the other. It seemed like a lifetime. What was I doing? He wouldn't want to see me after all the things I'd said to him this morning. With all of those pretty girls screaming his name, would he even acknowledge my existence?

I convinced myself to head back home. If I hurried, I could pick up the end of my shift and maybe make a few dollars. As I began walking across the lot, a car behind beeped its horn. I jumped and spun around to see a yellow cab.

A smile immediately appeared on my face and without a second thought I walked over and slid into the backseat. "I need you to take me to the Savannah Theatre on Bull Street."

The cabdriver nodded and pulled off into the night. My heart was racing. There was no turning back now. I didn't know what I was going to say to Tucker, but I would figure that out when I was looking him in the eye. This was the craziest thing I had ever done in my life. I had never been to a concert. I could never afford it. In so many ways, this was a dream come true.

Savannah was more crowded than usual. The streets were

flooded with visitors and concertgoers. My eyes scanned the front of the old building with the huge neon sign that read SAVANNAH. The giant marquee that spanned the entire front of the building read DAMAGED in large, red letters. My gaze drifted lower, taking in the group of people that crowded the street outside the theater. The men wore faded and tattered jeans with vintage-style T-shirts with catchphrases on them, just like Tucker. The women all wore next to nothing, hoping to catch the eye of one of the band members. Miniskirts and belly-baring shirts were the dress code for the night. I looked down at my dress and realized I was the most conservatively dressed. The excitement in the air was palpable. Everyone was smiling, and the hum of excited concertgoers could be heard from inside the cab. "Ten fifty-seven," the cabbie called over his shoulder as he rolled to a stop. I slipped him $15 and told him to keep the change. At this moment, money was the least of my concerns. I couldn't take my eyes off the outside of the theater as I slid out of the car. I don't think I had ever seen so many people in one place at a time.

I held the dirty ticket in my hand, clutching it for dear life as I crossed the busy street. I wasn't a crowd-type person, and I could feel my heart rate kick into double time.

I stood in line and stared down at the ticket. Maybe this was a mistake. Maybe I should just go home. The crowd inched forward. Why would he want to see my face ever again after what I'd said to him? My mind went back to the bar just a few blocks away. I had to risk seeing him again. I couldn't let him leave town thinking that I didn't care. I wasn't sure what was going on in my heart for this boy, but if nothing else—and despite the nagging guilt that I still felt because of it—I knew I cared. More than a little bit.

"Ticket." The lady behind the counter held out her hand.

"Oh . . . here." I held out my ticket.

"Front row, center. Enjoy your concert." She gave me a weak smile.

I beamed back at her. I felt like Cinderella going to the ball. In my new dress, I almost blended in with the crowd. I still felt as if I wore a big sign on my forehead that said WHITE TRASH, but it didn't matter. Tonight I was actually living instead of just surviving. It felt good. I knew Tucker didn't care about that, and I was here only for him.

I shuffled in the doors with a mob of fans, shouting and laughing with one another. It was crowded and hot, and I was beginning to get light-headed from all the excitement. Looking around me, I felt as if I had been abducted by aliens and dropped on a foreign planet. The women had expertly been made up as if they were walking a red carpet, and the guys all smelled as if they had been dipped in a vat of cologne and hair gel.

I made my way into the room and followed the others to the very front. I was practically on the small stage that curved across the front of the giant room. There was no way Tucker could miss me. I hoped I wasn't making a complete fool out of myself. More often than not, I did. The theater, a beautiful, historic fixture in the city, was a major tourist attraction. But the inside was unexpectedly modern, with rows of seating and an open area in the front that served as a dance floor for concertgoers. Heavy, crimson curtains flanked the stage, as if a dramatic play were about to take place rather than a rock concert.

The girls around me were giddy with excitement. All they talked about was having sex with Tucker or the Twisted Twins, as they called Chris and Terry. Hearing them talk about Tucker in this way made my stomach turn. *I shouldn't be here.* Obviously, I had no idea what being a rock star entailed. Why did I even care if he slept with a different woman every night? *I have a boyfriend.* Jax would never talk to me again if he discovered I'd run off, especially if he knew where to. And how much tip money I'd given up to be here, money we all sorely needed. A palpable sense of panic spread throughout every cell of my body. Suddenly I turned to leave, hoping that Jackson was passed out somewhere and I could make it back to the trailer before he woke up. *I knew this was a bad idea.*

Just as I began pushing through the crowd to make my great escape, the lights dimmed and everyone around me went off like firecrackers. The crowd was deafeningly loud. I spun around to face the stage.

A local singer took the stage. He wore a knitted, olive-green sweater and worn-out khakis. He would have looked as if he had just stepped out of a college classroom if not for his scraggly beard. He sat on stool in the middle of the stage with an acoustic guitar on his lap and began to play a quiet tune. His song was sad but somehow managed to put a smile on my face. The crowd hushed as his voice quieted to barely a whisper. It was magical to watch such a large group of people fall under someone else's spell. I became lost in my own memories of loss and pain as one song bled into the next. Before I knew it, the crowd was applauding and the man got up from his seat with a quick nod of his head and left the stage. The spell had been broken. I cheered along with the other fans, swept up in the excitement.

Then the Twisted Twins emerged from the darkness behind the stage, guitars in hand. They were clad in grunge gear that was ripped and torn. They wore more jewelry than I even owned, but somehow made it look masculine and even tough. They looked nothing like the men who had sat in my diner. A few moments later, another guy came out and sat at the drums. I had never before seen him. His hair was buzzed short and he was stockier than the other band members. He was shirtless and missing the trademark tattoos of his bandmates.

As loud as the crowd had been before, the sound paled in comparison to the noise they made as Tucker finally walked onto the stage. He had his jeans slung low and wore a baby-blue T-shirt that read GROUPIE.

He walked to the center of the stage and grabbed the microphone.

"Hello, Savannah!" He smiled, revealing those sexy dimples as his eyes scanned the crowd. They paused when they reached me, and for a second I forgot how to breathe. "Hello, sweetheart," he said quietly, just to me. The girls around me went wild, absolutely certain that he was speaking to them. I didn't care. I was too busy begging my heart to start beating again as I couldn't help but let a megawatt smile spread across my face.

The twins began to strum on their guitars. The room grew louder as the audience's anticipation mounted, then the crowd suddenly quieted down when Tucker stepped to the microphone.

Tucker began to sing, and I didn't understand how I hadn't recognized his beautiful voice sooner. The lyrics were beautiful, talking about staying with the person he no longer wanted for one more night. The song was incredibly catchy, and I felt myself swaying my hips with the crowd. It reminded me of our night of dancing, and I blushed when his eyes flicked down to mine, indulging in the fantasy of him and me. I wanted to be that girl he sang about, the love he lived his entire life for.

The song ended and blended perfectly into the next. He sang about having to say good-bye, a surprisingly upbeat tune given the subject. He danced a little as he sang, and I imagined my body pressed up against his as it was the night before.

I was lost in his voice, in the fantasy of it all. Music had always been a great escape for me, but this was surreal. Being front and center at a live concert, and at a show headlined by someone I knew, was magical. His heart and soul poured into the lyrics of his music. I listened as if I had never heard them before, the words taking on new meaning after knowing the kind of childhood he'd had.

When his eyes would meet mine, I felt as if we were the only two people in the theater, his words meant for only me to hear. I was happy. Genuinely happy, and I never wanted this moment to end.

The next song was slower, and Tucker sat down on a stool, taking a long sip from a water bottle before singing. The room dimmed and only a soft light illuminated him. He began to sing of being sad, his eyes closed as the room fell silent. I didn't recognize it. The crowd swayed around me as Tucker poured his heart out to us, judging eyes be damned. I wished I had the bravery it took for him to sit upon that stool and expose his soul to the world.

As the song ended, he slowly opened his eyes and grinned nervously. I cheered and clapped with everyone else. He stood and the next song began. Everyone clapped together with the beat as Tucker poured his heart and soul into each song, each lyric. The lights flickered and danced off him. He looked completely in his element.

The last song wound down and the lights brightened around us. Tucker shot me a wink and held up his finger to let me know he would be a minute. I was grinning like a fool now. It was as if I had stepped into someone else's life. I never wanted to wake up.

I was getting pushed and jostled by girls eager to meet anyone in the band that they could. Tucker's bandmates all took a moment to sign shirts and CD cases for the fans in the front row. It was amazing to see how dedicated their fans were and how open and exposed Tucker was. He reemerged, beaming from ear to ear, and thanked every fan he met. Suddenly, it dawned on me that the woman at the bar last night had wanted his autograph, not his phone number. I had always thought the worst of people, and it had never occurred to me that not everyone had an agenda. I'd been judging Tucker from the moment he stepped into the diner, and none of it was deserved. When he finally reached me, he smiled as he put a hand on either side of my waist and lifted me effortlessly over the metal barrier that kept the fans out. My skin burned under his fingertips, and warmth radiated throughout my body.

The crowd hooted and hollered as he set me down in front of him, his fingers never leaving my sides, and whispered in my ear so I could hear him over the crowd.

"I'm glad you came, Cass." His breath tickled my ear and sent a shiver down my body. I couldn't stop smiling; my cheeks hurt as if the muscles had never before been used.

"Why didn't you tell me?" I leaned in closer, standing on my toes so I could speak into his ear. I took a deep breath, taking in his coconut scent.

He motioned with his head for me to follow him. He grabbed my hand, entwining our fingers as he pulled me behind him. We worked our way around the rest of the band members, who were still signing autographs, and slipped through a door at the far side of the stage.

"I didn't want you to look at me like they do." He nodded his head toward the crowd on the other side of the door, the deafening sounds behind it now muffled.

"I wouldn't." I tucked my hair behind my ear as I let out a nervous laugh. "I would have been just as bitchy." One side of his lip curled into a smile but he didn't respond. "This is really amazing, Tucker. All of this success."

"We're just starting out really." He shrugged. "Still paying our dues."

"It's only a matter of time before you're playing the big stages all over the world."

"They're all the same."

"Still, better than being stuck in one place for the rest of your life."

"I don't want to talk about the band." Tucker tipped up my chin so I'd look into his eyes.

We were standing so close that I could feel the heat radiating off his body. The mood suddenly shifted to serious as my heart began to thud in my chest at his proximity. "I'm sorry about—"

Tucker pressed his finger against my lips. "It doesn't matter. Why would you trust some guy who rides into your life on a motorcycle demanding a beer? I told you I like the challenge, sweetheart." He pulled his finger away and quickly swiped his thumb across my lower lip. His eyes fell to them.

I smiled, hoping I wouldn't wake up from this dream anytime soon.

"It's nice to see you smile," he whispered as he leaned in closer. My breath hitched.

"Hey, man, that was a killer set." One of the Twisted Twins patted Tucker on the back as he walked past us.

Tucker hung his head and laughed. "Yeah, man. Thanks." His eyes followed his bandmate as he walked down the hall and disappeared. Tucker's eyes drifted back to mine, looking as if he were just busted with his hand in the cookie jar. "Did that asshole give you any trouble when you got home last night?"

"No." I shook my head, cringing at the memory of his standoff with Jax . . . and at his use of the word *asshole*. I didn't want him to worry about me any more than he already had . . . and I couldn't help but feel a lingering sense of loyalty to Jax, especially in light of my recent lies to him regarding my whereabouts.

"Does he do that a lot?"

"He does it enough." I sighed.

I watched the muscles in Tucker's jaw jump under his skin. "I should have kicked his ass in the diner."

"No, you shouldn't have. It would have made things worse for me."

Tucker's eyes narrowed at mine as he struggled not to let his anger get the best of him.

"When do you leave?" The question had plagued my thoughts since he'd stepped into the diner, though I would never have admitted it.

"We leave town tonight." His face turned serious.

The air rushed from my lungs as he spoke. I don't know why I cared, but I did. The harsh reality in those four words hit me hard, and the disappointment that sank into my stomach made me suddenly nauseated.

"I'm glad I got to meet you, Tucker." My words carried more weight than I cared to admit.

His fingers twisted in my hair and our good-bye hung heavy in the air. "I bet I could fill an album with songs about you . . . if we could just have some more time together. . . ." The subtle sadness in his voice did not escape me.

Everything had become too real. Maybe I should have just let him leave and pretended he was nothing more than a figment of my overactive imagination.

"I should get home. Someone is going to notice I'm gone. I just wanted to apologize for the way I acted earlier." I needed to escape. The hall suddenly felt narrow and I couldn't breathe. *I knew I shouldn't have come. What did I think would happen? That he would stay for me? For a girl with a junkie boyfriend and a dead-end diner job?*

He didn't say anything, just nodded and backed away. "I'll call you a cab. I have to stay here, help the guys, but I'd like to see you before I leave." His eyes looked sad, but he kept a small smile on his lips.

I knew I should have said no. I should have said good-bye and walked away, made a clean break. But instead I smiled weakly. "Third trailer on the right. My window is on the side."

He pulled out his cell phone and called for a ride home for me.

CHAPTER

Nine

$\mathcal{I}$T SHOULD BE here in a minute. I'll walk you out the back to avoid the fans," he said as he hung up his cell. He slid his hand onto my lower back and guided me through the hall to a service door. He paused before pushing it open. "I'm really glad I got to meet you, Cass." He was saying his good-byes. The thought tied my stomach in knots once again.

I swallowed hard and pushed through the door. I couldn't say good-bye. I knew I might not get a chance to thank him for making me smile tonight, but I couldn't find the right words. It was too hard.

Tucker followed me, waiting by my side for the cab to arrive. He slipped his hand around mine and laced our fingers together, but didn't say a word.

The cab pulled up and Tucker's grip tightened around my hand. I looked up at him, taking in his beautiful face one last time before pulling my hand away and slipping into the backseat.

Tucker handed the cabdriver some cash and gave him directions to my place. He paused to look at me before standing up and taking a step back. I stared at him through teary eyes as the cab pulled out of the dark ally. I had had my escape. And now it was time for me to go back to reality.

The driver occasionally glanced at me in his mirror but never said a word as I cried silently. I was thankful. I wasn't one to share my feelings with anyone, let alone a stranger.

The trip back seemed twice as fast as the one to the concert, and I was immediately filled with regret when we reached Aggie's Diner. I should have said something to Tucker, anything. I was afraid it would make our good-bye real. But it was happening whether I wanted it to or not.

I thanked the driver and slid out into the now-empty parking lot of the diner. The concert crowd had moved on, and life was back to normal. Sadness crept over me as I realized that, starting tomorrow, I would resume my old life exactly where I had left off a few days before. The fantasy was officially over.

I sighed as I kicked at the dirt, making my way through the fence to the trailer park. The neighborhood was quiet. My nerves began to get the better of me as I drew closer to my place. I had pissed Jackson off many times in the past, but there was no telling what he would do if he found out that I had lied to him to see another man, even if that man was a rock god, not a lover.

I found my hidden bag of clothing and quickly slipped my pants on under my dress. I glanced around before pulling the shirt down over me and wiggled free of my dress. I switched out my shoes and carefully opened my bedroom window, slipping the bag inside. This was it. Moment of truth. If he knew, I deserved what I had coming to me.

I ran my hands through my hair a few times and twisted it back into a bun. I took a few deep breaths before making my way to the front door and slipping inside. Jax was passed out on the couch, the television still on. I grabbed the remote and clicked the OFF button.

"Cass?" Jackson's voice called behind me, causing me to jump.

"Yeah?" I didn't turn to face him. I was terrified that he knew where I had been.

"How was work?" He stretched and yawned. I slowly turned to face him.

"Good. It was good. Not as many tables as I would have liked." I begged the tears in my eyes to go away.

He nodded and placed his arm over his face to fall back asleep. I let out the breath I was holding and made my way back to my bedroom with my hand over my chest, secretly feeling for the locket that lay under the material. I closed the door quietly behind me and slid down to the floor, hugging my knees.

I didn't feel good about lying to Jackson. I knew he wasn't the best thing for me, but he had always been there. He was the one constant I had in my life, and I had betrayed his trust. At the same time, I was starting to realize that there was more out there than this. I wanted to escape, to spread my wings. Unfortunately, Tucker was going to be gone before I knew it. It was foolish to get my hopes up for anything more, but I was dangerously close to letting him in, to entertaining the idea of what-if. But Tucker was a wild card, a rock star whose life was a constant adventure, and it was Jax who had never left me after all of these years, no matter how tough times had gotten. One thing was for certain—being alone terrified me more than any of Jackson's outbursts. I'd seen my mother fall to pieces when my father left her, and I didn't think I would be any stronger.

I stood and grabbed my bag from the bed, slipping it into its hiding spot in my closet. I took off my locket and carefully placed it inside the bag. I pulled off my work clothes and headed for the bathroom.

I took the longest shower I could stand in the cold water. It felt good after the warmth of the crowded concert. But it didn't wash away my guilt, which clung to me stronger than ever now that I'd lied to Jackson's face again. As I replayed the night over and over in my mind, I began to feel insecure. I wasn't sure anymore if Tucker actually liked me or if he just felt sorry for me. I shook the idea from my head and turned off the water, letting myself shiver a minute before drying off. I pulled on a pair of red flannel pajama pants and a red tank top.

When I got back to my room, I slipped under my covers and curled into a ball. Tucker would soon be gone. I didn't need to think about it anymore. Life would go back to being what it had always been: a big disappointment.

I dreamed all night that I was in a great concert hall sitting front and center. The lights were dimmed and a small spotlight lit the center of the stage. Tucker sat on a wooden stool in front of me, singing his heart out. I couldn't take my eyes off him as he let his own flutter closed, his face full of emotion that flowed out in the lyrics he sang. It was the only place in the world I wanted to be. I had had a taste of what life could be like and I wanted it.

I awoke to the sound of a gentle knock on my bedroom window. I sat up, terrified at first as I pushed the mess of still-damp hair from my face. I squinted in the dark, trying to make out the shadowy figure on the other side of the glass. My heart thudded in my chest as my eyes adjusted to the lack of lighting.

I slid across my bed and pushed the window open. "Tucker, I didn't think you would come," I whispered, a smile instantly lighting up my face.

He looked indignant, as if the option not to show had never crossed his mind. "I said I would, Cass. I'm a man of my word."

"Where I'm from, what a man says and what a man does are two different things."

"Maybe it's time to get a new view."

"I don't mind the view I have right now." I blushed at my own forwardness.

"Did anyone notice you were gone?" He glanced past me.

I shook my head no. I knew he was worried that Jax would lose it if he'd realized I'd ditched work. It was sweet of Tucker to care, but I could take care of myself.

He smiled and pulled a small sliver of paper from his pocket. "This is my cell number. I want you to call me if you ever need anything. Even if you just want to talk."

I took the small piece of paper from his fingers and held it against my chest.

He smiled, his eyes locked onto mine. "Oh, I almost forgot." He dug through his pocket again and pulled out a small, white square with the word *Damaged* written in big, bold letters across it.

I took it from his fingers and examined the concert ticket, furrowing my brow.

"We play in two nights at Tybee Island. It's not far from here. I was hoping you could make it?"

I had been to Tybee once when I was younger. The beautiful island had a giant pier that jutted out into the ocean. As a girl, it had made me feel as if I were on the edge of the world. "I'll try." I dug my teeth into my bottom lip. It would be almost impossible to make it to the island and back without someone's noticing I was gone.

He smiled and slipped his hand over mine. His touch sent a jolt of electricity that shot straight to my chest. "This isn't good-bye, Cass. This is only the beginning." His fingers slowly pulled back and he swallowed hard. "I have to go." His hand rubbed through his messy hair again.

There was so much more I wanted to say, but I couldn't find the words. "Two days." I smiled, wondering why my gut had suddenly twisted with sadness.

He flashed me another perfect grin, his teeth bright white in the dark. He turned and walked out of the trailer park. I watched him disappear through the fence and waited until the faint roaring of his motorcycle faded away.

I slid my window closed and fell back on my bed, clutching the ticket and the phone number to my chest. I glanced over at my bear, wondering how much money it would take for a cab ride to Tybee. It would cut into my savings, but part of me didn't care. I deserved another escape from my pathetic life. I took the ticket and slipped it into the hole in the back of my bear. I folded up Tucker's number as small as I could and placed it in the locket in my closet before settling back into bed and drifting off to sleep.

The arms around my waist tightened as his steady breathing blew across my cheek from behind.

"What time is it?" I groaned, not wanting to open my eyes to the sunlight that streamed through the window behind me.

"Too early."

I chuckled and snuggled farther into his grip. "You have to go back out to the couch before my mom wakes up."

"Just a little longer." He ground his hips into me from behind.

I blinked several times, waiting for the alarm clock to come into focus. "We're gonna be late for school."

"Then we better make it quick, sweetheart." Tucker pulled me onto my back and positioned his body over mine.

My alarm beeped angrily in my ear. I groaned and reached my arm out, trying desperately to make it stop. My fingers nudged it off the edge of the stand and it clattered to the floor but continued to beep.

"Fuck!" I pulled my pillow over my head, trying to block out the noise, but it didn't work. I sighed and pushed myself from the bed, taking a moment to steady myself before picking up my alarm and switching it off. I ran my hand over my face. I had to get ready for work.

I trudged to the kitchen and dug through the cupboards for some coffee. I prepared the filter in the coffeepot and poured in a heaping scoop of coffee. As I waited for it to finish, I rummaged through the cupboards for something to eat. I decided on a can of corned-beef hash. I emptied the contents into a bowl and popped it into the microwave. I watched the timer count down as I thought about the previous night. Tucker's face in my window, illuminated by the lone streetlight off at the edge of the park.

The microwave dinged and I jumped, glancing over at the couch. Jax stirred and I quickly grabbed the bowl. It was steaming hot and I cursed under my breath as I set it down on the stove below.

I grabbed a dish towel and slid it carefully under the bowl. Digging through the silverware drawer, I grabbed a spoon. I took a small bite, burning the roof of my mouth. "Ow! Jesus fuck!" I pulled open the fridge and grabbed the ketchup, squeezing it over my food. I picked up the bowl and headed into the living room, sitting down carefully on the squeaky recliner.

I stirred my food as I watched Jax sleep. My heart broke again as I thought about my dishonesty. He wasn't always so . . . mean. When he and I first met, it was in the ninth grade. My family had never had money, and my clothes came from thrift stores and church donations. I was incredibly self-conscious, knowing that my worn sweaters stood out from my peers' tight jeans and trendy tops that revealed just enough midriff to catch the boys' eyes. I just focused on staying under the radar, but trying to keep to myself only made me a prime target for bullies. One day in class my art teacher handed out a list of supplies for a project. When she reached my desk, she patted my shoulder and let me know, in a loud whisper, that she would help me get the items on my list if I couldn't afford them. The room suddenly buzzed with snickers, with one of my classmates muttering, "There's like five bucks' worth of stuff on this list. Seriously, Cass?" I just put my head down.

After the class ended and I slunk to my locker, a boy named Brandon came up behind me and knocked my books out of my hand as everyone stood around laughing. He told me not to worry, that Ms. Jenkins would pick them up for me since I was her favorite charity case. Jax came up behind him, shoving him hard across the hall. Brandon's head cracked off the white subway tiles that lined the corridor. Everyone fell silent. Jax grabbed my books and handed them back to me, apologizing for Brandon as his eyes scanned the crowd, daring someone else to say something. It was the first time anyone had stood up for me. Jax and I had never spoken before that day. He was popular and handsome, even though his family was every bit as poor as mine. The girls seemed to fall all over themselves in his presence, and it was easy to see why. His eyes were a bright and vibrant green, his hair was cut short, and he looked amazing in anything he wore, even if it was a hand-me-down or thrift-store find. But the sexiest thing about him was his confidence, his I-don't-give-a-shit attitude.

We were inseparable after that moment. He taught me how to fish, and I taught him how to get free snacks from the vending machine at the mall. He stood up to the many men my mother brought into the house, even once punching one in the nose for trying to cop a feel. I used to joke that he was my knight in shining armor. I truly believed he was sent by some higher power to protect me, just like in the Disney movies I used to watch as kid. I didn't realize that I would eventually need to be protected from him.

When his mother developed a cocaine habit, he began staying over more and more. My mother didn't care. She was thankful to have a man helping out around the house again. She took me to get put on the pill at sixteen. Having one child was too much responsibility for her, and she certainly couldn't handle a grandchild. We were barely scraping by, but she was still optimistic that things would work out for us.

Eventually, Jackson stopped leaving altogether and became a permanent fixture in our home, a two-story row house on the outskirts of Savannah. My father had left us just before my seventh birthday, with only the clothes on his back. My mother left his belongings strewn about the place as if he had just stepped out for coffee. Jackson and I were joined at the hip. My mother made him sleep on the couch, but I would sneak out of my room at night just to lie by his side whenever I would have a nightmare. He would hold me, stroking my hair until I would drift back to sleep. Some nights, I would sneak out just to be in his arms. My heart would race just from his holding me, but like many things, it soon wasn't enough. Our cuddle sessions became make-out sessions in which he taught me how to kiss like the women on television. Jax was much more experienced in life than I was, and that included sexually.

When I became sick with the flu over my seventeenth birthday, he took care of me, missing school for a week to make sure I was okay. He even took me to an urgent-care clinic to get medicine, reassuring me that he would pay for it. When I finally began to feel better, I decided to let him know just how much he meant to me.

"You don't have to do this." Jax smiled devilishly as his fingers traced the waistband of my jeans, leaving my skin on fire in their wake. He had been begging me to sleep with him since we began dating.

"I want to." My voice cracked.

He laughed, his eyes lowering so he could take in my body before they met my gaze. His tongue shot out and ran over his lower lip. "You are so fucking hot."

His words were like lighting a fuse. I pressed my lips hard against his, pushing my body into him. He groaned as his hands found my hips, gripping them tightly as he struggled not to move too quickly. My lips moved against his just the way he had taught me, causing him to groan into my mouth.

"Cass, I need to know if you're serious. I won't be able to stop after much longer."

I tried my best to look confident as I trailed my hand down his stomach and over the bulge of his jeans. That was all the answer he needed.

I don't know if I ever truly knew what love was, but I knew that Jackson would be there for me. That was all I needed in that moment, and all I thought I would ever need until I met Tucker: the security of knowing Jackson would always be there for me.

But then bills began to pile up and Jackson worked two jobs to try to keep us afloat. He washed dishes at a chain restaurant in town and also fixed cars. He was a great handyman. Unfortunately, his little beat-up car had broken down for good, and he no longer had a way to get to work. My mother styled hair out of our living room, but few people we knew could afford to get their hair done. I worked bagging groceries at the local Piggly Wiggly, but people rarely tipped and it wasn't enough to make a dent in our bills. We needed to make a change if we wanted to keep ourselves above water.

Jackson found us this trailer and got us a good deal on the rent. I started working at the diner and was able to make just enough to keep a roof over our heads. A leaky roof, but shelter nonetheless. We both dropped out of high school in order to get more hours on the job. College was never an option, and it no longer made sense to spend eight hours a day in classes. Shortly after we settled into our new home, Jax began to run with the locals. He took up selling drugs as a way to help support us. I hated the idea, but the money was better than from any other job we could find locally. Eventually, he gave in to temptation and began to use himself, burning up any profit he made.

My mother always hid her feelings in a bottle of alcohol or pills. She soon became Jax's partner in crime. Life didn't change overnight. I think that is why I didn't protest against it sooner. Everyone was looking for an escape from reality. I couldn't blame them. Getting high occasionally didn't seem like such a bad thing. Unfortunately, getting high in the evening soon became using first thing in the morning. Jax grew distant, finding his companionship in a pipe instead of with me. Soon we barely spoke, and when we did, we would usually argue. It took three solid months until drug abuse became physical abuse. By then I was already in too deep.

I stood in the doorway, pleading with him not to buy more drugs. I knew he was getting angry and was not in his right mind, but I stood in his way.

"Please don't do this anymore, Jax." I braced myself in the doorframe as he inched closer, sweat coating his skin.

"Baby, I just need to catch a buzz." He ran his hands over his face, clearly frustrated.

"You need to get clean. I can help you."

"I don't need your fucking help, Cass. I'm not a fucking kid." His eyes narrowed as he folded his arms over his chest.

"Of course not, babe. I just want things to be like they used to be." I reached out to touch his face and he knocked my hand away with such force

that I lost my footing and fell out of the doorway and onto the ground. My elbows bled after colliding with the stones below.

Jax was over me in a flash, panic in his eyes. "Fuck, Cass. Are you okay? Why do you have to keep pushing my goddamn buttons all the time. Look what you did!" He pulled me against his chest, hugging me for the first time in weeks.

I reluctantly looped my arms around his waist. It was the touch I had been craving from him. I needed that from him, from someone. "I'm sorry," I whispered into his shirt. I didn't believe he meant to hurt me. I was standing too close to the ledge. I justified it as an accident and was able to look past it.

I took a small bite of my food as Jax stirred.

"That smells good," he mumbled as he rolled over onto his side. He had removed most of his clothes last night and was only wearing a pair of dark gray boxers. The air conditioner hadn't worked since the first month we moved in, and it tended to get unbearably warm. His chest was covered in tattoos, though the designs were not nearly as beautiful and intricate as the ones on Tucker's skin, I now realized. I ducked my head, embarrassed that I was thinking of him while looking at Jax.

I had lost my appetite. "Here, take mine. I'm not really that hungry." I stood and walked toward him, holding out the bowl.

"Thanks, babe." He took the bowl and gave me a smile. I smiled back at him and turned to the kitchen to get my coffee.

"You want some?" I grabbed a mug from the counter and paused.

"Sure," he called to me, and I flipped over another mug.

As I poured the coffee, Jax snuck up behind me and slipped his hand around my waist. My body stiffened.

"Yeah, I want some," he breathed into my ear.

"Not now, Jax." I shoved him back with my hips and picked up our mugs. I turned to face him and handed him one.

"Jeez, what the fuck? You used to like it." His eyes combed over my body. I moved my free hand over my chest. I'd never said it out loud, but I'd never cared for sex with Jax once he began using. I knew it was what I had to do to keep him happy, and that was a good enough reason for me to continue. But it didn't take long before he was never happy no matter what went on in the bedroom. Over the last few years, his touch had become synonymous with nothing but pain.

The front door banged against the wall as Jax entered. I rolled over to look at my alarm clock to see it was already after three in the morning. He yelled my name as he stumbled down the hall, falling through the doorway to the bedroom. His fingers fumbled with his belt as he grinned at me wickedly.

"Not now, Jax." I groaned, pulling the pillow over my head.

He stumbled forward as he undid his button and fly, shoving his jeans over his hips. "What do you mean not now? I just scored us enough money to cover the rent and I don't deserve anything for it?"

I lifted the pillow from my face as I felt the bed sink down as he crawled over me.

"You're just going to spend it on getting high anyway," I snapped, wishing I could get just a few more hours of sleep before my shift.

His face contorted in anger as my words sank through the fog of his high. His hand came down sharply across my cheek, causing me to scream out in shock. Waves of pain radiated through my face as I struggled to push him off my body. Even high, he was twice as strong as I was. That was the day Jax stopped asking for what he wanted and decided that he could just take it from me. That was also the day I stopped living and began surviving.

"I have to get to work." I walked past him and made my way to my bedroom. He followed me, perching against the doorframe.

I slid off my pajama bottoms and pulled my tank over my head, keeping my back to him.

"I know I have been a fucking prick lately."

I nodded but didn't turn to face him. I grabbed my uniform from last night and pulled it on quickly, sitting on the edge of my bed to tie my sneakers. I felt sick. Suddenly he wanted to be nice, now that I was thinking of someone else? I pushed past him to leave. He grabbed my arm and I flinched.

His hand slipped off me and he grimaced. "I'm not going to hurt you, Cass." He looked down at his feet.

"I know," I said softly. "I have to get to work." I turned and made my way down the hall, not looking back.

CHAPTER

Ten

"HOW WAS YOUR night?" Larry was drying his hands with a dingy rag as I entered through the employee door.

"Fine." I didn't meet his gaze as I walked to the waitress station.

"Marla made a killin' last night." He was now leaning against the menu holder, judging me with his eyes.

"I had something I had to do. Laundry has been piling up." My eyes flicked to his and I glanced back down at the bin of freshly washed silverware.

"Yeah, well, you need to stop airing all of your dirty laundry in the diner. Jax is driving away business."

"I'm sorry, Larry. I'll do my best to keep him away."

Larry didn't say anything else, just walked into the kitchen and got ready for the day. I sighed, letting my shoulders sag as I hoisted the heavy gray bin and made my way to a table.

I had rolled a few dozen pieces of silverware when Larry came out of the kitchen with two plates of food. He set one down in front of me, and I gave him a small smile. I picked up a fork and poked at the yolks of my eggs.

"It's none of my business, but Jax . . ."

I shot Larry a glare.

"I know he don't always do the right thing, but he sticks around. That other guy"—Larry motioned with his fork out toward the parking lot—"he ain't the stayin' type." Larry cut a bite of ham and shoved it in his mouth, egg yolk running down his chin.

I nodded as a lump formed in my throat. I knew that. Tucker was going to be on the road, leaving this town, leaving me in his dust. I never expected anything different from him. So why was I suddenly so sad?

The bell chimed above the door. My first customer had arrived. I cleared my throat and went to the kitchen to start a fresh pot of coffee while she found a seat. I rushed back onto the floor with menu in hand.

"Welcome to Aggie's Diner. My name is—"

The woman held up her hand to stop me from talking. "Coffee. Black" was all she said, and her eyes glanced over the menu. Her hair was a deep gray and curled perfectly back into a bun. Heavyset, she had an air of superiority about her. What a bitch.

I bit my tongue and stormed off to the kitchen to get a fresh cup of coffee. I brought it out to her, resisting the urge to spill it over her lap. She gave me a smile and I tried my best to smile back.

"Have you decided?" I asked as she took a small sip from her mug and made a sour face.

"Wheat toast and strawberry jelly, please." She held her menu out for me to take but stared straight ahead. At least she used her manners.

I headed back into the kitchen. Larry had already cleared our breakfast plates and was washing them in the sink. I slipped past him and grabbed some bread for toast. He didn't say anything to me. I felt incredibly uncomfortable and worried that maybe he would tell Jax about Tucker. Not that there was really anything to tell . . . but I knew Jax wouldn't react well to news that I'd been friendly with another guy. The toast popped up, jarring me from my worried thoughts. I grabbed a few packs of strawberry jelly and made my way to my customer.

I stopped as I entered the dining area, my eyes locked on one of the Twisted Twins. He smiled, holding out a brown box. I gave him a confused look and walked to my table to drop off the toast.

I brushed my hands over my apron as I made my way to the twin. "What's this?" I looked at the box as if it might explode. He smiled and nudged it toward me. His eyes flicked to my customer, who had her back to us. I took it and he smiled, turning to leave as quickly as possible.

"Thanks." My fingers ran around the edge of the cardboard as I looked around. Larry was still in the kitchen.

I made my way to the ladies' room and locked myself inside. I sank to my knees and carefully pulled back the flaps. Inside was a beautiful bright yellow sundress. My eyes danced over the silky material as I pulled it to my chest and hugged it tightly against me.

I glanced back down at the box and saw a white envelope. Picking it up, I let the dress slip through my fingers onto my lap. I tore open the envelope and pulled out a handful of cash.

"What the fuck?" I pulled out a small sliver of paper.

> I wanted to make sure you had money for a cab.
> No excuses not to come. -Tuck

I smiled as I brought the note to my face, inhaling the light scent of coconut that lingered on the paper. I was touched by the gesture, but I didn't want his money. It felt like charity. I worked my ass off and didn't need any handouts.

I made up my mind that I was going to call him. My hand went to where the necklace should be. I sighed. With Jax in my room this morning, I didn't have a chance to grab it.

I stuffed the envelope of money into my apron and tucked the dress back into the box, folding the top closed as I made my way out of the bathroom. I slid the package under the waitress station and closed the curtain underneath so no one would see it.

My customer was glaring at me over her cup. I grabbed the pot of coffee and quickly made my way to her table. "Can I top you off?"

She held out her mug but didn't say anything. I poured her coffee and gave her the best smile I could manage before leaving her to herself. Sitting back at the far table, I continued to roll silverware as I let myself daydream about what the concert would be like at Tybee. I hadn't been to the beach in years. It was by far my favorite place in the world. It felt a million miles away from the trailer park. The water was always warm, clean. Looking out at the ocean, I always felt so free, as if I could just close my eyes and let the water carry me off to somewhere far away.

"Miss? Miss?" My customer was raising her voice in aggravation. I pushed up from my seat.

"I'm sorry. Is there something else I can get you?" I made my way quickly to her table.

"Just the check."

"Of course." I grabbed the pad out of my apron and tore off the ticket, sliding it onto the table. "Thanks again." I smiled and walked into the kitchen. I grabbed a mug and poured myself a cup of coffee, sinking back against the counter as I took a long sip.

I heard the bell above the door chime and my heart skipped a beat as I set down my mug and pushed open the kitchen door. I sighed as the mean woman made her way outside. I turned back into the kitchen, locking eyes with Larry.

He looked down and shook his head.

"Don't fucking judge me, Larry." I grabbed my coffee and headed back into the dining room, where I could be alone with my thoughts.

I made my way to the dirty table and grabbed the plate and the mug in one hand and grabbed the cash. She had left just three cents more than her bill. Just fucking great. She'd also left behind a mag-

azine, which I folded in half and slid into my apron. Was this supposed to make up for my tip?

I stormed into the kitchen and dropped the dishes in the sink.

"Holy fuck, Cass. You break it you're paying for it!" Larry had a
warning glare in his eyes.

I leaned against the sink, calming myself before I picked up
the plate and a rag and began to clean it. The door chimed and I
looked at Larry. He shook his head and went back to his kitchen
prep work. I threw down the rag and made my way into the dining
room.

It wasn't Tucker, and once again I let my heart fall in disappointment. The day continued like this. The customers seemed
meaner than usual, but I barely cared. I couldn't concentrate on
anything. All I could think about was the pretty yellow dress tucked
below the waitress station. I wanted to try it on and see what it
looked like. I wanted to see Tucker's face when he saw me in it. I
wasn't a pretty girl by any means, but it would be hard to look less
than spectacular in a dress like that. I smiled to myself.

"Clock out," Larry called from the cash register.

"But I still have to—"

"Just go home. That goofy smile you've been wearing all day is
starting to scare the shit out of me." He waved his hand toward the
door with a disgusted look on his face.

I laughed and grabbed my secret brown package, making my
way out the back door as quickly as possible. I let out a small giggle.
My hand shot up to cover my mouth as Larry shook his head in disgust.

My cheeks hurt from smiling and I wished I could hold on to
this feeling of happiness forever. But I wasn't that naïve. I knew
eventually I would wake up from this fairy tale, but I was determined to try to enjoy it while it lasted. I sighed as I made my way
through the trailer park fence. I continued past my place and
slipped between the next row of trailers.

I climbed the steps of an old green-and-white single-wide and knocked on the door. After a moment and some choice swear words, the door flew open.

"Hey, Marla. I was wondering if you might be able to take my shift tomorrow?" I smiled.

She narrowed her eyes and ran her hand through her tangled, bleached mane. "What are you up to?" She stepped down a step and crossed her arms over her chest as she blew out a puff of cigarette smoke.

"Nothing. I just need a favor. I have a mountain of laundry to catch up on and we're in desperate need of groceries." I felt sick as the lies poured out of my mouth.

"Yeah, all right. For an extra twenty." She raised an eyebrow and held out her hand.

I gritted my teeth and dug through my apron, pulling a twenty out of the white envelope.

She smiled and squeezed her fist tight. "You got yourself a deal." She walked back inside and slammed the door closed behind her.

I cursed her under my breath as I made my way back to my trailer. I made sure no one was around as I slipped my window open and slid the box inside.

I opened the front door and closed it quickly just as something came flying in my direction and smashed against the door. I pulled it back open to see my mother standing inside threatening Jackson. "What the fuck, Mama? You almost fucking killed me!"

My mom smoothed her hair as she shuffled her feet anxiously. "I didn't mean to, baby. I was aiming for Jax's head."

"Fuck you," Jax screamed from the kitchen.

"What the hell is going on?" I stepped between them as they yelled more profanities at each other.

"I just need a fix, baby, and Jax is holding out on me!"

"This is about dope?" I turned to look at Jax and back to my mother. I shook my head and took off down the hall to my room, slamming the door as hard as possible. The arguing continued as I held up the yellow dress to my body, spinning once and watching it fly out in the wind.

"*That is a perfect dress for our tea party, baby.*" *My mother always knew how to make me feel like the belle of the ball.*

I spun in a circle as I held up my pink polka-dot dress and watched the skirt fly out around me. "*Do you think you can do my hair like a princess, Mama?*"

She looked at her watch, frowning at the time. "*Daddy is gonna be home real soon. We don't want to be late for your own birthday party, do we? It's not every day a princess turns four.*" *She smiled widely as she twisted a long, blond strand of my hair around her finger.*

The front door banged off the wall and I took off down the hallway, dragging my pretty new dress behind me.

"*Where's my birthday girl?*" *my father yelled from the entry of our home. I jumped as I reached him, leaping into his arms. He caught me, spinning us around before wrapping an arm around my mother's waist and pulling her in for a kiss on the head.*

"*How was work?*" *she asked as she smoothed her vibrant blond hair and plastered on a dazzling smile.*

"*Johnson said if I keep up these hours, I'm on my way to a promotion.*"

My mother squealed, then clapped her hands over her mouth in shock.

"*Things are finally looking up for us. Let's go out and celebrate.*" *He set me on the floor and ran his hand over my hair. I quickly smoothed it down just as my mother always did to her own.* "*Get your dress on, birthday girl.*"

I pulled off my uniform, double-checking the lock on the bedroom door. I began to hum "Loved" by Damaged as I slipped the slinky dress over my head. It fit me like a glove.

A loud banging shook the door. "Cass," Jax called from the hallway. I pulled the dress over my head and shoved it into the box, throwing it into the closet. I ran my hand over my hair as I opened the door in my bra and panties.

"Hey." He smirked as he stepped closer.

I backed away and crossed my arms angrily over my chest. "What do you want?"

"Don't be mad at me, baby. I did her a favor. I didn't give her no dope, like you asked." He smiled.

He was right—why was I mad at him?

"That's because he used it all himself!" My mother was behind him in the hallway now, screaming. I rolled my eyes and shoved Jax backward out of my room, closing and locking the door. I couldn't take it any longer. Every day was more of the same. People always made promises that things would get better, but it only seemed to ever get worse. I was sick of the disappointment. Sick of the fighting.

"How was I supposed to know he was skimming the books?" My dad slammed his fork down on his plate.

My mother's eyes danced from me to my father as I took another bite of macaroni and cheese, still wearing my princess dress from my birthday party three weeks prior. I refused to take it off, except to bathe, not wanting the magic to end. I was certain that if Cinderella hadn't lost her shoe, she would still have been a princess come midnight.

"We spent three times the money we would have on that party. You said you were getting promoted, not fired." My mother clenched her jaw as she spoke, trying not to raise her voice.

My father ran a hand through his hair and slammed back his chair.

My mother reached her hand over the table, placing it on mine, and smiled brightly as tears filled her eyes. "Everything is gonna be just fine, baby. I promise."

"I know, Mama." But even then, a part of me already knew it wouldn't be.

CHAPTER

Eleven

I GATHERED UP MY laundry and shoved it in a basket along with Jax's pile of clothes, throwing the magazine my customer had left behind on top of the pile. I slipped the tiny locket around my neck and hid it under my shirt. As I made my way down the hall, the house was quiet again. When I reached the living room, I realized they were now in the back room, most likely getting high.

"I'm going to do laundry," I called back down the hall, not bothering to wait for a response.

I was glad to be under the cover of darkness so I could play with my necklace as I walked to the Laundromat on the far side of the trailer park. The ridiculous grin was plastered firmly back in place as I thought about the concert at the beach. I knew it was stupid of me to keep this fantasy going, but I finally had something to look forward to. Finally, I had a reason to wake up. It didn't matter what I thought of myself as long as Tucker looked at me as if I were perfect. I'd never felt wanted and I was determined to enjoy it as long as it lasted.

I pulled open the heavy door to the Laundromat and shoved past the people loading their machines. *One day I will have a set of these machines in my home*, I thought as I stuffed my clothes into the washer. I got some quarters from the change machine and started the load. I chewed on my lip as I held an extra dollar in my hand.

"Fuck it."

I made my way outside to the pay phone. I carefully pulled open the locket and unfolded the tiny slip of paper with Tucker's phone number on it. My heart beat out of my chest as I pressed the buttons on the phone and it rang in my ear. After four rings, I pulled the receiver away from my ear, disappointed.

"Yeah?" Tucker sounded exhausted.

My smile spread.

"Get off the phone," a woman called from the other end of the line.

My heart caught in my throat and I hung up the phone and covered my mouth with my hands. It felt as if I had just been punched in the stomach. I knew better. I fucking knew better than to believe this guy had given a second thought about me. I could feel my eyes well with tears as I struggled to swallow my emotions down. He was no one for me to cry over. I barely knew him. I put my head against the blue box surrounding the phone, hating myself.

The phone rang and I nearly jumped out of my skin. I stared at it in disbelief.

I picked it up and slowly raised it to my ear.

"Cass? Cass, are you there?" He sounded as panicked as I felt.

"Yeah." My voice was barely audible. I cleared my throat to try to speak again. "I'm here."

He sighed heavily in my ear. "Thank God. I'm sorry. That wasn't what you think."

"It doesn't matter what I think." I shook my head. I was being stupid. There was no reason for Tucker not to be able to do what he wanted with whomever he wanted.

"It matters to me, sweetheart."

I didn't know how to respond to that. No one had ever cared about my thoughts, my feelings. At least not since I was a little girl—not since Jackson had changed. In fact, it seemed the people I cared about the most only went out of their way to hurt me.

"Cass?"

I took a deep breath. "I'm here."

"She was here with the guys. They've been driving me crazy trying to get me to party with them, but I was trying to sleep." I heard him yawn.

I felt terrible. I assumed the worst of him. I always did. It was my way to keep from getting hurt. You will never be disappointed if you don't have high expectations. I'd learned that lesson long ago.

"Did you get the package?"

"Yeah . . . yeah . . . The dress is . . . beautiful. Thank you. But I can't take your money, Tucker." I dug my teeth into my bottom lip as I twisted the phone cord around my fingers.

"I know you could pay for it, but that wouldn't be fair. I invited you. You're my guest. It wouldn't be right for you to pay for the trip."

What he said made sense. I had assumed the worst again. He was just trying to do the right thing. I nodded to myself as I untangled my fingers from the cord and fidgeted with my locket. Just talking to him made me feel like a completely different person.

He yawned again.

"I'll let you get your rest."

"Will you be there tomorrow? I'd really like to see you again."

"I'll be there." I was beaming and had to turn the other way as people filed out of the Laundromat and passed me.

"Bye, Cass."

"Bye," I whispered into the receiver, and waited for the click on the other end before hanging up.

I tucked my locket into my shirt, making sure to conceal it before heading back inside to finish my laundry.

I switched my clothes over to a dryer and sat down on one of the long wooden benches that lined the far wall. I focused on the television mounted in the corner of the room. The local news was playing but I couldn't focus too much on anything they were saying. A hurricane was forming off the coast and they expected it to make landfall next week, but the weather was the last thing on my mind. I grabbed the magazine and flipped through the pages. One dog-eared page was titled, "Doing Damage." I stared at a picture of Tucker with his arm around a leggy brunette, flanked by his band members. His other hand was grabbing her thigh and pulling it around his hip.

> If you haven't heard of Damaged, you soon will. The small Tennessee band has been rising in the charts and the hearts of women across America. One such lucky woman reveals all, from late-night partying to whether or not Tucker White is as smooth in the bedroom as he is on the stage.

"Hey, Cass."

I snapped out of my daze and locked eyes with Tom Fullerton. He was as well-known among the users in our area as among the local cops. He had a drug habit and a nasty pattern of stealing. My hand shot to my chest to make certain my necklace was hidden from view. He looked rough. He wore a red polo shirt, untucked and wrinkled. His jeans were filthy and torn, and I was certain he didn't pay extra to make them look that way. His under-eye circles were so dark and purple it looked as if he had been on the losing end of a boxing match. His hair was an overgrown, black, greasy mess. His eyes looked dead.

"Hello?" He waved with irritation. "Can you fucking hear me?"

"Yes," I snapped, turning my eyes back to his.

He smiled and wobbled on his feet. "What brings you out so late all by yourself?" He ran his hand over his jaw and his eyes raked over my body.

I glanced around the Laundromat, biting my tongue to keep myself from giving him a smart-ass reply. "Laundry," I said flatly.

He chuckled a little, amused by my response. He leaned over me, the smell of mildew and alcohol assaulting my senses. "You let Jax know I said hi." His eyes grew serious. "I'll be seeing him soon." The smile flashed across his face again and he turned and left. The door slammed behind him and I let out the breath I was holding.

I glanced around the room. Three other people remained in the room, but none of them looked in my direction. They didn't want to get involved in any trouble. Fucking cowards.

I shoved off the bench in a huff and checked my laundry. The clothes were slightly damp and I slammed the door, letting the cycle finish. I just wanted to go home and sleep. Tomorrow couldn't come soon enough. I was becoming addicted to running away from my life.

Getting a taste for what life was like outside this godforsaken place only made me want to escape even more. I hated having to babysit my mother and living in constant fear that I would say the wrong thing to Jax and be forced to endure the brunt of his anger.

My life had become a precarious balancing act of trying to survive financially and survive the beatings. It was hard to believe that Jax was once the boy who made me happy. He'd been my knight on a white horse.

"You have to flick your wrist. Like this." Jackson's arms looped around my waist as he put his hands over mine, steadying the fishing rod. I giggled and leaned back against his chest, feeling safe in his arms. He was only sixteen but he seemed to have everything figured out.

"It's no use. I'm never gonna catch anything on this damn thread." I slumped, ready to give up.

Jax lifted the rod and forced me to stay put and try again. "You're never gonna catch shit if you don't even try." His arms drew back with mine as we cast the line again. Water rippled around the bobber as it bounced on top of the water.

"I appreciate you taking the time to teach me this. Maybe one day we

can run away together, live off the land, start a new life. We could be who-ever we want."

"I wouldn't want to be anyone else right now, Cass." He kissed my neck from behind, causing me to shiver.

"I'm serious. Haven't you ever wanted to just start your life over? You could be anyone you wanted."

"No, Cass." His voice grew irritated. "There's nothing wrong with who we are."

Just then, the rod bowed in our hands and I screamed as it nearly ripped from our fingers.

"We got one!" Jax was more excited than I had ever seen him. His fingers worked quickly to wind up the line. A fish sprang from the water and dangled in the air.

"My hero!" I turned and kissed Jax on the cheek.

I wiped a wayward tear from my cheek and quickly glanced around to make sure no one was watching me. The fairy tales we were told as children were all lies.

For a while, I clung to the dream, but drugs quickly destroyed it. I even fantasized that my knight was still out there somewhere and just hadn't found me yet, leaving my fairy tale still unfinished. I laughed at the absurdity of it.

"I'm home." I flung my purse on the counter and pulled open the fridge, practically starving after my shift at the diner.

"Babe, I was thinking we could go fishing like we used to." Jax appeared from the hall holding a fishing pole and wearing a floppy green fishing hat.

I giggled at how silly he looked in only a T-shirt and boxers. "You might want to put some pants on first."

He looked down at himself before his eyes fixated on me and he smiled. "Deal."

I grabbed a yogurt from the fridge and ate it quickly while I waited for him to get dressed. I couldn't wipe the goofy smile off my face. I missed having carefree moments like this with Jax. I was always so busy with work it seemed as if we hardly got to spend any time together.

"I'm not gonna wait all night. It's gonna get dark soon!" I waited for a reply but none came. Worried, I threw my trash away and headed down the hall and found Jackson slumped on the floor.

"Jax?" I pushed on his shoulder and he startled awake. "What the hell is wrong with you?" I looked down at his lap and picked up a small baggie. "What is this?"

"Just sampling the product." His eyes looked empty.

I dropped the baggie back onto his lap and ran from the room, thinking if I ran fast enough, I could escape my problems. Unfortunately, they always seemed to find me.

My thoughts went to Tucker, but I quickly pushed him to the back of my mind. He felt pity for me, nothing more. No one ever did, and I shouldn't expect anything different from him just because he was some sort of rock star. I had to convince myself of that. If my world was going to change, it was going to be because of me and me alone. No one was going to give me any handouts. I needed to work harder and make my dream of owning my own home a reality. It was possible to make something of your life from nothing, and I was hell-bent on proving it.

The dryer buzzed and I quickly grabbed my basket and pulled the contents out of the hot machine. I folded everything as fast as possible, making sure to hide my white dress with purple flowers in the middle of a stack.

I would never be able to explain where the dresses came from if Jax found them.

Glancing up at the clock, I realized it was late enough now that he and Mom should be passed out. I smiled and made my way back across the dusty roads to my trailer.

The concert, the beach, and Tucker were only a few hours away now. He might not be my savior, but for now he could at least be my escape, my fantasy.

Propping the basket on my hip, I opened the trailer door and listened for any signs of life inside. There was nothing but the sound of the television in the living room. I sighed and traipsed down the hall, ready to call it a night.

"Fuck," I cursed under my breath at the sound of water sloshing around in the bucket that sat in the middle of the hall as I smashed into it with my knee. That brought me back to reality quickly.

I tossed the basket on my bedroom floor and peeled off my clothes, then collapsed on my bed.

CHAPTER

Twelve

I WANTED TO SLEEP the entire day away, but I was too excited. I stretched and pulled myself from my warm bed. It was nearly lunchtime.

I hadn't been to the ocean since I was a kid and wondered if it would be everything I remembered. Making sure the house was silent, I slid off my bed and rummaged through my closet. I pulled out the plain cardboard box and held it to my chest.

Would it really hurt to let my mind get caught up in a fantasy? I slid the box back into the closet. I knew it would hurt. It was going to crush me when I woke from this dream. I stood and rubbed the head of my teddy bear. I carefully unhooked my necklace and tucked it inside for safekeeping.

I slipped out of my bedroom to take a quick shower. The water was freezing and I was forced not to linger as long as I would have liked. This day was going to drag on forever.

I then stood in front of the bathroom mirror, examining my bruises. My arm had a yellowish-green ring around it. It was still tender to the touch but not nearly as sensitive as it had been the day before.

"Cass! I'm hungry," Jax grumbled as he rapped on the door. I jumped and grabbed my towel, securing it tightly around my chest.

"Okay," I yelled back, trying not to let my voice shake. I gave myself one last glance before opening the door and sliding by him. "Just let me get dressed and I'll find you something." I tried to close my bedroom door behind me, but his hand caught it and held it open. I glanced over my shoulder, trying to avoid his eyes.

"No hurry." His eyes traveled down my body as he reached out and tugged on the corner of my towel.

I pulled back from him and smiled weakly. "It's a bad time of the month."

His eyes narrowed and he let out a small laugh. "I'm not touching that." He put his hands up and walked away.

I sighed and slammed the door, letting my back fall against it. My lies where piling up, and if I wasn't careful, the house of cards I was building would fall.

I searched my laundry basket and picked a green tank top and a pair of cutoff jean shorts. I avoided the magazine, not wanting to destroy the image I had built of Tucker in my mind. I wanted to know more about the girl and if she had meant anything to him, but I wasn't sure I would like the answer. I slipped on a pair of panties and slid my clothes on over them.

"Cass," Jax yelled from down the hall.

I ran the brush through my hair quickly and hurried out to the kitchen.

The cupboards were practically bare. "Tuna?" I asked, holding up two cans.

He waved his hand dismissively. "Whatever."

I grabbed the mayonnaise from the fridge and quickly prepared our food. There wasn't any bread, so I grabbed a pack of saltines to eat it with.

I took our bowls into the living room and held his out for him. He grabbed his, and as I turned to go sit on the recliner, he reached out and captured my wrist. I turned back quickly, waiting for him to scream or swing at me.

"Sit." He smiled and patted the cushion next to him. I gave a weak grin and sat down next to him. His attention went back to the news.

"You see this storm coming in?"

I nodded and began to eat my food.

"Gonna be lots of people needing repairs." His eyes met mine.

I smirked. "That's great. We could use the extra money."

He nodded again. We ate in silence as my stomach retched. He was trying. I pushed my food around with a cracker.

"You gonna eat that?" His eyes were on my bowl. I shook my head and handed it to him. He continued to talk about the stories on the news, but I couldn't focus on his words. When he wasn't strung out, I could still see the boy I first fell in love with. My heart sank.

I took the empty bowls to the sink and leaned over it, trying to clear my head.

"You got some money I could borrow?"

I shook my head, squeezing my eyes closed. Nothing had changed. I stomped down the hall to my room and pulled ten dollars from my bear.

I didn't bother to look at him as I crumpled it into a ball and tossed it at him.

"Where did you have this hidden?"

I didn't answer. He stood quickly and grabbed my face roughly. I let out a whimper as his fingers dug into my flesh.

"If I find out you're hiding shit from me, you will fucking pay. Do you understand me?" He looked murderous.

I nodded my head as tears began to stream down my cheeks.

"Good." He pushed my face back and I quickly touched my cheek. I could feel the bruises forming. He fell back onto the couch as if nothing had happened, his eyes glued to the television.

I turned and bolted out the front door. I didn't look back. I didn't want him to see me crying. I felt like a fool. Why would he change now? He didn't see his drug use as a problem. The only problem was that I didn't just accept it.

I made my way into the diner through the front door. The bell chimed above my head and I quickly wiped my cheeks as I glanced around the room.

Larry raised his eyebrow at me and I gave him a quick nod. His eyes followed me as I made my way to the coffee machine and prepared a fresh pot. He disappeared into the kitchen.

"Change your mind about tonight's shift? No refunds." Marla grabbed the pot and slid a mug under the machine to fill it for a customer.

"Nope. It's all yours." I didn't look at her. I wasn't in the mood for anyone's bullshit. I also didn't want to talk myself out of going to the concert.

She pulled the mug from the machine and slipped the pot back in its place. Why didn't anyone ever ask me if I was okay? Just once, I wanted someone to be concerned about me and not himself.

I yanked the pot from its resting place and slipped my mug under the slow trickle of coffee.

Larry pushed through the kitchen door carrying a steaming plate of eggs and took it to the corner booth. I watched him as he turned in my direction and ran his hands through his greasy gray hair. He pointed to the table and walked back to the kitchen. I watched him as my mouth hung open. I grabbed a roll of silverware and made my way to the table. I was starving.

I savored every bite of the delicious comfort food even though my jaw was tender. Marla stood over me as I cut up the last few bites of my ham steak. She took the coffeepot and topped off my mug.

"Thanks." I emptied a few sugar packets into the black liquid.

"Big night tonight, huh?" She smiled, and all the blood drained from my face as my heart began doing a hard-rock drum solo. She patted my shoulder with her free hand. "I always hated laundry." She turned and headed off to her one customer. I blew out a long breath. I was a lot of things, but adding liar to the top of that list was a heavy burden to carry.

Everyone knew what Jackson put me through; no one cared. With fresh bruises forming on my face and my eyes still swollen from my tears, that fact was more clear to me now than ever before. It was time for me to care for myself. If I didn't do something to make myself happy, no one else would. *I need this.* I squeezed my eyes shut.

"Good?" Larry grabbed the plate from the table, flicking the dishrag over his shoulder.

My eyes shot open and I nodded, scared for a moment that he could see what kind of person I was written all over my face. I tried to justify running around on Jackson with all of the things he did to me, but I knew it still made me a bad person. I didn't want anyone, even Larry, looking at me that way.

Larry turned and made his way back to the kitchen, oblivious of the inner turmoil I was feeling.

"Thanks," I called after him. His hand flew into the air to signal he had heard me as he disappeared back into the kitchen.

I watched the customers come and go as I let myself get lost in my daydreams. I didn't want to go home, but I knew I would need to in order to get my dress.

I walked across the dusty lot and through the fencing that kept us in like caged animals. I hoped I could get in and out of the house without a fight.

Jackson was probably high by now and shouldn't be too much trouble. I slipped in through the front door, holding it so it wouldn't bang shut.

I tiptoed down the hall and slipped into my room unnoticed. I could hear my mother in her room. I shook at the thought of her and Jax getting high while I prepared to run off, leaving them far behind for the night. I slipped on my work clothes and took my yellow dress, fitting it into a bag that I could drop out my window. I grabbed my necklace and carefully hooked it around my neck. I took a minute to examine myself in the bathroom mirror. With a sigh, I was ready to leave. I was going to do this.

Two deep breaths and I rounded the corner into the hallway. No one stopped me, no one was concerned where I was or where I was going. I slipped out the front door into the bright light of the sun, taking a moment to breathe in the warm country air. I moved quietly around the trailer and grabbed my bag, glancing around to make sure no one was watching.

I walked as fast as I could to the pay phone at the diner. My cab was on its way. I smiled nervously as I slipped in through the employee entrance to the restaurant and into the bathroom.

Yanking off my clothes, I pulled the bright yellow dress over my head and shoved the sandals onto my feet. I freed my hair from my ponytail and ran my fingers through it. The stupid grin I wore whenever I thought of Tucker was now permanently plastered on my face. I took the bag of work clothes and shoved it under the bathroom sink. No one would ever look under there. I was the only one who ever cleaned it.

I opened the door and glanced down the hall to make sure no one was watching. When I was sure the coast was clear, I made a dash for it. I ran across the parking lot, not stopping until I was under the giant oak tree that stood next to the main road.

The shade did little to keep the heat at bay, and I wished I had stayed inside the cool restaurant a little longer, but I couldn't risk getting caught.

CHAPTER

Thirteen

I COUNTED THE MONEY I had left from Tucker and slipped it into my little purse. I never used the thing, which was an odd shade of baby blue, but it was all I had. I snapped it closed and slipped the strap over my head so it crossed my body. I wasn't used to carrying around cash and it made me incredibly nervous.

The cab pulled up and I practically ran for it. I wanted to get as far away from this place as possible.

"The pier at Tybee, please." I looked out the window as we took off down the road. Everything seemed different. I watched the scenery pass as I wrung my hands together on my lap.

"Going to the concert?" The driver's eyes were on mine in the mirror.

I nodded and looked back out the window.

"Lots of good bands tonight. You're lucky."

He had no idea. I just hoped my luck wouldn't run out anytime soon.

The rest of the trip we didn't speak. We listened to the radio instead, and the station was playing songs from all the bands that would be performing tonight. My heart skipped a beat when Tucker's voice filled the small space.

I didn't recognize the song, but it was absolutely beautiful. When he sang, "Come away to the water," I couldn't help but feel as if he were singing to me. I wished I could have made this trip with him, my arms wrapped around him on his motorcycle.

We crossed the Intracoastal Waterway, and I knew that in minutes we would be on the island. I tried to focus on the scenery and not let myself get too nervous. Fort Pulaski sat back to the right. I had always wanted to go there, but my father had told me that we would do it some other time. That time never came.

We soon passed the lighthouse and dolphin tours. My heart was pounding out of my chest. As the Sugar Shack went by, we turned to drive along the coast. This was it. The island was small and could be crossed in minutes. I began biting my nails nervously as I watched ahead.

We pulled into the small parking lot next to the pier. The crowd was overwhelming. I glanced at the meter and handed the driver a stack of bills.

"Have fun," he called after me as I pushed open the door and took in the sight. The salty smell of the ocean engulfed me, and I had no idea where to go from here.

I walked toward the giant wooden structure that jutted out into the ocean. I made my way under the pavilion where tourists gathered to eat pizza and ice cream. An arm wrapped around mine and I jumped, spinning around when I thought I had been caught.

"There you are. The yellow was a good call." An older woman eyed me with a scowl on her face.

"Aren't you . . . ?" I recognized her angry face immediately. The old woman from the dinner the other day. She'd left me a measly three-cent tip.

"I'm Dorris, Tucker's manager." She held out her hand for me. I took it and shook it limply. Tucker had said that Dorris had saved him from his childhood. I wondered why she'd left the magazine for me to read. Was she trying to scare me away from him?

"Don't give me that look. I had to make sure you weren't

some two-bit floozy wanting to take Tucker's money. It's so easy for these boys to get distracted." She turned and began to walk down the wooden steps. I followed after her, still unable to process this revelation. "Your coffee sucks, by the way." She glanced over her shoulder at me. "The service wasn't much better." She let out a small laugh.

I opened my mouth to say something but couldn't form the words.

"Let's go, dear. We don't have all damn day." She waved her hand, motioning for me to catch up to her. I walked faster, trying to keep pace.

We made it across the busy street to the Tybrisa hotel. It was four stories tall and white, with blue-railed balconies lining the front.

She stopped in front of the doors. She fumbled in her pocket and pulled out a key card, holding it out to me. "Don't do anything to get him worked up before the concert. He needs his head in the game." With that, she turned, shaking her head as she made her way down the street.

I smiled like an idiot as I held the card to my chest and looked over the hotel. My nerves crept back in.

I slowly stepped inside and made my way to the stairwell. As I rounded the corner, two hands found my waist and pulled me into their body from behind. I squealed and pushed against him.

"It's me," Tucker whispered in my ear, holding me firmly against him. The smell of coconut filled the air.

"What are you doing?" I twisted in his arms to face him.

"I can't let anyone see me. They'll never leave us alone." He smiled. "I'm glad you came." He pulled me tighter against him and wrapped his arms around my back.

I hesitated, not used to being hugged; it seemed foreign and unnatural. I let myself relax and slipped my arms around his neck, inhaling his scent. I loved the smell of coconuts because it reminded me of the beach, of freedom. I hadn't put two and two together that the smell of him was ingrained in my mind as my escape until I was actually here.

"Don't you have a room?" a voice boomed from behind us. I pulled back from Tucker, embarrassed, but his hands held firm on my back, keeping me in place. My eyes danced over the black T-shirt that clung to his chest. He'd paired it with dark, wash-distressed jeans. His hair seemed slightly shorter, and I wondered if he had gotten it cut since I had last seen him.

"Worry about your playing, Chris, and not my social life," Tucker shot back.

Chris let out a deep laugh and headed to the lobby of the building. "I just played a redhead like a fiddle. Does that count?"

I looked at Tucker and let out a small giggle.

"That dress looks amazing on you."

I felt my cheeks flush at his compliment. "Thank you. I love it."

He smiled and brushed my hair back from my face. He cocked his head to the side and ran his fingers along my jaw. His expression grew concerned. "What's this?" He pushed my head to the side so he could get a better look at the purpling bruise.

"It's nothing." I turned my head back and let my hair fall down over my cheeks.

"I'm going to fucking kill him." Tucker clenched his teeth and his body became rigid against mine.

"No . . . no . . . no . . . You're not. You're going to calm down and get ready for this concert."

He shook his head as I spoke, running his hand through his hair.

"Dorris is going to be pissed," I said under my breath.

"What? Don't worry about Dorris. She's not nearly as mean as she looks." He laughed a little and his eyes locked on mine. He relaxed slightly. "Come on." He slipped his fingers in mine and pulled me up the stairs. I hesitated and he turned to face me from several steps up. "What?"

"I don't think it's a good idea for me to go into your hotel room." I shrugged.

"It's the only place we can get away from all of those people." He rolled his eyes and grinned.

I shot him a warning glare but began to follow him again. We went all the way to the fourth floor. He opened the lock and held the door open for me.

"Wow, look at this view!" I walked over to the window and stared over the ocean.

Tucker walked up beside me and with his fingers tilted my chin toward him. "Breathtaking."

My whole body shivered with his words and my knees threatened to give out.

He clenched his jaw as he ran the pad of his thumb over my fresh bruises. "I'm not going to let this go."

"It's not your problem." I shook my head, looking to his shirt. He tilted my chin a little higher so I would meet his gaze.

"I don't have a choice. From the first moment I saw you, I didn't have a choice." He leaned in closer, filling the small gap between us with his delicious tropical scent.

I started to pull back. "But why? Why me?" I envisioned the brunette in the magazine with her body wrapped around him. I wondered how many more women had been in her position.

"You come off so strong and brave, and it's obvious you're hurting. Someone is hurting you and no one is there to protect you."

"Tucker, I don't need someone to protect me."

"Yes, you do, Cass. Everyone needs someone to care about them. I know you're strong. It's the first thing anyone would notice about you, but I know that if someone doesn't take the time to show you how great you are, that hard edge will begin to take you over. I've been there.

"I became so good at pushing people away that I forgot who I was and let others' hatred consume me." He paused, looking into my eyes with such intensity that I suddenly felt exposed, naked. "You still have this light in your eyes. The way you scrunch your nose when you smile, the way your eyes widen at the littlest things.

Even your smart-ass comments are you trying to bring humor into something when you're only feeling pain. I see so much of myself in you. It breaks my heart to picture you lying in bed at night and feeling like you're all alone."

"Tucker," I whispered as his lips brushed against my bruised cheek so softly I thought I had imagined it. My eyes fell closed and I melted against him, drinking him in.

He pulled back, still holding my face, and it took me a moment to open my eyes. His expression was serious. "I won't let him hurt you again."

I nodded and he wrapped his arms around my back and pulled me against his body. I let my hands slip around his waist, gripping his T-shirt in my fists. It felt good to be cared for even if I didn't think it would last. I've had many empty promises made to me in my life, and I found it hard to convince myself that I could trust this one. But I wanted so badly to believe Tucker, and I began to feel that maybe he was someone I could let myself believe in.

"It's time," Dorris called from the other side of the door, knocking on it rapidly.

Tucker pulled back from me slightly and pressed his lips against my forehead, letting them linger. "Let's go." He smiled and slipped his hand in mine, pulling me toward the door. I was in a daze. I wasn't sure if I had been scared of hurting Jax or if I was scared of his hurting me physically when he found out about what I had been doing. I braced myself for the wave of guilt to consume me . . . but this time, it never came.

We made our way down the stairs and out into the evening sun, which was partially blocked by the hotel. I still didn't know what I was doing here, but I didn't care anymore. I wanted to be where Tucker was. I would deal with the consequences later.

CHAPTER

Fourteen

HE MUFFLED SOUND of the band off in the distance seemed out of place on the quiet beach. We made our way across the parking lot, where the rest of Damaged joined us to walk up through the crowd of people. Pushing through all the fans was no easy feat.

The wooden pier was old and warped, and panic set in as I worried about the pillars giving way, sending us floating away into the ocean. I pulled back slightly, and Tucker turned and shot me a smile, squeezing my hand. I could faintly hear the sounds of seagulls squawking in the background over the laughter and small talk of the crowd. Someone dumped an entire container of french fries on the path, and birds swooped in for a bite, causing girls in heels and short miniskirts to scream and squeal. They ducked for cover in the arms of their dates, who were more than happy to take advantage of the situation by copping a feel. The entire display made me uncomfortable, and I wrapped one of my arms over my chest, wishing I had not ventured out in public. I was much happier when I wasn't in a crowd.

As we reached the end of the pier, Dorris put her arm around me and guided me to the front of the crowd, while the band pressed forward to the very end, which was shaped like an oversize gazebo jutting out above the water. The band had a roof overhead, but all of us eager fans had no protection from the hot sun that beat down on us. I could feel the sweat begin to bead on my forehead.

"Thanks for coming out, Tybee! I'm Tucker, and this is Damaged." He gave a dazzling smile and a wink.

The girls went nuts around me. I couldn't look away from him. I didn't glance at the ocean. I was in awe.

He began to sing and the crowd fell silent, swaying to his voice. "'I'm here to wipe your eyes . . .'" His eyes locked on mine, and my heart fluttered and kicked into high gear in my chest. "'I won't let you down.'"

My hand went to the tiny silver heart that hung from my neck. He smiled.

"He seems to like you." Dorris leaned closer so I could hear her. "You better not hurt him."

I rolled my eyes at her threat but didn't say anything. I had no intention of hurting Tucker. I was more scared of what he would do with my heart if he knew he had it. As our eyes met, I couldn't help but feel that this was the only place in the world I wanted to be. I knew in that moment that I had stumbled and tripped through my life before, but now, for the first time, I had finally fallen hard. My heart raced when I looked at Tucker, and somehow I suddenly knew it would be impossible for me to ever look at anyone else the same way.

Damaged flowed seamlessly into another song, this one more upbeat. The crowd began to dance around us. Tucker danced as he sang, and the crowd went wild, emulating his moves. He was enjoying himself and it was amazing to watch. I flushed as I remembered some of those moves from the dances we'd shared at the bar. He was so confident, so commanding. His passion for his music was infectious.

The sun had all but disappeared behind the buildings, shooting slivers of light cascading across the sky as it descended. Small lights set up around the band illuminated the show. Tucker peeled off his shirt, revealing his toned body and those tattoos I'd noticed before. The women in the crowd went wild at the sight of him half-naked, and an unfamiliar feeling boiled inside me. It was jealousy. I didn't like other women looking at him that way.

I blushed when my eyes danced from his chest to his face and he was smiling. He had caught me staring, and he was completely oblivious to any other women around us. I put my hands to my mouth and yelled with the rest of the crowd.

Damaged performed one more song before their set was over and it was time for the next band. They hung out in the crowd for a good twenty minutes, signing everything from pictures to body parts. I lingered to the side, not wanting to interfere with Tucker's rock-star moment, even though every ounce of my being wanted to leap on him like an animal and claim him as mine.

When he was finished, Tucker grabbed my hand and pulled me through the crowd toward the parking lot. As the rest of the band continued on to leave, Tucker pulled me to the side and down a staircase that led directly onto the beach. I glanced at Dorris as she made her way through the food pavilion. She would be pissed when she noticed we were gone, but I didn't care.

We slipped under the pier and Tucker spun around, planting my back against one of the large wooden pillars. His lips hovered over mine as his hands trailed down my back, pulling my body tight against his. His fingers dug into the skin of my hip.

He groaned, pushing his body harder against me. My hands trailed up his bare, muscular arms and over his shoulders, coming to rest on the back of his neck. I'd never been looked at the way Tucker looked at me; it made my knees weak. My hips involuntarily pushed back, desperate to get closer to him. I wanted nothing more than to kiss him, but his mouth never touched mine.

Tucker pulled back, our breathing ragged and mingling, as if his air were keeping me alive.

"I was dying to touch you the whole set." He grinned, sending butterflies fluttering through my stomach. The rapid beating of my heart in my chest drowned out the music on the pier above. He leaned his forehead against mine. "I keep thinking about dancing with you in that bar."

It was too dark for me to see his face but I could tell from his tone that he was smiling. I let my fingers slide onto his back, my nails trailing down his spine.

"Come for a walk with me." He took a step back and flung his T-shirt over his shoulder, holding out his hand for me to take.

I wasn't sure my knees wouldn't buckle under me, but I pushed myself from the pillar and slipped my hand in his, ready to follow him out of the darkness and into the moonlight. He walked me down to the water.

I slipped off my sandals and carried them so I could let the water lap at my toes. "It's warm." I smiled at him as I dug my toes into the wet sand.

"Come on." He cocked his head to the side and tugged on my hand. I followed happily as we made our way down the dark beach. Others were there, but none recognized him in the dark.

"Where are you taking me?"

"It's a surprise."

I couldn't remember the last time a surprise was something good. It made me nervous.

"You'll like it. I promise." He squeezed my hand, sending a charge of electricity through every inch of my body. "You see it?" He pointed out into the water. The moon bounced off a giant line of sand out in the sea.

"What is that?" I stood on my toes to try to get a better look.

Tucker let go of my hand for a minute to slip off his shoes and socks. He grabbed my sandals and placed them with his shoes. He dropped his T-shirt on the pile before taking my hand back in his. "A sandbar. Let's go." He tugged me toward the water.

I hesitated.

"I won't let anything happen to you, Cass."

His smile was all the convincing I needed. I happily followed him into the dark water. I felt free as my toes sank into the sand below. I wasn't scared of the vast unknown when I was with him. He could have pulled me into a volcano and I would happily have followed. It was surprisingly shallow between the beach and the sandbar as I dragged my feet along the bottom to see if I could kick up a few shells.

He pulled me onto the small, secret beach and wrapped his arms around my waist from behind. It felt as if we were on our own deserted island.

"This is amazing."

He buried his face in my hair and took a deep breath. "Yes, it is."

I placed my hands on his as our bodies began to sway to the rhythm of the band off in the distance. Suddenly I wished I knew more about this man who had lifted me out of my shitty routine and made me realize that maybe I deserved something more than my trailer-trash life. "Tucker, tell me more about you, about your life."

His hands grew tense around my waist, tightening momentarily before he answered. "Not much more to tell. My life now just consists of one gig after another. Not much time for anything else."

I nodded, but I was far from satisfied. Everything about him was an enigma. I wanted to know about his family, why he got into music, the stories behind his tattoos, how he came to be who he was . . . and why he gave a damn about me. When I'd first met him, I'd thought he would be like all of the others, but he was different from anyone else I had ever met.

"You ever been in a serious relationship?" I asked, holding my breath. I knew his childhood had been tragic, but I couldn't imagine he didn't have any happy memories. Even I had a few.

He let out a deep sigh. "Don't you read the gossip magazines?" he joked, but I knew he was just stalling.

I turned around in his arms to face him. "You don't have to

tell me anything you don't want to. I just wanted to know more about you."

He smiled and brushed a wayward strand of hair from my face. "I want to tell you everything, Cass." He took a deep breath. "Her name was Cadence. We started dating in the tenth grade. She was wild." He laughed quietly to himself. "She had the mouth of a sailor. By that time I was spending every free moment with the guys, practicing. She didn't care. She sat in my garage for hours just watching us rehearse."

"What happened?"

Tucker cleared his throat as he focused off at the water. "We started playing gigs anywhere we could. Mostly local bars and clubs. Terry found a guy to make us some horrible-looking fake IDs." Tucker laughed. "We would sneak out a couple times a week and play until the bars closed, all while trying to make it to school every day. Cadence loved it. She would perch at the end of the bar and be the loudest one screaming. She would have a few shots, no big deal, but eventually she needed something to counteract her late-night drinking. . . ." He didn't need to say anything more. He placed his hand on the back of my head and pulled me into his chest.

I rested my head against him and let my arms slide around his waist. "I'm sorry." I really was. I knew exactly what it was like to have the person you love be completely changed by drug abuse. Here Tucker was surrounded by thousands of fans, but no one really had any idea who he was. No one knew the pain he carried with him.

"Nothing to be sorry about. I'm happy with how my life turned out. I would do it all over again knowing I would be standing here with you one day."

I pulled back from him and gazed at his face. He was smiling down at me, and I knew he was telling the truth. He was content with his life and didn't need or want any pity.

"I could stay here forever," he whispered.

That brought me back to reality. "Oh, my God. I have to get

back. It's at least a half-hour drive to my place." Panic began to set in as I thought about Jax's figuring out I was gone. There would be hell to pay, and my mother didn't deserve to be on the receiving end of it in my absence.

Tucker let out a deep sigh. "Okay. Let's go."

We made our way back through the warm water and to the beach. Tucker grabbed his shoes and handed me my sandals. He slipped his shirt over his head. We walked straight to the parking lot ahead instead of taking another leisurely stroll on the beach. The mood had shifted considerably. I didn't say a word. Nothing would make this situation any different. My life was waiting for me back in Eddington. My mother needed me and I wouldn't abandon her the way my father had. I hated that I had become the parent in our situation, but she needed me and I wouldn't let her down.

Tucker led me to his hotel so we could clean the sand from our feet and call a cab.

When we reached his room, Dorris was standing outside with her arms crossed over her chest. She was livid. "You wanna explain your little disappearing act to me?"

Tucker squeezed my hand and slid his key card into the door. He stood back so I could enter, then turned to Dorris. "I'm taking Cass home. I'll see you in Florida." With that, he shut the door in Dorris's stunned face.

I'm sure mine didn't look much different when he turned to face me. "You're taking me home?"

He grinned as he walked past me toward the bathroom.

I followed him.

"I don't have another concert for two days, and I still owe a visit to that asshole." He shrugged as he turned on the faucet in the tub. He held his hand under it for a minute, ensuring it was a good temperature, before gesturing for me to clean my feet.

"You can't, Tucker. You won't be there for the repercussions."

Anger flashed in his eyes. "I wasn't planning on leaving him in any shape to lay a finger on you ever again."

"Tucker . . ." I sat on the edge of the tub and dangled my feet in the pool of water. It was perfectly warm, like the ocean. I didn't realize how much I'd missed that feeling—the simple comfort of warm water.

He propped himself on the edge of the tub beside me, letting his feet dip into the warm water.

"You're not that kind of person."

"What kind of person would I be if I let him hurt you?"

He'd be like every other person in my life. I struggled for something, anything, to change the direction of our conversation. "Tell me something else about you." I needed to know more. "What's it like to play to crowds of screaming girls?"

"The first time we played a gig that people actually paid to see, it was surreal. I couldn't believe that people knew me by name and sang along to the lyrics of my songs. It was . . . terrifying."

"I couldn't imagine."

"Don't get me wrong. We lived up to the rock-star image. There was a different party every night, in a different city. The girls were always different but also exactly the same. No one cared who you were as long as you were in a band."

I nodded, not knowing how to respond. I didn't want to picture Tucker with women hanging all over him.

"It's crazy, going from feeling like the most important woman in your life regretted even having you, to every woman throwing herself at you and telling you she loves you. Eventually, I realized none of them did. Not any of them." He sighed and ran his hands through his hair. "Money, fame, fans . . . none of it really means anything. It doesn't make you happy. I mean, I love my music, but if you don't have someone to share that stuff with, you'll still be lonely." I felt his eyes on me. "Tell me something about you, Cass."

"There's nothing to tell."

"What do you want to be when you grow up?" He chuckled.

"Happy."

He sighed, reaching over to take my hand in his. "You don't have to put up with him. I could help get you out of there."

"No, Tucker. I have to do it myself, and I can't leave my mother behind." I pulled my hand free from his and placed it on my lap.

"Come on. Let's get you home, Cinderella." He grabbed my hand again, helping me from the tub.

He handed me a white towel and I dried my feet and slipped my sandals back on my feet. He did the same and threw a few items in a backpack before leading me out of the room.

Dorris was still in the hallway, looking even more pissed off. If that was even possible.

Tucker grabbed my hand and kept walking. "I'll be there, Dorris," he called over his shoulder.

If she didn't like me before, she definitely hated me now. We hurried through the stairwell and out the back door of the building. His motorcycle sat close to the door.

"Here." He slipped my arms through the straps of the book bag and pulled it tight. "Okay?"

I nodded and he smiled, turning to grab a helmet and putting it on my head. He pushed a few strands of hair from my face and secured the straps. I felt like a bobble-head. He grabbed his helmet and slid it on his head before straddling the bike and standing it upright.

I hoisted my leg over the giant machine and slid my arms around his waist, squeezing him tightly. His hand met mine and he rubbed over my knuckles with his thumb. "Let's get you home."

We took off into the darkness, snaking our way through the crowd. The ocean air mixed with the smell of coconuts made it easy to forget that I was going home to a broken-down trailer. I laid my cheek against his back and closed my eyes.

Tucker pointed out landmarks as we drove. He told me one day we would have to go there. The idea warmed my heart, even though I knew he probably wouldn't be around once his tour took him to Florida.

CHAPTER

Fifteen

WE PULLED INTO the dusty lot of Aggie's Diner. My legs were sore from the ride, but I didn't want to move my body from Tucker's.

His hand found mine again, rubbing it gently. "I'm going to get a room down on the river walk. The Bohemian, overlooking the water. If you need me . . . if you need anything . . . *please* come." I could feel his heart rate quicken under my fingers. "I will have to leave for Florida tomorrow. I don't know when I can make it back here. . . ." His voice trailed off.

I nodded my head against his back, fighting off the lump that had formed in my throat. I held him as tightly as I could for a few minutes before I forced myself to pull away.

He followed, propping the bike on its kickstand. He took off his helmet and set it on the bike, running his hands through his hair a few times. He stepped toward me, smiling at how ridiculous I looked. He unbuckled my helmet and set it on the bike behind him. Taking a step closer, he pushed the book bag from my shoulders and let it fall to the ground behind me. His hand slipped behind my neck, into my tangled hair. His eyes were a vibrant shade of blue that reminded me of the ocean.

"If I never see you again, I want you to know that the time I have spent with you has meant more to me than you will ever know. I've never been able to talk about my life with anyone. I never realized how much I needed that, needed someone who really understands what I've gone through . . . needed you."

"I was so mean to you . . ." My voice trailed off and he let out a quiet chuckle, pressing his forehead against mine, his eyes falling closed. I inhaled deeply, relishing the smell of coconut . . . of freedom. My heart wrenched in my chest as his fingers tightened into a fist in my hair and he pressed his lips against my bruised cheek. I put my hands against his chest as his frantic heartbeat pulsed against my fingertips.

He pulled his mouth back but kept his head resting against mine. I slowly stepped back, and he let his arms fall to his sides. I turned and walked across the parking lot toward the diner, forcing myself not to break into a run as the tears threatened to fall down my cheeks.

As I reached the employee entrance, I turned back to look at Tucker one last time. He was staring at me, his hands shoved deep in his pockets. I gave him a small smile before pulling open the door and slipping inside.

By the time I opened the bathroom door, I was no longer strong enough to hold back my sadness. I sobbed as I pulled my bag of work clothes from under the sink and began to undress. I held the yellow dress to my face and inhaled the faint scent of coconut that still lingered on the fabric. I missed him already and I barely knew him. He had turned my entire pathetic existence upside down.

I shrugged my work clothes on and folded my dress, placing it in the bag along with my sandals. My fingers went to the delicate piece of metal around my neck. The tears grew heavier as I fumbled with the tiny clasp and tossed it in my little blue purse. I made sure everything was in the bag and tied it closed. The faint roar of his motorcycle drifted away as a second round of tears began to fall.

I knew he wouldn't be around forever; I just didn't realize how much it would hurt me when he left.

I turned on the sink and splashed my face with cold water several times before I was able to get my emotions under control. My face was red and blotchy. Not that anyone would notice.

I left the dingy diner and made the trek across the dusty parking lot. My fingers traced my lips where his had been. They still tingled from his touch. I wondered how long it would last before I couldn't feel him, couldn't smell him. Before he became a memory that I couldn't even be certain was ever real.

I looked up at the door of my dilapidated trailer.

"This is our new place?" I made a face at Jackson.

"It's not that bad. It just needs a little TLC, that's all. We can fix it up while we live in it."

I stepped inside the front door and inhaled the musky smell. "I don't know Jax. This looks pretty run-down. Maybe we can find something toward the city."

"Baby, you're looking at this all wrong. Sure she could use some fresh paint and a good scrubbing, but it's got a good foundation." He turned me toward him. "It's like us."

"Smelly?"

He laughed and rolled his tongue over his lower lip. "No." He grabbed his shirt and pulled it to his nose to sniff it. "No. It's had a rough life but with a little love it can be good as new again."

"Awww!" I threw my arms around his neck and hugged him. "This is a new beginning then."

He smiled and kissed me on the cheek.

"Get a room!" my mother yelled at us as she brought in a box from outside.

"I got us a room. I got us a whole house." Jackson laughed.

It was time to go back to reality. I snuck over to my bedroom window and tossed my bag of clothes inside. Smoothing my hands over my apron and pushing my hair back from my face, I stepped inside. I wanted to run the other way, run to Tucker, but if I got caught missing in the middle of the night, I would pay.

Jax sat on the couch in a pair of basketball shorts and nothing else. He nodded at me as I entered. I smiled and walked across the living room toward the hallway.

"How was work?" he called after me, stopping me dead in my tracks.

"Fine," I replied without turning around.

He flicked through the channels on the television and didn't say anything else. I let out a heavy breath and made my way back to my bedroom.

"I'm home, Mom," I called down the hall. I heard her mumble something as I closed my door. I grabbed the bag of clothes from my bed and shoved it into my closet, burying it deep beneath my boxes. Most people had skeletons in their closets. I had pretty little dresses that I had to hide from the world.

I changed into shorts and a tank top before leaving my room. Pulling open the fridge, I searched for something to drink. I grabbed a bottle of beer and closed the door with my hip as I twisted the cap off the bottle.

"Grab me one?" Jax's words were slurred.

I rolled my eyes and pulled the door open to grab him a bottle. "This case is almost empty." I wasn't talking to anyone in particular. Jax didn't bother to respond.

I carried the beers into the living room and handed him his bottle. He snatched it without looking up. I tilted my bottle to my lips and began to drink as much as I could before having to come up for air. I had warned myself not to develop feelings for Tucker, but somehow he had gotten under my skin. Another long sip and my bottle was empty. I made my way back into the kitchen and grabbed another from the fridge.

"What's up with you?" Jackson raised an eyebrow at me as he drank his beer.

"Nothing. Can't I ever just have fun and relax?" I was snapping at him, and if I didn't watch it, I would be dealing with an angry drunk.

"Fuck you, Cass" was all he mumbled before turning his attention to the television.

Tonight was going to be hard. I had hoped that Jax would treat me with a little bit of kindness, but clearly that was asking too much. I grabbed an extra beer from the fridge for Jax. If he couldn't be nice, maybe he could just pass out instead.

I handed him his drink and sat on the far end of the couch, keeping distance between us.

"You've been different lately," he said, pointing the top of his bottle in my direction.

My heart was pounding out of my chest. I focused on the television as I took another drink. "I'm the same as I've always been. You're the one who's changed."

"I grew up. The world ain't some fucking fairy tale, Cass."

I rolled my eyes and didn't answer. What did he know? There was a whole world out there of good people who cared about others and didn't treat them as if they were nothing. Tucker was out there. "Want another beer?" I asked, and jumped up from the couch.

Jax looked at me as if I were crazy. "Now you're talkin'."

I shot him a smile and made my way to the fridge. I waited for his eyes to focus on the news before grabbing his beer and keeping my old one in my hand. I took my seat on the couch and held out his bottle.

He twisted the cap off and flicked it across the room. "What more do you need out of life than this?" He laughed and put his hand on my thigh. I tried not to flinch as he drank the entire contents in one long sip.

He grabbed a cigarette and fumbled with the lighter. I took it and lit the cigarette for him. He inhaled and let his lips fall open, sending the burning cigarette falling down onto his stomach.

"Ouch! Shit!" He jumped up and brushed the hot ashes off his bare skin. I jumped up and grabbed the cigarette from the floor. He snatched it from my fingers and took a long drag, eyeing me. "Bet you thought that was pretty funny, huh?"

I shook my head and made my way to the kitchen to grab him another drink. He had to be at least eleven beers in, and I knew it wouldn't be long until he passed out cold. I just needed him to do it before his temper got out of control again.

It seemed as if, these days, he lived his life to make mine miserable. And if I didn't do something about it, no one would. I was tired of living my life afraid of what Jax would do next, or even worse, finding my mother dead from an overdose. I needed to get out of this situation. I needed to leap, and hopefully Tucker would be there to catch me when I fell. And if he wasn't . . . I'd just have to figure things out on my own. All I knew was that Tucker had opened my eyes to a world outside this trailer park, to feeling that I was worth something. I wasn't going to let those feelings die in this hellhole.

I handed Jax his beer, and he collapsed back onto the couch. His cigarette hung between his lips with the ashes still clinging to the end. His eyelids were at half-mast as his lips turned up into a grin. "You used to be prettier." He laughed.

"Oh, yeah?" I rolled my eyes as I fell back onto the couch with a loud sigh. This was a side of Jax I hated. The side that felt the need to rip me apart and let me know how much of a nothing I was. "You used to be nice."

He laughed and took another drink. "I could have done better." His words slurred together and it was almost impossible to understand them.

"I was thinking the same thing." I tipped the bottle of beer to my lips and drained the remainder down my throat.

"Why are you always trying to piss me off? Huh? You like it when I punish you?" His fingers squeezed my thigh.

"Stop it, Jax!" I tried to pry his fingers away but he held on tight.

"You telling me what to do, Cass?" He set his beer down on the floor and began to pull down his shorts. I tried to stand, but his hand pushed me back onto the couch. He leaned his body over mine.

"Stop it right now!" my mother yelled from behind us as she came out of the hallway.

Jax relaxed back into his spot on the couch, adjusting the band of his shorts. "We were just playing, Anne." He took a long drag from his cigarette and blew the smoke in my face.

I took the opportunity to get as far away from him as I could. "You're such an asshole," I said between gritted teeth as I folded my arms over my chest.

My mom got a drink from the fridge and stumbled her way back down the hall.

Jax just laughed, his eyes growing heavier. "That mom of yours is a fucking zombie."

"Yeah, well, maybe you should stop feeding her drugs."

"Maybe you should loosen up and try it. You might not be such a fucking bitch."

"No," I spat. "I'll never be like you."

I looked over to my left and saw that Jax had already fallen into a peaceful slumber. His breathing grew heavy and the cigarette still rested between his lips. The ashes had fallen onto his chest and caught in a clump of hair. I thought about leaving the cigarette there, letting fire destroy all of my sadness. But I could never do something like that. I pulled the cigarette from between his lips and took a long drag from it before dropping it into my empty beer bottle.

CHAPTER

Sixteen

I GOT UP FROM the couch as carefully as I could, determined not to wake the sleeping giant. I was certain my frantic heartbeat could be heard throughout the trailer park. I tiptoed back down my hallway and carefully maneuvered around the water bucket to my room. I was crazy for even considering going to Tucker. Jackson was not the kind of man you lied to or cheated on. There would be no forgiveness, no talking things out. If he discovered what I was doing behind his back, I would be lucky to make it to a hospital.

I pushed the thoughts to the back of my mind as I took my clothes off and slipped on a prettier tank top and cutoff shorts. I ran a brush through my hair several times until it lay perfectly straight down my back. I was either going to live or sit around waiting to die.

My mind was made up. I had never felt as happy as I did when I was with Tucker. I needed more. He was my addiction, and I needed to see him again before he left my life. I tiptoed through the house and opened the front door. The door squeaked against its hinges and I bit my lip and squeezed my eyes shut. There was no sound from Jax. He was out cold and would stay that way until morning if

I was lucky. I smiled and slipped through the open door, pulling it closed behind me. I waited for a few minutes to see if he would follow, but he never came.

This was it. I practically ran out of the trailer park and across the parking lot of the diner. I grabbed some change from my pocket and slid it into the pay phone. I carefully pried apart the locket and unfolded the tiny scrap of paper with Tucker's phone number on it. My heart was thudding out of my chest as I carefully punched in the numbers and waited for it to ring.

Tucker answered after the first ring, and my heart was now lodged in my throat, making it nearly impossible to speak.

"Cass?" His voice was filled with nearly as much excitement as I felt. "Everything okay?" His tone now turned more concerned.

"I'm fine," I managed to whisper as I twisted the phone cord around my finger. "Can you . . . come pick me up?"

"I'm leaving now." He hung up before I could even say goodbye. I smiled as I clicked the receiver back into place and headed for the giant oak tree at the edge of the lot. I sat down at its base and leaned my back against it. It was taking all of my strength to not take off running back home. But I didn't; the potential consequences paled in comparison to the overwhelming excitement I felt knowing that Tucker was on his way. For the first time, I felt that he wasn't looking at me with pity; he was looking at me with actual empathy. He got it. And he needed me to heal as much as I needed him.

His parents seemed as if they were cut from the same cloth as mine. I knew there was more to the story, and I hoped that with time he would share it with me.

I wouldn't allow myself to think about Jackson. Instead, I thought about what life would be like when I was finally able to get myself out of this place. I had to stop wavering between thinking this was what I deserved and desperately longing to make something better of my life. I'd been saving for years to make a better life for myself, and I had to make it happen. Now that I'd been reminded of how it felt to be truly happy, excited, and free, it was no longer a matter of if, but when. I knew everything would have to change to get myself there, and I knew now that it would be a mistake to take Jackson with me. I would never look at him and feel what I felt for Tucker on that pier. I couldn't go through life knowing what that felt like and never have it again. Jackson wasn't the same man he'd been before, even though he'd been with me for so long, and despite my knowledge that this fling with Tucker would likely end soon, I knew Jackson just was not going to be my future—any more than I'd let this trailer park be my future.

I couldn't even make myself consider this cheating on Jackson; not really. There hadn't been anything between us in longer than I wanted to admit. Not sexually, and not even emotionally—at least not on my part.

The distant growling of Tucker's motorcycle pulled me from my thoughts. I wasn't going to think of the future and what could be in store for me. All I wanted to think about was tonight. The roaring of the engine grew closer and I pushed myself up, brushing the dirt and grass from my bottom.

As the headlight on Tucker's motorcycle turned on me, I shielded my eyes until he was parked in front of me.

My feet couldn't carry me to him fast enough.

He represented everything I wanted in life. He was freedom, he was a fantasy. A dream that played inside my head since I'd learned how cruel this world could truly be.

I slid my leg over the back of his bike and grabbed the spare helmet from his hand. I slipped it on and laced my arms around his body, holding on to him for dear life as we took off out of the parking lot. In a blink, we left that dirty trailer park in our dust and made our way to the city. At every light, Tucker's hand rested on one of my legs, rubbing my chilled skin. He left a trail of heat in the wake of his fingertips. We only slowed when we went over the cobblestone streets. Tucker pulled off the side of the road at the City

Market. Hundreds of bodies filled the streets as live music played off in the distance.

"This is amazing!" I took in the surroundings as I slipped off my helmet. Tucker did the same and ran his hand through his messy hair. I slipped my leg over the bike and stood waiting for Tucker. He propped the bike up on its kickstand.

"It only gets better." He got off the bike and took my hand as we rounded a public fountain that was still alive with children trying to escape the balmy evening. We began to weave our way through the crowd. We made our way past the band and made a beeline for a place called Café that sat off to the right. The hostess out front greeted us with a warm smile.

"Two hard Savannah sweet teas, please." Tucker pulled out a wad of cash from his pocket and handed a twenty to the woman.

"Coming right up." She smiled brightly and took off to prepare our drinks.

We took a seat on the wooden bench just outside the restaurant, taking in the sights and the sounds. The crowd applauded as the band finished their version of "Hotel California."

"'Freebird,'" Tucker yelled over the crowd members who were screaming out song suggestions. I laughed and ducked my head as the band began to play his requested song.

"Here are your drinks." The hostess was in front of us with two plastic cups and Tucker's change. He waved the money away and took our drinks, holding one out for me. We both took a sip, and my cheeks puckered from the strong concoction.

"Oh. Shit. We have to hurry!" He glanced down at his watch before taking my hand and pulling me from the bench.

"Where are we going?" I let him pull me through the crowd to a carriage drawn by two massive horses. His grin grew wide as I took in the massive wooden cart. "Oh, no!" I pulled back from him, but he held on to my hand tight.

"You're not scared of a couple of ponies are you?" His lips curled up into a playful smile.

"They're huge!"

He stepped closer and took my other hand in his. "I know they're not white and technically we're not riding on them, but this is the best I could do on short notice." His eyes searched mine, and I felt my heart clutch in my chest.

This was my fairy tale. Even if it was for just one night. I put my fears aside and nodded, unable to contain my smile, not that I wanted to.

I let him pull me closer to the cart as a woman set out a small ladder for us. I hesitantly climbed it and slid across the black vinyl seat. Tucker followed, and the woman removed the ladder as the carriage jerked into motion.

Tucker slipped his arm around me and pulled me into his side. At that moment, I feared nothing. Not the massive horses, not what waited for me in the morning, not even Jackson.

We sipped our drinks as we toured the cobbled streets, weaving our way around the squares as our tour guide told us of the history of Savannah. It was hard to focus on anything she said with Tucker so incredibly close. We were transported to another time and place. It was perfect. We even passed by the Savannah Theatre where I'd watched Tucker perform only a few days before. It felt as if an eternity had passed. So much had happened in these few days that it could have spanned a lifetime. We learned of the city's burning down three times and being rebuilt as new. I thought of what it would be like to let everything I had been through go, nothing left but ashes. Let the memories go up in smoke and start again.

"What are you thinking about?" Tucker ran the back of his finger down my cheek and along my jaw.

"How people change, life changes, but it all still stays the same."

"It's not always a bad thing."

"I feel like it is my fate to be stuck in that trailer, and no matter what I do to get myself out, I will somehow end up back in there."

"I don't believe in fate."

"Really?" I turned toward him with a smirk. "What do you believe in, Tucker White?"

"Karma."

"Karma?" I raised an eyebrow.

"I think it was karma that brought you into my life."

"Then tell me, what is it I did to deserve Jax?"

"You don't. That's the bad karma *he* is putting into the world. One day it is going to pay him back for everything he has done to you." Tucker pulled my head against his chest and rubbed his hand over my back.

"I wish karma would hurry the hell up."

He laughed and kissed the top of my head.

Much too soon, our ride came to an end, and we pulled back into the City Market. The ladder reappeared next to the cart and Tucker climbed down, holding out his arms for me. He grabbed me by the waist and slowly lowered me to the ground in front of him.

"Thank you." I was breathless, staring into his blue eyes, which sparkled in the streetlights. He leaned closer and placed a soft kiss against my forehead.

"Anytime." His fingers looped in mine and we made our way farther down the Market. "Hungry?"

The smell of pizza was heavy in the air, and I realized I couldn't remember the last meal I had eaten. I nodded and he pulled me into a corner pizza parlor called Vinnie Van Go-Go's. The hostess led us to a little bistro table outside and left us with a couple of menus.

"This place is amazing. I had no idea it even existed."

"Sometimes we don't know what we're missing until we find it." Tucker smiled over his menu.

My cheeks flushed and I looked down at the menu, trying to calm my rapid heartbeat. "What are you hungry for?" Everything on the menu looked amazing.

Tucker sighed. "I guess pizza will do for now."

The waitress approached us with a bright smile. "Can I start ya'll with something to drink?" Her eyes darted between us and came to rest on Tucker as they narrowed. She looked as if she recognized his face but couldn't quite place him.

"Beer?" He didn't even glance in the server's direction.

I smiled and nodded.

"Two Buds would be good." He flashed her a quick smile.

She beamed from ear to ear as she took off to fill our orders.

"When do you leave for Florida?" I asked, addressing the huge elephant in the room.

"Can we just not talk about that tonight?"

The waitress returned with our drinks and placed the bottles in front of us. I picked up my bottle and took a long swig.

"Have you decided on what you want?" She was batting her eyelashes at Tucker, but his eyes stay fixed on mine.

"I know exactly what I want." He grinned and shot me a wink, sending the butterflies in my belly into a frenzy. "Medium cheese."

"I'll get that to you in a few minutes." She disappeared inside the building.

Tucker and I stared at each other for what felt like an eternity, pausing only to sip our drinks. Finally, Tucker broke the silence, digging in his pocket and taking out a small, black square and holding it out for me. "I picked this up for you today."

I took the small phone from his hand and pulled my eyebrows together in confusion.

"I want you to be able to get ahold of me whenever you . . . want to." He cleared his throat. "It has my cell programmed into it."

"You didn't have to—"

"I had to," he said, ending the conversation, just as the pizza arrived.

I smiled and slipped the phone into the back pocket of my shorts. "Thank you."

The waitress set a metal contraption in the center of the small table to put the pizza on, raising it off the surface. She placed two metal plates in front of us and asked if we needed anything else. Her question was directed to Tucker and held more than an offer of food service. He smiled politely and told her no. She left us alone.

Tucker slid an oversize slice of New York–style pizza onto my plate before taking one for himself.

It was quite possibly the best pizza I had ever eaten in my life. It could have had something to do with the company I was keeping. I watched his jaw flex as he chewed and licked the sauce off his fingers, sending my thoughts into overdrive.

"You could be here with any girl you wanted. Why me?" I suddenly needed something solid to cling to.

"I don't want to be with just any girl. I want to be here with you." He smiled as if it were a silly question. "You understand what it's like not to have everything handed to you on a platter. You know what it is to work hard, to struggle. No one else out there cares about that side of my life."

"I want to be here with you, too," I said quietly, then resumed eating. A comfortable silence—but a silence nonetheless—settled over us.

"What is your greatest memory?" I asked after a few minutes, trying to lighten the mood.

The waitress returned to check our progress, and we ordered two more beers to go as Tucker settled the bill.

"The day I went home with Dorris."

The waitress returned quickly with our drinks and Tucker's change, along with a slip of paper containing her phone number. I glowered at the back of her head as she left our table. Tucker smirked and crumpled the paper into a tiny ball, leaving it on top of a tip in the center of the table.

"It was just days before the holidays. All I wanted for Christmas was to be wanted. Dorris had been coming in to visit me, but she always left alone. I was beginning to think that she didn't want me, I wasn't good enough."

"Tucker." My heart was breaking for the child in him that I never knew.

He smiled and reached across the table, slipping his hand over mine. "I was too young to understand that adoption is a long process." He shrugged.

"What was it like, getting a new family and being able to start your life over?"

"It was one of the scariest things I had ever gone through. I had all of these new toys, new clothes . . . everything was different. It was like I stepped inside someone else's shoes. I sort of did, actually. Dorris had a son who was killed in a car accident when he was six years old. She left his room untouched for four years before she decided to adopt a child."

"Oh my God."

"Yeah . . ." He blew out a long breath and picked up his beer to take a sip. "She's the one who named me Tucker. That's what my birth certificate says now. I got a new name with my new toys and clothing." He shook his head. "I became a new person."

"What was your name? Your birth name?"

"Nathaniel, after my father."

"I like it."

"What about you, Cass?" He leaned forward in his seat, his eyes locked on mine. "What's your greatest memory?"

I grabbed my drink and took a long sip. I was too terrified to let him know exactly how much meeting him meant to me, so I searched my memories for a happier time.

"My father had given me a teddy bear for my birthday."

"A teddy bear? That's your greatest memory?" He grinned.

"It's all I have to remember what life was like before it all went to hell." I nodded and the smile left his lips.

"Well, we'll have to make you some new memories then. Let's get out of here." He stood and held out his hand to me. I slipped my fingers in his and he pulled me from my seat back toward the busy street.

We made our way to the first block, where the band continued to play. The music slowed as they began "I Won't Give Up." Tucker pulled me into his arms in the middle of the street, and we began to dance slowly in the center of the crowd.

"'Even if the skies get rough, I'm giving you all my love.'" He sang so quietly into my ear that no one else could hear. In the middle of this crowded place, we were sharing a moment that was just for us.

My heart completely melted. There was no turning back. There would be no forgetting him when he was gone. I would be hopelessly lost, chasing a fantasy for the rest of my existence. I slid my fingers into his messy hair and guided his lips to mine.

"Cass . . ."

"I trust you." I mumbled against his lips. I kissed him softly at first, letting my lips brush lightly across his, but the need to be closer to him, to cherish this moment, took over. Without a care in the world, I parted my lips and ran my tongue over his mouth. He groaned quietly and deepened our kiss.

Without warning the crowd erupted into cheers; the song had ended and everyone's attention had turned to us. Tucker laughed and I buried my face into his chest to avoid their stares.

"Come on." Tucker looped his arm over my shoulders and pulled me in the direction of his bike. As we reached it, I grabbed for the helmet, but he stopped me.

"Let me see your phone."

I shot him a confused look but slid the phone from my pocket and placed it in his hand.

He grinned and slid the things from his pockets and secured them, along with the phone, under the seat of his bike. He grabbed my hand and pulled me back the way we came. "Come on."

"Where are we going?" The giant fountain came into view and I tried to unweave my fingers from his. He let go and wrapped his hands around my waist. "Oh, no, no, no!"

My pleas fell on deaf ears as he dragged me into the spraying shoots of water. I screamed and squealed as we made our way to the center. He wrapped his arms around my drenched waist and pulled my body against his, instantly warming me in the chilly water.

Time slowed as his hand pushed my sopping-wet hair from my cheek and he leaned closer, brushing his lips against mine. My eyes fell closed as I let my body relax into his, sliding my hands up his slick arms and over his shoulders. My lips fell open as I breathed in his warm breath and the scent of coconut that would make me think of him forever.

The sound of the music nearby filled my ears as I held on to Tucker as if he were the source of life.

"I take back everything I said before. You are my greatest memory." His whisper could have been shouted from the mountaintops. It rang through my body and settled in my heart, where Tucker was now permanently lodged. He tightened his grip around me in a hug like none I had ever before experienced. I felt safe, complete, and genuinely happy for the first time I could remember in longer than I cared to admit.

"I don't care about where you came from or who is waiting for you at home. Tonight is just you and me, Cass. No one else matters."

"No one else." I pushed my wet lips back against his, feeling more safe in his arms than anywhere else.

"Come on." He pulled me from the slightly chilly water back to his motorcycle, holding out a helmet for me. I smiled and slid it on over my soaked hair.

He climbed onto the machine and started it. The bike roared to life like an angry monster. I slipped onto the back without hesitation, squeezing my body tight against his to keep myself warm as we weaved through the streets.

Luckily, we didn't have far to go. We were only a few blocks from the Bohemian. The hotel spanned two levels, making it accessible from the riverfront but also from Bay Street. The hotel boasted a fine-dining restaurant where people could eat while taking in the river.

We pulled up to the upper level, and he parked the bike just off the main road. Tucker gathered our things from the seat compartment and we hurried inside, both still dripping wet.

CHAPTER

Seventeen

E SLIPPED INSIDE and made our way to Tucker's room without any complaints about our condition, although the two receptionists gave us a stern look. We laughed as we stepped inside the room. It was magnificent. We were on the top floor, just below the rooftop bar. The entire hotel was reminiscent of a pirate ship, with reclaimed wood for the headboards, crimson velvet linings, and beach glass adorning the light fixtures. One wall was a massive window overlooking the sparkling river below, where ships were docked for tourists to climb aboard. The side tables even looked like old treasure chests. I ran my fingers over the faux-fur blanket that was draped over the bed as I made my way to the window.

"This is amazing." I was shivering as I stared out at the boats below.

Tucker came up behind me and wrapped his arms around my waist. "You are freezing." He placed tiny kisses over my shoulder, sending bolts of heat everywhere he touched. "Come on." He tugged at my arm to lead me to the master bathroom. Floor-to-ceiling tile made the space feel cavernous. Tucker grabbed a white, fluffy robe from the wall and held it out for me. "I can send our stuff out to be dried." He grabbed a second robe from the wall for himself.

I took the robe and nodded as he left me alone. I closed the door and quickly began to peel the damp clothes from my body, leaving them in a heap on the floor as I slid on the oversize cotton robe. The floor was surprisingly warm under my feet, and I wondered if they did something special to make it that way.

I ran my fingers through my hair and gave myself a quick glance in the mirror before gathering my wet clothes to give to Tucker.

"Thanks," I said as I entered the main bedroom area. Tucker was also donning a matching white robe. I could feel the heat already burning its way down my body all the way to my toes. His hair was even wilder than usual, but it suited him.

He made his way to me and took my clothes from my hand. He deposited them in a tiny dry-cleaning bag and called the front desk to have them picked up. Within a few minutes a man was at our door for them.

As Tucker made his way back to me, he stopped to turn on a radio on the dresser. "I'll Take Care of You" began to play around the room from hidden speakers in the walls. He stopped a few feet short of me and held out his hand, inviting me to dance with him. I smiled and placed my fingers in his as he pulled my body flush against his. Our hips swayed to the music, and a touch of sadness was in the way he held me, as he was gripping me tighter than usual with his fingers desperately holding me in his grasp. I could feel another good-bye approaching, and it shattered my heart into a million pieces. I clung to him with just as much need. I didn't want any of this to end. The skin of his neck was still damp and I buried my face into the crook of it, drowning myself in him.

"I love dancing with you." His hands slid up and down my back as we slowly turned.

"You know what they say about a man who dances well, don't you?" I joked.

"Would you like me to show you?" He pulled his face back, smirking.

"I think I'd like another dance." I pulled his cheek against mine and closed my eyes.

The song ended and faded into the next. Frank Sinatra lightened the mood as he bellowed "The Way You Look Tonight." I smiled as Tucker began to sing the words in my ear, tickling me with his breath. His mood changed considerably as he pulled back and spun me around before pulling me tight against him once more. I giggled and stared into the fathomless depths of his eyes as he continued to serenade me.

We spun around the room as if it were a ballroom and my robe a fancy gown. As Tucker sang the last line, his forehead rested against mine, and I could taste the sweet mint of his breath blowing against my lips. "'Just the way you look tonight.'"

Our eyes fell closed, and for what felt like an eternity, we held completely still, not wanting this moment to end. My hands loosened from his neck and slid down to his chest. His breathing became more ragged as his hands slid to my neck and his fingers traced my collarbone, sliding over my shoulder, brushing aside the robe to the fading green and yellow bruises on my arm.

I dug my teeth into my lower lip as I searched his eyes for answers to unasked questions.

"I won't hurt you," he said quietly, and waited for my response.

"I trust you, Tucker."

He nodded in understanding as his lips crushed into mine. His fingers frantically searched my skin as my robe fell down my arms, catching at the elbows. I slipped my fingers inside his robe and ran the pads of my fingers over his bare, tattooed chest and down the ridges of his abdomen. His muscles flexed under my fingers as his tongue expertly coaxed mine into a deeper kiss. I slid my hands back up his body and pushed his robe loose from his shoulders. He groaned and his lips left mine, trailing hot kisses down my neck as his hand rose to cup the weight of my breast. His thumb slid gently over my nipple, causing it to grow hard under his touch. His tongue slid against the hollow of my neck as his other hand moved to my lower back, pulling me tighter into his arms. My back arched to meet his need, and I could feel just how much he wanted me through the fabric of our robes.

He walked me backward until the back of my knees pressed against the edge of the mattress. The music of "I Really Want You" filled the room to drown out our heavy panting and frantic heartbeats.

Tucker pulled back so he could look me in the eye as his fingers quickly undid the belt around my waist. My robe fell open and slipped down my body to pool at my feet. It looked as though I were standing on a cloud. That is exactly how I felt. Tucker ran his fingers over my cheek and traced the line of my jaw.

"You can say no at any time. I won't ever make you do something you don't want to." He swallowed hard as if waiting for me to tell him to stop, but I couldn't. Every fiber of my being wanted him. I needed to feel him against me, inside me.

"Please don't stop." I reached between us and slowly pulled with shaky fingers at the belt that wrapped around his waist. His robe fell open and joined mine on the floor at our feet. His eyes finally broke from mine for a split second as he took in my naked body. I did the same, taking in the artwork that covered his torso in bright, vibrant colors.

"You are perfect." His words were reverent and delivered with a sudden, hungry kiss. We both tumbled back onto the bed behind me. His fingers wrapped with mine as he pressed them into the mattress on either side of my head. He settled in between my thighs. His hips slowly rocked against me as his mouth found mine again. I squeezed his hands as I matched his movements. My lips parted slightly and his tongue found mine.

"Are you sure?" He was breathless.

"You are the only thing in my life I've ever been sure about."

He slowly pushed against me. I moaned into his mouth as he filled me, stilling my hips as my body adjusted to his size.

"I'm hurting you." He pulled his mouth from mine and searched my eyes.

"No . . ." I pushed down onto him until he filled me completely, my body and my heart. My back arched toward him as we became more frantic and consumed by this driving desire. He rolled his hips against me as he released my hands, and we clung to each other, desperate to get closer.

All that mattered was here and now.

Our bodies moved perfectly together as if made for each other. I'd never felt so cared for and completely consumed by someone. It was overwhelming. My body pulsed in time with our heartbeats as we slowed our pace. My fingers fisted in his hair as Tucker pushed his lips softly against each of my bruises. I let my eyes fall closed as I burned into memory what it felt like to have him against my skin.

"Look at me, Cass. I want to see you."

I slowly opened my eyes and locked onto his intense gaze. Ripples of pleasure pulsated through my body as my nails dug into his flesh. His mouth covered mine, drinking in my moans as we came together, writhing in passion.

When it was over, we were both panting and covered in a thin veil of sweat. Tucker's body collapsed on top of mine as he held me tightly in his arms.

But then all of my sadness and regret washed over me as I struggled to simply let go and just live in the moment. The pain of my real life was crushing, and I knew deep down I had made a mistake by stepping out of it and letting myself believe I could have more. My heart hurt in my chest as it pounded against Tucker's body. I could feel tears forming and I squeezed my eyes closed, begging them to stay at bay until I was on my own. I'd let it go too far. I felt too much for him and I wouldn't be able to just forget about him now. I didn't just have sex with Tucker, I had made love to him.

"Please don't regret me, Cass." His voice was barely audible as he ran his thumb over my cheek, catching the stray tear that had betrayed me. His words unleashed a floodgate. I didn't regret being with him. I regretted letting him into my heart and knowing he would be ripped out soon. It was all suddenly too much to take.

His arms wrapped around me and he held me tightly against his body as I sobbed into his shoulder. I knew I should say something, anything, to make him understand, but there were no words. There was nothing to say.

I suddenly thought of Dorris, and his band, and I realized that he was already on his way out of my life. Nothing was going to change that. Even if Tucker wanted to stay with me, it dawned on me that I could never let him jeopardize his career for me. He needed to tour and become the famous rock star he was destined to be. I would only get in the way of that. He needed to focus. Our lives were on two different paths, and I was thankful that at this one moment in time those paths intersected. But if I truly cared for him, then I knew I couldn't stand in the way of his dream.

Instead of telling him my heart ached because I didn't want to lose him, instead of telling him my every thought was consumed by him, I simply had to let it go. A knock sounded at the door, and I pushed him from my body and scrambled from the bed, then picked up my robe from the floor. I put it on and tied it, then opened the door to find our freshly dried clothing in a bag just outside. I grabbed it and hurried into the bathroom to change. I just had to get out of there. It would only become harder and harder to leave.

Tucker was soon on the other side of the door knocking. "Cass, I'm sorry. For whatever is hurting you. I'm sorry." His voice shook with the words, and I hated myself. I slowly opened the door, avoiding his eyes. He had dressed in a hurry, too. This had to end now. I was already in over my head, and if I didn't push him away now, I wouldn't be strong enough to say good-bye.

"It's too late for you and your white horse. I can't be saved." I swiped a tear from my face and pushed past him. He grabbed me by my upper arm to stop me. I swung around and glared at him.

His fingers slowly released my arm as his eyes burned into mine. "Fine. I'll take you home." He ran his hands through his hair before grabbing his keys and wallet from the dresser.

He was pissed, confused, and the mood in the room had completely changed. I couldn't wait to get out of there. I had finally stopped floating and landed, hard, on solid ground. Now I just needed to be home in my own bed. That was reality. The trailer park. This was all just a cruel joke being played on my heart.

We made our way to Tucker's motorcycle in complete silence. He held out his extra helmet to me, but his eyes did not meet mine. I wanted to apologize and throw my arms around him, but I couldn't. I was broken. I needed to do what was best for Tucker, even if he ended up hating me for it. I slipped the helmet over my head and silently wept to myself as I slipped onto the back of his bike and wrapped my arms around his waist. He tensed but quickly relaxed and took off into the night. His speed was frightening, but I didn't say a word. The sooner this was over, the better. The city faded to black as we made our way into Eddington. My heart seized as I thought about our final good-bye. It had to be done, but it didn't make this any easier. For me at least. As much as I knew that there was something special between us, I was also sure there was a Cass in every city along his tour. But he was the only Tucker for me. No amount of punishment from Jackson compared to the pain I was putting myself through at this moment.

As we pulled to a stop under the giant oak tree, I clung to Tucker for an extra minute before forcing myself to let go of him, physically and emotionally. I removed my helmet and handed it to him as he removed his and stood in front of me.

"I'm sorry." My words shook as a sob escaped my lips.

He reached out and took my hand in his, shaking his head. "I'm not sorry, Cass. You have no idea how much this time with you meant to me." He grabbed the small phone he had given me earlier from his pocket and slipped it into my hand.

"I can't." I pushed the phone back toward him, but he refused it.

"I need to know you're safe. I'll feel better if you have it." He sighed and kicked at the dirt under our feet before running his hand through his hair again.

"Thank you." I wasn't just thanking him for the phone. I was thanking him for the time, the affection, the happiness that I bathed in when he was by my side. I tried to keep my guard up and protect myself from feeling something, anything, but I wasn't strong enough. Tucker had worked his way into my heart and it was killing me to push him away.

"It doesn't have to end this way."

"Yes, it does, Tucker."

He nodded and got back onto his bike. He gave me one last glance before he slid his helmet on and revved the engine. I stepped back a few feet to avoid getting caught in his cloud of dust as he took off. I watched as he made his way onto the road and his taillights faded into nothingness. Just as I faded back into nothingness, too.

My heart had shattered into a million shards, and every tiny piece was piercing my soul. I couldn't imagine ever being able to forget about him, to move on. I slowly made my way across the dark, deserted lot toward the trailer park. For the first time, I wasn't filled with fear. I didn't care if I came face-to-face with Jax. I didn't care about anything anymore.

I took a deep breath and pulled open the door to the trailer.

CHAPTER

Eighteen

AX WAS SPRAWLED on the couch with his arm over his face. I slowly stepped inside, careful not to wake him. As I crossed the living room, his arm shot out and he grabbed me by my wrist.

"Where were you?" His voice was gravelly from sleep.

"I was out smoking a cigarette." My voice shook and I closed my eyes, cursing myself for not being stronger.

He let go of me and adjusted himself on the couch to get more comfortable. "I thought you quit?"

"I did. I just gave up right now. Go back to sleep."

He mumbled something under his breath and rolled over into the back of the couch.

I sighed and walked back to my bedroom. As soon as I got inside, the floodgates opened and I sobbed uncontrollably as I hugged my teddy bear to my chest.

I pulled the phone from my back pocket, dying inside to dial Tucker's number and tell him how sorry I was. I needed to hear his voice. I clutched the phone to my chest as my emotions completely consumed me.

Tucker was probably on his way to Florida. I had treated him like complete shit and made him feel as if he were nothing to me, someone I could just sleep with and then cast aside. He only left the phone for emergencies. I repeated this in my head several times before burying the phone in the depths of my closet, determined to never use it to call Tucker.

It would only make things worse. I needed to get over him.

I stripped off my clothes and made my way into the bathroom. A warm shower would have been nice, but the water wasn't too cold. I slathered my bath sponge with soap and began scrubbing the salty coconut scent from my skin. I could smell him, feel his touch. His words echoed inside my head and my heart was in jagged pieces. My tears mingled with the shower water and ran over me to cleanse myself of my sins. I scrubbed harder as my chest heaved, desperate to wash him away.

I always thought that I had gotten the short end of the stick. That I didn't deserve the life that was handed to me. But now I'd earned it. Now, standing in the trailer that Jax had bought for me, my home, I couldn't deny the truth: I'd lied and cheated on Jackson. No matter what he had done to me, I still felt guilty. I didn't want to be that kind of person.

I let the soap wash from my body and pool at the drain before shutting off the water and opening the shower curtain. A shiver ran down my body and my thoughts went to the fountain in Savannah. I forced the tears to stay inside as I grabbed a towel hanging on the rack and quickly wrapped it around myself.

I didn't bother dressing; instead, I collapsed onto my bed and curled into a tight ball. I forced my eyes shut and prayed I would soon fall asleep. Anything was better than reality. I needed to see Tucker. I knew it would hurt more when I woke, but I didn't care. I just wanted to see his smile.

I finally cried myself to sleep and dreamed of the carriage ride. My body was tucked safely into his side as we toured the town. The world stopped spinning for us then. I could feel every bump of the cobbled roads, the smell of the pizza in the air mingling with the delicious coconut scent of Tucker. I could hear the band singing "Hotel California" off in the distance: "You can check out anytime you like, but you can never leave." That was true about my heart. Tucker was gone, but he was still with me. I couldn't shake him. I could feel his fingers laced in mine as if our hands were molded for each other.

I awoke with swollen eyes and a dampened pillow, partly from my wet hair and partly from my tears. I silenced my alarm and slowly unwrapped myself from my towel, then grabbed my work clothes and dressed quickly. I put on my locket and tucked it away under my shirt. The small piece of cold metal was a constant reminder of Tucker. I knew it would be best to burn everything he'd given me and try to move on, but I decided I deserved the hurt I felt from thinking of him. And the hurt was better than feeling emptiness, feeling nothing at all.

I slipped on my sneakers and made my way to the living room. My mother was in the kitchen making a fresh pot of coffee.

"What are you doing up?" I asked as I grabbed two mugs from the cabinet. She didn't answer, just shook her head. I patted her on the shoulder and filled our mugs. I held her mug out to her, but her hand was shaking violently. I knew she would end up with burns if I gave it to her.

"Come on." I motioned toward the small table. She sat down and I slid her mug in front of her while I took a minute to relax with her.

"What's with you?" she asked as she took a small sip.

"Nothing. Tired." I raised my mug and began to drink.

"You've been crying."

I slammed my mug down harder than necessary, which made the hot liquid splash onto my hand. "Ow . . . fuck! I'm fine, Mom. You don't get to pretend you care if I cry now. It's too late for that."

I stormed from the kitchen and left the trailer as quickly as possible.

If someone had asked me yesterday, I would have said it was

impossible for me to feel any worse, but I was wrong. My mother was actually sober this morning and cared about my well-being and I shut her down. *What have I done?*

I didn't turn back. I made my way through the empty parking lot toward the diner.

"Good morning, Larry," I called out as I entered through the employee entrance.

"What the fuck is good about it?" he called from the kitchen. "Not a damn thing."

I couldn't argue with him on that. Everything was wrong. I grabbed the bin of clean silverware and a stack of napkins to begin some of my side work. I glanced up at the table Tucker usually sat at. My heart cracked a little further. I swallowed hard and got busy with rolling. Time would make this go away. I sat in silence, reliving my memories because I couldn't bring myself to turn on the radio. I might hear his voice and lose all control over myself. Instead, I tried to think back to a time when Jackson wasn't the monster he was now. It was almost impossible.

"Oh, God. What is that smell?"

Jackson frowned as he pulled out a chair at the table for me. "I cooked." He was beaming from ear to ear.

"You cooked?" I slid into the seat and he pushed me forward before joining me on the other side of the table. "Well, what is it?" I grabbed my fork and pushed around a hard, brown piece of something.

"It's macaroni and cheese."

"Which part?" I joked.

"I added a few ingredients. I made it with love."

"Is the black part supposed to represent your heart?"

"Funny. No. I gave my heart to you a long time ago."

But those memories seemed like a lifetime ago, and I knew now that they hardly made up for what I had to go through now.

Larry came through the kitchen doors with breakfast in hand. My stomach panged at the smell. I hadn't realized how incredibly hungry I was. I was so thankful I had Larry. He could be an asshole, but deep down I realized that he cared. He just didn't know how to show it. Just like my mother. I knew it was dysfunctional, but I also knew that now more than ever I had to grasp at any happiness life would give me, and those moments were few and far between. But when my thoughts drifted to Tucker, the tears threatened to fall again.

"Thanks," I whispered, and picked up a piece of toast. I could feel Larry's eyes on me but he didn't say anything.

I forced myself to eat a few bites. I knew my stomach was craving more, but my heart had wedged itself in my throat.

"So . . . ah . . . you gonna be staying your whole shift today?" he asked as he dipped his bread into the yolk of his egg.

I cleared my throat and nodded, unable to speak just yet.

"That's good."

"Aggie's been askin' about ya. She wants you to stop by our place sometime."

"Sure." I stared down at my plate of food, wishing I could fast-forward time.

"I know your situation ain't what you hoped for." He cleared his throat. I nodded in agreement. "We can't always have what we want or what we think is best, but things work out for us in the end."

"Nothing has changed, Larry. I'm sorry I haven't been around lately but it won't happen again."

"All right. If you want to talk about it—"

"Larry, I am not about to share my boy problems with you."

"Jesus Christ, Cass. I was gonna say Marla knows a thing or two about men. She sleeps with a different one every night. Sometimes two." Larry laughed, then took a drink. I managed a smile.

We ate the rest of our meal in silence. I knew he'd been referring to Tucker. It was better if I didn't say his name.

I just needed things to go back to normal. It wasn't a good life, but it was mine, and I suddenly missed the simplicity of it. In a perfect world, I would have run into Tucker's arms and never looked back at this godforsaken place, but that wasn't reality. I had a mother to take care of and bills to pay.

I pushed myself from the bench and held out my hand for Larry's plate. He laid his fork on top of the half-eaten mess and pushed it a few inches in my direction. I grabbed it, along with my own plate, and made my way to the kitchen.

Customers began to trickle in not much later, and I was finally able to get my mind to relax and think of something else. By the time a woman gave me a dirty look and mumbled something about good help being hard to find, I felt as if things might get back to normal.

Still, every time the bell chimed above the door, my heart seized for a fraction of a second. I wanted it to be Tucker. I wanted him to come and whisk me away and for me to never look back. It was selfish, but the daydream kept me from breaking down altogether.

By lunch, my body was begging for a break, but I was glad not to have time to take one. When the bell on the door chimed, I snapped my head up and saw that it was Jackson. My stomach instantly tied itself in knots as I waited to find out if he'd discovered what I'd worked so hard to hide.

His eyes caught mine, and he nodded, a slight smile tugging at the corners of his mouth. I managed to force a small grin and hurried to deliver a cup of coffee to one of my customers, then walked over to Jax.

"Hey," I said with a heavy sigh as I nervously smoothed my apron and looked anywhere but in his eyes.

"I'm hungry and I need some money." His hand ran over his stomach and he stifled a yawn with his fist. I grabbed a menu from the hostess stand and turned to find him a table.

"Come on then." I walked a few tables back and stopped in front of an empty booth.

He slid into his seat and held out his hand for the menu. Habit, I guess, as he knew the menu as well as I did. "You gonna join me?"

I set the menu down on the table before turning to walk over to the coffeemaker. "I'm too busy," I called over my shoulder.

In truth, my tables were taken care of, and besides the occasional drink refill, I could spare a few minutes. I couldn't bring myself to do it. To look him in the eye while he was sober and lie to him was not how I wanted to spend my afternoon. I grabbed the coffeepot and made my rounds, taking extra time to make sure everyone was satisfied.

Jackson waited patiently for me to return so he could tell me what he wanted to eat. I took down his order with shaky hands. I used to dream of these rare days when he wasn't completely loaded and I could catch a glimpse of the boy I fell for years ago.

Thinking back to how I felt about him then, it still paled in comparison to what I had been feeling the past few days with Tucker. Still, I hoped things could change with Jackson. They had to change.

"I was thinking of going down to the creek later tonight. Maybe we could try our hand at catching dinner again?"

I gave him a sad smile. He was still in there, the guy who'd protected me and stood by my side when my own family didn't seem to care. I knew he was still there. And I needed to be the same for him. I needed to stand by his side when his life was falling to pieces. I nodded my head, hoping he wouldn't want to make idle chitchat.

I made my way to the kitchen and gave Larry the ticket for the order, lingering in the back to wash a few dishes. Marla made her way in while tying her apron low on her hips.

"You look like shit, darlin'." She grabbed a still-wet coffee mug from the rack and made her way back onto the floor.

"What is she doing here?" I shot Larry a raised eyebrow.

He cleared his throat and focused on cooking Jax's burger. "You haven't been here even when you are here." His eyes flicked to mine for a brief second. He was right. I had been in my own world lately, and if I wasn't careful, I was going to end up losing my job. I couldn't imagine where my life would go from there.

Larry set the plate of hot food on the line and I grabbed it, determined to make things get back to normal as quickly as possible.

I took the food out to Jackson and placed it in front of him before sliding into the bench seat across from him.

"Mmm," he moaned as he picked up the burger and took a large bite. I grinned as he pulled it away from his mouth, leaving ketchup in the corners of his lips.

"You are worse than a baby." I laughed and unwrapped his silverware so I could wipe his face with the napkin.

He gave me a lopsided grin. "That's why I have you to take care of me."

I stole one of his fries and gave him a weak smile. I could make this work. If this Jax stayed around, I could learn to forget about Tucker . . . eventually.

Larry came out of the kitchen and leaned against the waitress station. He nodded once at me, and I looked down at the table.

"So . . . what are your plans for the day?"

Jackson raised an eyebrow as he shoved a handful of fries in his mouth.

"I heard they're hiring dockworkers . . ." I stopped talking as Jackson's face grew hard.

He was now glaring at me with a clenched jaw. "I'll look into it." He took another bite. I waited for a threat but it didn't come.

"Good. I think I would like to try fishin' again."

"Yeah?"

"Yeah, why not? As long as you pull them off the line. I could fry them up for dinner. It would be nice to have a meal around the kitchen table again."

"You want some?" He held out his burger, dripping grease all over his hand.

I leaned over the table and took a small bite.

"It's good, right?" He smiled and wiped his hand on his shirt.

The bell chimed and my head snapped toward the sound. Tom Fullerton staggered in. My eyes shot to Jax, growing wide. This wasn't going to go well. I knew Jax probably owed Tom drug money, and this was not the kind of guy who forgot about your owing him something. Marla and Larry immediately began watching the local troublemaker.

His eyes met mine and his lips twisted into a sneer when he saw Jax. I tapped Jax on the hand and motioned with my head so he would look behind him. He dropped his burger on his plate and turned to face Tom, who was now standing next to our table.

"I believe we still got some business we need to handle." Tom grinned at Jax, then turned to me. "Good to see ya again, Cass."

Jackson's eyes shot to me with anger as if I had been sneaking around with dirty Tom.

"I saw him at the Laundromat." I rolled my eyes.

Tom found humor in our little exchange. "Three nights ago. I thought she would have made it clear that we needed to speak."

I glanced over at Marla, who had her brows drawn together in thought. Larry looked at her and shook his head. I had been lying to all of them so much. Marla and Larry knew it now, and I hoped that they would keep Jax in the dark.

"What do you want?" I leaned in closer to Tom and kept my voice low so we didn't disturb any of the customers.

"I want the money this fucker owes me."

"There's a time and a place for these sorts of things, Tom."

"I want my fucking money and I want it now!"

I rolled my eyes and looked to Jax. "How much?" I had some saved and he couldn't have gotten himself in that much trouble. What kind of drug dealer sells on credit anyway?

"Six hundred." Tom crossed his arms over his chest.

The air went out of my lungs. Six hundred dollars?

"I'll get it to you," Jax said, looking at his plate.

"How? How, Jax?" I couldn't keep my voice at a whisper any longer. I could see my dreams being yanked away from me and it hurt. It physically made me ill as I mentally counted the money I had saved in my bear.

"Shut up, Cass, and let the grown-ups talk," Tom said with a chuckle.

"Fuck you!"

"Hey, that can be arranged," Tom shot back.

Jax grabbed the front of Tom's shirt and pulled his face down to his. "Don't fucking talk to her like that. I said I'll get you the fucking money."

"I'm tired of fucking waiting," Tom shot back. "When?"

I didn't wait for his answer. Tom was a lot of things, and crazy topped the list. I got up from the table and made my way out the front door. I broke out into a run as my feet hit the dirt. I wanted to leave this place and never look back, but instead I headed for my trailer. This was my punishment. I let the tears fall freely down my cheeks as I slipped inside the trailer and headed for my bedroom. I grabbed my old, tattered bear and squeezed it before slipping my hand inside the hole in the back and pulling out my savings. I counted it once to make sure it was all there. Six hundred and forty-five dollars. I would be starting over completely.

"Cass?" my mom called from down the hall.

"Not now, Mama."

"Cass, I'm hungry."

"You're gonna have to wait!" I yelled back at her.

I shook my head and slipped the money inside my apron, giving the bear a quick kiss on its nose. This wouldn't make up for what I'd done to Jackson, but it would help to ease my conscience. I knew now it would be forever before I could escape this place. This was where I belonged and I couldn't fight it any longer. There was no escaping fate.

CHAPTER

Nineteen

I MADE MY WAY back to the diner with a broken spirit and my life savings. Jackson and Tom were now in the parking lot arguing. Tom had his hand on his waist, and I knew he was letting Jax know he had a weapon. I didn't know if he would use it, but I would never doubt what someone is capable of while under the influence of drugs. On many occasions I had watched drugs turn Jackson into a heartless monster. I jogged to Jackson's side. I hated myself for what I was about to do. My dreams, my new life, all riding on this money, and I was about to hand it away because of drugs. A habit that wasn't even mine.

"Stay out of this, Cass." Jax gave me a stern look, but I knew he was worried about what Tom would do with that gun. He was worried about my safety. I knew I needed to protect Jax, even if it meant giving up on my dreams and living in this nightmare forever. I glanced around the dirty lot as I forced myself to accept reality once again.

"How 'bout you come over here, Cass?" Tom smiled as he pulled the small, silver gun from his waistband and gestured for me to move closer. I glanced at Jax, pleading with my eyes for him to do something. He didn't move, and Tom wasn't pleased I didn't do what I was told. His arm shot out and he grabbed the hair at my nape and pulled me in front of him. He pressed the barrel of the gun to my chest with shaky hands. The cold metal rested beside the locket that held my secrets.

"What do you think, Jax? It's not exactly an even trade, but I think she is a start."

My stomach rolled and my knees gave way beneath me. I was held firmly in place by my hair.

"Jax!" I screamed.

"Don't fucking hurt her! I'll get you your fucking money."

"When?" Tom pushed the gun harder into my chest, letting Jax know he wasn't playing games.

"Here." I grabbed the wad of cash from my apron and held it in front of me as my stomach twisted in knots. My knuckles turned bone white as I gripped the small stack of cash, wanting desperately to run in the other direction.

Jax looked completely shocked as his mouth fell open and his eyes locked on the bills in my hand. Tom grabbed the money with a huge grin, finally releasing his grip on my hair. I fell to my hands and knees as Tom began to flip through it and count it as I had a moment before. My heart sank as he slipped it into his pocket.

"Pleasure doin' business with ya, Cass." He smiled as he began to walk away from us.

"Tom," I called to his back, causing him to stop and look over his shoulder. "Don't ever fucking come around Jackson again. He doesn't need any more of your kind of friendship."

Tom just laughed and shook his head as he continued across the lot, carrying my future with him. My heart was in the pit of my stomach as the realization of what I had done began to sink in. It was more than money to me. It was a way to save my family. It was the only reason I got up each day and worked as hard as I did. Now I had nothing.

First I had pushed away Tucker's love, and now I had locked

myself into a self-perpetuating nightmare. I finally let out the breath I had been holding and pushed to my feet.

Jackson grabbed me under my arms and helped me up. "Where the fuck did you get that?"

I knew he was preparing for a fight, and I needed to get myself away from him as soon as possible.

"You're welcome." I walked around him toward the diner. Fresh tears threatened to fall as my head throbbed.

"Cass!" The tone of his voice was frightening and I stopped dead in my tracks. "Thanks."

I nodded and hurried inside the restaurant to take care of my tables. Marla was shooting daggers with her eyes, and Larry just shook his head and slipped back inside the kitchen. Everything had righted itself in the world, except Jax was no longer the scariest thing in the trailer park.

I continued with my shift like a zombie. I couldn't allow myself to feel anything or the sadness would take over. No one wanted a sad, blubbering waitress.

When my shift ended, I wasn't sure if I was relieved or more stressed. I dreaded going back to the trailer, but that was the only place I had to go.

"Cass, why don't you let Marla handle the side work tonight?" Larry said from the kitchen door.

"No, it's okay. I can handle it."

"Just go home."

"I need this job, Larry. I can't lose it on account of him."

"Your job will be here tomorrow. Go on home."

I was relieved and saddened that I would be coming back.

I closed out my final check and made my way into the darkened parking lot. My fingers absentmindedly played with the locket hidden beneath my shirt. I couldn't keep drifting off in these memories. Others were starting to notice and soon Jackson would as well.

I was too absorbed in my thoughts to notice the movement by the fence. Tom stepped out from the shadows and wrapped his arms around my waist from behind. His nasty scent assaulted my senses as I struggled to pry his roaming hands from my body.

"I'm looking forward to the next time Jax gets in debt with me. You know, I take *other* forms of payment." Tom laughed into my ear as I gagged on the bile that was rising in my throat.

"There won't be a next time. Keep your filthy drugs away from my family." I tried to struggle, but my arms were pinned to my sides.

He laughed again. "I like it when you struggle."

"Fuck you, Tom!"

"Are you giving consent?"

"I wouldn't give you water if you were on fire!"

"I'm on fire right now for you." He panted as he struggled to keep me locked in his grasp.

I bowed my head and threw it back with all of my might. Tom's hands fell from my body as he cursed and yelled. My flight instincts kicked in and I took off in a mad dash for my trailer.

I slipped inside to find Jackson on the couch with a beer in hand and my mother sitting in the recliner fidgeting with her hands. I could tell she was not feeling well, and she was also very much sober.

"Hey," I said quietly as I walked across the room toward my bedroom in a daze.

"What happened to you?" Jackson jumped up from the couch and followed me to my room.

"*You* happened!" I slammed the door and began to pull off my work clothes, praying he wouldn't bust it down. As I pulled off my shoes, I could hear the faint sound of music over the loudness of the living-room television. I listened as I wandered around the room to hear it better. It was Tucker's and my song. I realized it was coming from the closet and began to pull out clothes and boxes. I grabbed the cell phone in my hand and looked at the screen.

"Tucker." I sighed. I held it to my chest for a moment debating whether to answer. I stared at my bedroom door, preparing for someone to come bursting through. I clicked the ANSWER button and held the phone to my ear. "Hello," I whispered so quietly I wasn't sure he could hear me.

"Cass." Tucker sighed, and it tugged at a string that he had tied directly to my heart. I closed my eyes and leaned back against the closet door. "How are you?"

"I've been better."

"What happened? Did he hurt you again? I will fucking kill him if he hurt you, Cass." His voice was panicked now.

"No. It's not like that." The tears were threatening to fall again and I had to swallow several times to push against the lump in my throat. Tucker sighed loudly into the phone. His words made me feel safe even though he was so far away. It was comforting to know someone cared, even if he wasn't with you.

"Cass . . . I can't leave things like this between us."

I squeezed my eyes shut, knowing I would have to explain myself. "I never regretted it. It was . . . it meant more to me than you will ever know. It's just too much, you know?"

"It will never be enough." His voice was full of sadness, and I wished I could wrap my arms around him and make him feel better. All I cared about now was taking away his pain, even if it caused me more. "I can't stand not knowing if you're safe. The thought of that bastard putting his hands on you and no one there to stop him drives me crazy. Come on tour with me. It's insane that we aren't together right now."

"I can't." The words tumbled out of my mouth before I could think.

"Why not? What is so much better about *him*?" I could hear the anger in his voice as he mentioned Jax.

"Nothing." It was the truth, but I needed to set Tucker free. Doing so meant giving Jax yet another chance, and making sure my mother was safe and had a roof over her head.

"I can't leave my mother, Tucker. She needs my help. I'm all she has."

"You don't have to be her parent, Cass. That's not fair to you."

"It's the way it is. She needs me and so does Jax. I won't just abandon them. I'm not that kind of person." I held my breath as I waited for him to say something, anything. "I wouldn't take back what happened between us for anything, Tucker."

"Then why did you run?"

"Tucker, the sky is the limit for you. My limit is the tattered fence around this trailer park."

"Please don't talk like that."

"Tucker, you know that I'm only holding you back. . . . I can't do that to you. . . ." I could hear footsteps coming down the hall, and fear washed over me. "I have to go."

I hung up before he could respond. My heart immediately felt empty and I felt the pain of sadness in my chest. I wiped the tears from my cheeks and rehid the phone deep inside my closet. I finished pulling off my clothes and slipped on an old T-shirt and shorts.

I walked out to the living room and sat on the couch, eyeing my mother. A few seconds later, Jackson emerged from the bathroom and took the seat next to me. His arm extended behind me and he pulled me into his side. I wanted to pull away, but the closeness felt good in a moment when I felt so fragile. My eyes fixed on the television, which was now showing a college football game. I let my eyes fall closed and imagined I was in Tucker's arms.

I passed out immediately from exhaustion, not dreaming of anything. It was some very much needed rest. I awoke lying on the couch, pulled into Jackson's arms. I almost woke him when I gasped, expecting to see Tucker's face instead of my boyfriend's. Guilt consumed me once again for thinking of another man while in Jackson's embrace. No one deserved that type of deceit, not even Jax. I couldn't help but feel so conflicted it made me nauseated. I pushed Tucker to the back of my mind, vowing to keep his memory hidden like the pretty little dresses I buried in the back of my closet. Jax stirred and his arms tightened around me. I could feel his excitement from our closeness. I slowly pulled my body from his, not wanting to be pressed against him when he did wake up. I couldn't sleep with him after what I had done with Tucker. Maybe one day I would be able to forgive myself and move on with my life, but that day was not today.

I slid off the couch and landed less than gracefully on the floor. Jax groaned and rolled over so his back was now facing me. I breathed a sigh of relief and pushed off the floor. I needed coffee and I needed lots of it.

I stumbled into the kitchen and began to prepare a fresh pot, and my mother came down the hallway.

"Morning." She was smiling as she took a spot at the kitchen table. I raised an eyebrow at her but didn't respond. All these years I needed a mother and was forced to deal with my problems by myself. Now she was coming around and I could barely say two words to her. I knew her newfound sobriety wasn't by choice, but because Tom Fullerton was keeping his distance from Jax after their heated skirmish. In time he would show his face again and my mother would be a lost cause. There was nothing I could do now. I had no savings, no way out.

I poured the coffee and took the steaming mugs over to the table. She was shaking and looked to be in physical pain. I sat down and took a small sip from my cup.

"More tea, Mama?" I held the plastic teakettle adorned with pink roses in front of my mother.

"Of course, dear." She smiled brightly as she tucked a long strand of my hair behind my ear. My tiny hands shook under the weight of the pot as I poured sweet tea into her glass, spilling drops onto the table.

"Let me help you, sweet girl."

"Thanks, Mama."

"That's what I'm here for, baby."

"You okay?"

She looked like absolute hell, but she wasn't high. She nodded once and tried to steady her hands so she could drink.

"How is work?" She was making an attempt at small talk, and for some reason it pissed me off. It wasn't fair. All these years. Why now? Now, when I had secrets I couldn't possibly share. I cringed as I selfishly wished today of all days she were lost in a drug-induced daydream. A part of me even wished I had kept my savings a secret. I would feel less guilty about what I had done to Jax if drugs were still their number one priority. But now everything had changed—and stayed the same. Locking me into a twilight zone of never-ending misery.

"It's work, Mom. You should try it sometime." I rolled my eyes and took a long sip from my drink. She looked down at her mug and nodded once. I felt like such a jerk. I knew she was hurting. On the inside and the outside, but I couldn't help but be angry at her. I pushed back from my seat and made my way to the counter to freshen my coffee.

"Everything okay with you?"

I leaned against the counter and forced myself to calm down before answering. "You don't get to ask that now, Mom. You don't get to just pretend everything is okay. It's not. It's not okay." The tears threatened to fall again, and I mentally cursed myself for being so weak.

"You're right." She got up from the table and walked down the hall to her room, slamming the door behind her. I sighed and let my shoulders sag as the sobs rippled through me. I completely lost control of my emotions and simply wept.

I grabbed a rag and began to angrily wash the dishes in the sink as my tears continued to fall. It was therapeutic, and the trailer would be a little cleaner when I was finished.

I scrubbed everything harder than necessary and even ran the rag over the counters and the table for good measure. By the time I had finished, the tears had stopped and I felt that I could finally speak to my mother. I laid the rag over the faucet and wiped my hands on the back of my shorts to dry them.

The trip down the hallway felt like the walk down death row.

My mother wasn't a bad person. She suffered from a broken heart. The drugs and the depression were just a side effect. She was trying. I knocked on her door and waited for a response. She didn't say anything, so I leaned my ear against the door and listened. I could hear a few muffled sniffles. I turned the handle and pushed the door open to see her curled in the fetal position on her bed.

"Mom . . ." I sat down next to her on the bed and leaned my back against the metal frame.

"I'm sorry, Cass." Her fingers stroked my hair gently. I didn't pull away, didn't respond.

"You ever feel like you just want to get away from this place? To leave and find somewhere new to live?" I paused but she didn't respond. "I guess that is what's been bothering me. Things with Jax are just . . ." I shook my head and started again. "Things have been bad here for a long time. I know he isn't in his right mind when he's using, but that doesn't mean I should have to deal with it, ya know?"

Her fingers continued to comb their way through my hair.

"I had saved some money." My heart sank as I thought of what was left of it. "But it's gone now. I can make it back though. It will take some time, but I can fix it." I turned to glance at her over my shoulder.

She had a small smile on her lips and it encouraged me further. I twisted back so she could continue to play with my hair and I wouldn't have to look her in the eye as I spilled my soul.

"Jax is wrong for laying a hand on you, baby." Her words didn't change the past. They didn't make any of this better, but my heart finally didn't feel as if it were being squeezed. I nodded and ran the backs of my hands over my eyes.

"I met someone," I whispered, terrified of her response.

"Is he kind to you?"

"Yes." I smiled at the thought of Tucker. "He was. He's gone now."

Her hand rubbed over my head in gentle strokes to comfort

me. "Men are hard to keep around. It's in their nature to roam. Jax ain't been the best to you, but he's here." She was trying to make me feel better, and I knew she was thinking of Daddy and how he'd abandoned us.

"You can't just leave us. What will I tell Cassie?" I could hear my mother's voice shake as I hid in the darkness of the hallway.

"Tell her I'm going to find a better job. I'm not going forever. I'll come back for you when I get things settled in New Orleans."

"Take us with you." She was begging and I wanted to run out and beg with her, but fear trapped me in that hallway.

"I told you, I can't. When I get things set up, I'll come back for you. I'll send money every chance I get. This isn't forever."

"It feels like it's good-bye." A sob broke free from her throat as my father's footsteps grew distant and the front door opened and closed. I tiptoed into the kitchen, dimly lit by the light over the stove. When my mother's eyes caught mine, they were swollen and rimmed in red from her tears.

She picked me up into her arms, rocking back and forth.

"Where did Daddy go?" My own eyes began to water, not fully understanding the situation.

"Daddy went to work in a faraway land so he could get a big castle for his princess to live in."

I waited up night after night for my father to return. Every night my mother would tell me stories of how great he was and that it wouldn't be much longer. But that day never came. We never got our happily ever after.

"Maybe it'd be better if Jax wasn't."

She didn't respond.

I pushed up and cleared my throat. As I moved for the door to leave her room, she finally spoke.

"I'd like to hear more sometime. About this boy."

I nodded and left her room, pulling the door closed behind me.

It felt good to finally tell someone about Tucker, even if I didn't say his name. I'm not sure I could have without breaking down. I could help my mother get better and maybe she could help me get through this heartache.

I made my way down the hall and tiptoed by Jackson, who was still out cold. I slipped out of the trailer and made my way to the diner. I had a glimpse of who my mother used to be, and I wasn't going to let that slip away. At least that part of my plan could still happen.

I stepped into the front door of the diner and made my way to the stack of pamphlets and business cards that sat on a side table near the door. I thumbed through them until I found the pamphlet labeled "Narcotics Anonymous." I folded the paper in half and slipped it into my back pocket before searching for Larry. He was in the kitchen cleaning off his grill.

"Payday!" I shot him a smile, and he mumbled something rude under his breath. He walked over to his desk in the corner and dug through a few envelopes before pulling out one labeled "Cass." He held it out to me and I grabbed it eagerly, but he didn't let it go.

"That boyfriend of yours needs to stay away from here, Cass. He causes nothing but trouble." He gave me a stern look. I nodded and he released the check.

"Thanks, Larry." I knew the check would barely be anything, but every bit would help.

I skipped back to the trailer feeling that maybe things could get better. I deserved a better life. And if Mama was willing to sober up, then I could help us leave this place.

I made my way into my bedroom and dug my secret phone from my closet. After listening to make sure no one was around, I dialed the number on the front of the pamphlet. I found out that NA had several groups that met a few times a week. They met in the back room at the church out on Maple Street, a few blocks down the highway. We could walk there with no problem.

I was overjoyed. I couldn't wait to tell Mom. Jax was a different story. I knew he could benefit from the meetings, but he would think I was calling him weak and that could end badly for me.

One problem at a time. I wiped my finger over the screen of the phone and noticed a little icon with a red number 1 above it. I touched it with my finger and it opened a message folder.

I can still smell you all over me. I can't stop thinking about you. —*Tuck*

My heart did a somersault as I reread the message. I chewed on my lip as I typed out a quick reply.

When is your concert?

I held the phone in my hand as if it would do a magic trick. I couldn't believe I could sit here and talk with Tucker whenever I wanted. It beeped, startling me, and I clicked the icon.

Concert's tonight. I wish you could be here.

My pace quickened.

Maybe next time.

I hit SEND and wished I could take it back. I shouldn't have said that knowing I would probably never get to see him again. It wasn't good for either of us. I tucked the phone away in the closet and went to the bathroom to brush my teeth and hair. There was an NA meeting today and I wanted to make sure my mother was there. I got ready as fast as I could, avoiding eye contact with myself in the mirror. I was torn between missing Tucker and hating myself for falling for him. I knew time would make all of this go away, but the waiting was killing me. An hour felt like a lifetime. At least now I could focus on my mother.

I splashed cold water on my face and let it run down my neck as I closed my eyes and forced Tucker out of my thoughts.

When I left the bathroom, I ran into Jackson in the hall. He didn't appear to be completely wasted out of his mind, but he was certainly not suffering the pain of withdrawal like my mother.

"Hey." He smiled and his hands slipped around my waist as we turned to switch places. The hallway was incredibly narrow.

"Hi." I smiled and surprised myself as my cheeks burned from a slight blush. He had a playful tone to his voice, a welcome sound. He slipped into the bathroom and glanced back at me, winking before closing the door. A tiny spark ignited in my belly and I smiled. Maybe this wouldn't be as hard as I thought. I made up my mind that I would ask him to go to the meeting with us later. The worst he could say was no. That was a lie. The worst he could do was hit me, but I shook that thought from my mind and made my way to my mother's bedroom.

I knocked and waited for a response. When none came, I pushed open the door. She was sleeping in the middle of her bed with her knees pulled to her chest and covered in a thin coating of sweat.

"Mom," I whispered, and shook her shoulder gently. It took a few more tries before her eyes flew open. She stared through me as if she had no idea who I was before her eyes focused and she pulled completely from her nightmare.

"Cass." She rubbed her hands over her face several times before sitting up. "What's wrong?"

"Nothing. I just . . . I have somewhere I want us to go."

"I can't go anywhere, Cass. I look a mess." She combed her fingers through her tangled dark-blond hair.

"It's fine, Mom. You look fine." I smiled and grabbed her hand to help pull her up. She began to follow me out into the hall.

"Where are you taking me?"

"There's a meeting out at Cobbler's Church." I bit nervously at my nails.

"A meeting? You know I'm not into that organized religion."

"It's not a service. It's an NA meeting."

Her feet stopped moving and I turned to face her.

"I don't need . . . I'm fine, Cass." She crossed her arms over her chest in defiance like a child.

"You're not fine, Mom. None of us is fine and we need to heal. This family is broken. I need you to help me fix it." I had put it all out there for her. I hoped she would take the olive branch and help me make things better. I knew if she didn't, this family would crumble, and I couldn't hold it up any longer on my own. I was tired. I had no fight left in me. And now I had so far to go to earn back the money that had just paid off Jax's drug debt.

I waited as she thought over my words. I knew she felt horrible and would rather curl up and be miserable, but her feet began to move forward and she pushed by me into the living room.

"Well, we better get moving then," she said.

The smile on my face could have lit the entire city of Savannah. My heart felt as if it were fusing back together and was no longer lodged in the pit of my stomach.

At that moment Jax came into the room. "Where are you headed?" He gave my mom a look of confusion.

She didn't respond.

"We're going to a meeting at the church. An NA meeting. You wanna come?" I stepped toward him, the smile on my face growing smaller, but still there.

He laughed long and hard in my face before waving his hand at me. "You go. Have fun." He sank down on the couch and flicked through the channels on the television.

I knew it was pointless to argue, so I turned back to my mother and ushered her through the door. I would work on Jax later. For now, I needed to make sure, at the very least, she got better.

CHAPTER

Twenty

"M Y NAME IS Anne and I'm an addict." She fumbled with the tissue in her hand as she let that confession sink in. "I'd always taken a liking to prescriptions. What was the harm? If a doctor could give them out . . ." She glanced at me as she cleared her throat. "I began taking them for the pain in my hands. I used to be a hairdresser." She smiled but it quickly faded.

I thought back to when my mother used to do hair in our home. Back when my father still lived with us. I'd never realized her addiction spanned so much of my life. I reached over to her and clutched her hand in mine, encouraging her to continue.

"I began using . . ."

"Continue, Anne. We're all here for you."

She nodded and wiped her nose. "I began using heroin with Jackson, my daughter's boyfriend." The floodgates opened and she sobbed uncontrollably.

The man turned his attention to me. "Did you know?"

"I caught them using together. They were so messed up they didn't even know who I was."

"That wasn't the first time, Cass," my mother confessed.

As we left, I realized that the meeting had gone surprisingly well. My mother spoke but didn't open up as much as I'd hoped. Still, for her first meeting, it was amazing progress. I kept telling myself that the most important thing was that I'd gotten her there. She cried a little and I did, too, but mostly out of relief. It felt once again as if things were going to get better.

Eventually, we would be able to build on our relationship. I wanted that more than anything else. After cashing my paycheck, we stopped by the store and loaded up on hard candy to help her with her cravings.

The man running the meeting had pulled me aside and let me know things were going to get a lot worse before they got better. My mom would be craving an escape hard, and she might take out her frustrations on those closest to her. I guess that included me. I didn't care. I could get through anything if it meant she would be better.

We walked slowly back to the house, taking in the breeze from the pending storm. The hurricane had veered off course and would be going into the Gulf. We would still get a few strong showers from the outer bands, but that was nothing to worry about. The real worry was the new hurricane forming out in the middle of the ocean. Still, it wasn't something to think about for a while.

"Tell me more about this boy." Mom shot me a smile as she sucked on a strawberry lollipop.

"He's just a boy." I popped a piece of candy into my mouth.

"You wouldn't have mentioned him if he didn't mean something to you."

Her questions were making me nervous. If Jax ever found out about Tucker, I would regret it.

"Anything you tell me will stay between us, Cass. I know how Jax is."

"I met him in the diner. He's gorgeous . . . and doesn't bat an eye at my attitude."

We both laughed.

"So, where is this Prince Charming?" She grinned.

I rolled my eyes at her choice of words. "Gone." I kicked at the dirt on the ground as we made our way into the diner parking lot.

She didn't ask where or why he had gone. She didn't need to. We didn't say anything else on the subject.

We repeated this routine over the next eight weeks. Mom slowly forced me to open up to her about Tucker, and she listened attentively, offering no advice but no judgments either. I stuck by her side and made sure she kept herself sober. It was no easy feat.

Jackson was far from clean and sober. I had started saving again, and my bear was finally starting to fill out a little more in the midsection. Things were looking up. I continued to text with Tucker and sneak secret phone calls whenever his schedule allowed. I tried to ignore his calls, but a part of me still believed in us somehow. He needed to know I was okay, so I continued to talk with him every day, even if I knew it was going to make things harder on us. Last I heard he was in Pennsylvania, performing at the York Fairgrounds. I tried to distance myself from him as much as possible, but my heart refused to let him go. I would have to deal with this later. One puzzle piece at a time.

"You work today, Cass?" Mom was gathering laundry to take to the Laundromat.

I looked up at her and smiled. It was nice to see her getting out on her own. She was far from healed, but she was making progress, and I couldn't be more proud.

"I'm leaving in a few minutes." I grabbed a piece of her sober candy from the dish on the counter and popped it in my mouth. I think I was becoming addicted to sugar. A small price to pay to keep her healthy.

"I'll see you later then." She smiled as I made my way out the door.

I snuck into my room and checked the messages on my phone. *I need to talk to you. —Tuck*

I slid the phone into my pocket and headed outside.

Jackson didn't even acknowledge my leaving. He was too engrossed in the news. The last hurricane heading our way had fizzled out as it ran up the length of Florida. By the time it hit us, it was a weak tropical depression. Nothing to sneeze at. Now there was another and everyone was up in arms about it. I wasn't worried. If it was coming, we could do nothing to stop it. We couldn't afford to evacuate.

I slipped behind the trailer and dialed Tucker's number. My stomach did flips as it rang.

"Hey, sweetheart."

"Tucker . . ."

"I know. You're not my sweetheart." He sighed heavily into the phone.

"How's Pennsylvania?" My eyes scanned the trailers around us as I made sure no one was watching me.

"We're in New York now. Got in at about midnight yesterday. You wouldn't believe how chilly it gets here. Be nice to have someone to snuggle up to at night."

My heart sank into the pit of my stomach.

"I saw the storm is gonna miss you. I was worried."

"The weather has been crazy though. I think I caught something." I placed my hand over my stomach.

"You all right?"

"I'll live." I sighed. "Just a stomach flu."

"You haven't been well for weeks. You should see someone. I wish I was there to take care of you."

"I can take care of myself."

"Clearly . . . Shit, Cass. I have to go. We need to get on the road."

"All right." I tried not to let my sadness show.

"See you later, sweetheart."

"Bye." I tucked my phone into my apron and quickly made my way around the trailer.

My stomach growled as I crossed the parking lot, and I hoped Larry was in a kind mood and had prepared us breakfast. I hated to have to pay for it. I needed to save as much as possible.

"Hey, Larry," I called through the diner as I made my way to the pan of clean silverware.

Larry popped his head out of the kitchen door and held up his spatula. "About time," he called, and slipped back inside his little room.

"I'm not late," I called after him.

He reappeared with two plates of breakfast he had waiting for us. I smiled at him and made my way to our booth.

"You used to come in early. I miss the free labor."

I laughed and shot him a playful glare.

Larry no longer seemed like the bitter and mean old man he had been before. He had a tough life and dealt with it much the same as I did. We weren't all that different.

We ate in silence, and for once I cleaned my plate. Life wasn't all that bad. Sure, I still had to help Jax out with his addiction, but even he seemed to be doing better these days. We hadn't had any major fights in weeks, though the stress of taking care of all three of us was still taking a toll on my body—I was more exhausted than ever.

When I came back from the kitchen, Larry was still sitting in the booth, staring out the dirty window. "Everything okay?" He never spent more time than necessary outside the kitchen. He waved his hand to dismiss my question, but I could tell he had something on his mind. "What is it?" I slid into the booth and propped my head on my hands.

"You're a good kid, Cass. You used to have such a chip on your shoulder, and with your life no one blamed you. You've changed a lot, and Aggie and I are proud of you." He pushed himself from the bench and walked to the kitchen, leaving me sitting with my jaw hanging open.

That was the nicest thing Larry had ever said to me. My eyes welled up with tears. Happy tears. Why was I such an emotional wreck lately? It didn't seem to matter what my mood was, I was always crying over something. My shift flew by and I found myself being more understanding and patient with the customers. It was amazing how a little kindness changed your perspective on life. And as I attended more meetings with Mom, I realized that they were helping me let go of a lot of my anger. I was beginning to understand why I was the way I was.

After work, I met my mother in the parking lot and we headed off to the old church. The meeting was crowded as usual, and all there had a chance to introduce themselves and tell their story.

"Would you like a chance to speak?" the man directly across from me in the circle of chairs asked as he adjusted his glasses.

"Oh, no. I'm just here for my mom." I looked down at my hands, wishing the room would swallow me whole. I hated speaking in public, especially about something so personal.

"There's no judging here." The entire room was focused on me now.

"My name's Cass. My mom and my boyfriend are addicts." The room collectively responded by saying hello. I laughed nervously as I focused on my fingernails.

"Your boyfriend is an addict? Why do you think that is?"

What an odd question. I'd never tried to make sense of it. Things are the way they are. "Um . . . well, I guess a lot of bad things had happened. Sometimes you can't always make things better, ya know? Sometimes people look for things to fix their feelings."

"That's good, Cass. But I was wondering why you think you sought out another addict to be your companion in life?"

"Oh . . . uhh . . . He found me really. He stood up for me, always kind of protected me."

"But when the drug abuse began? You didn't think it would be better to distance yourself from him? To protect yourself from him?"

"Jackson never left me. I wouldn't do that to him."

"Interesting. I had assumed you found comfort with another addict because of your mother. I'm not so sure that is the case. Cass, where is your father in this picture?"

"He left when I was little." I felt my face turn red as everything clicked into place. Jax took the place my father abandoned. It never mattered if Jax was the right guy for me, he was filling a void in my heart.

The next day at work, my mind drifted from thoughts of my father, to Jax, and—as much as I tried to block them out—to thoughts of Tucker. My apron pocket vibrated and I jumped from my seat and made my way to the restroom to check my messages.

I miss you. —Tuck

I miss you, too. I clicked SEND and waited for another message.

It felt good to hear your voice today. —Tuck

Don't do this, Tucker.

We are coming to S. Carolina. I'll be there late tonight. —Tuck

My heart raced as I read his message. He was coming back. Suddenly, the thought of pushing him away seemed impossible. Every bone in my body craved him.

Really???

I wasn't sure if I should tell you. I don't know if I could handle being so close and not seeing you.

My stomach was now doing flips and I felt as if I were going to be sick. We'd pressed our luck before, and we might not be as lucky as we were in the past. It wasn't fair. I wanted to see him more than anything else, but I couldn't. It wouldn't be fair to Jax.

I can't.

Are you all right? Did something happen?

No, I'm fine. Really. Please don't worry.

It's impossible not to worry when I have no way to see you.

I'm sorry, Tucker.

I shoved my phone back in my apron and left the bathroom. I felt the familiar vibration of the phone but forced myself to ignore it. I finished my shift as if nothing were bothering me. I was good at pretending. By the time it was over, I wanted to run home and prove myself right. Jax was getting better. Life was getting better.

As soon as I was in the comfort of my own room, I changed out of my work clothes and slipped on something more comfortable. I felt physically ill when I checked the messages on my phone.

Please. I need to see you. —Tuck

Cass, please don't do this to me. —Tuck

I'll be staying at the Marriott on Hilton Head Island. —Tuck

I put the phone into my closet without responding. Tucker didn't deserve this. I should have told him weeks ago I couldn't speak to him anymore. As much as he said he cared about me, I always knew we could never be anything serious. He was a rock star. He deserved better. I curled up in a ball on my bed and forced myself to sleep.

I didn't dream of Tucker. I almost never dreamed at all anymore. I knew I would never get what I wanted, but I was making the best of what I had. It was all I could do.

When I got up the next morning, I pushed myself to my feet and made my way to the kitchen to make some coffee.

I jumped as Jax's fingertips slid against my spine. I hadn't even heard him come up behind me.

"You okay?" He leaned over my shoulder.

I shook my head. "I just don't feel well." I turned on the water and began to wash out a few bowls.

He leaned back against the counter. "Maybe you should take the day off. You work constantly. You could use a break."

I stopped what I was doing and looked at him. He was being sincere and thoughtful. I hated myself for moping over Tucker. Grabbing the dish towel, I dried off the bowls. "You're right. I should just stay home. We could do something fun. Go for a picnic?"

"Yeah, I mean, whatever you want to do." He ran his hands over his face and he pushed off the counter.

I begged my tears not to fall. This was what I had always wanted. The old Jax. He was finally coming around.

When he had disappeared, I wiped my hands on my shorts and made my way back to my bedroom. I pulled on a dark tank top and a pair of jean shorts. I grabbed a twenty out of my bear and slipped it deep in my pocket.

"I'm gonna go get us food for later," I called, and made my way out into the sunshine. It certainly didn't seem as if a storm was coming. I tilted my head to the sky and let the rays warm my skin.

I made my way out of the trailer park and up to the main road. It was only a five-minute walk to Stewart Grocery, our local grocery store. It was a perfect day for a walk. There was no humidity hanging heavy in the air. In fact, there was a pleasant breeze.

The highway was slightly busier than usual with people wanting to evacuate for the hurricane before a mandatory evacuation notice was put into place. The storm wasn't set to make landfall on the eastern coast of Florida until tomorrow, but the outer bands should be hitting us late in the evening.

I made my way into the small store and glanced around. The shelves were practically bare. That was usual whenever a storm was approaching. I found the bread aisle and settled on a bag of rolls because the normal loaves had long since been cleared out. My stomach growled as I grabbed a jar of peanut butter and some strawberry jelly. Jackson's favorite. Next, I made my way to the beverage aisle and picked up a bottle of wine. It wasn't anything fancy and only cost $5, but it tasted fruity and I knew it would be a nice touch. I picked up a peach on my way to the register to eat on the way.

I checked out and made my way back into the sunshine with a smile on my face. When Jax and I were kids we would sneak out all the time and have little picnics together. It was the only time I felt as if I escaped my life. All that mattered was him. A lot of things had changed since then, and we both knew that being adults did not fix any problems. If anything, things got harder. A lot harder.

"Jax!" I hoisted the grocery bags onto the kitchen counter and made my way down the hall. "Jax?" I knocked on the bathroom door, but all I heard was a mumble. I slowly opened it, not wanting to disturb him, but to let him know what I had gotten for our trip.

"Oh my God!" Jax was on the floor, slumped to his side. Orange, stretchy tubing was still around his arm, and he held a needle in the opposite hand.

He slowly turned his head toward me. "It's just a little. I'm fine. We can still go," he mumbled and then his vision went unfocused as his high took over.

I slammed the door behind me and ran into my room. To hell with what was fair to Jax. This wasn't fair to me. I couldn't believe I'd let myself be fooled by Jax. Again.

Suddenly, the delicate sense of hope that had been keeping me afloat—keeping me from Tucker—for the last few months shattered, along with any remaining sense of loyalty that I felt to Jax. It suddenly became all too clear to me that Jax had no real desire to change, and even the force of my will couldn't resurrect that boy who once took me fishing, once made me feel safe.

I grabbed all of my things from my room, shoving cash into my purse. I pulled out my phone to send Tucker a message.

I am on my way.

I made my way to my mother's room and handed her the phone. "If you need anything, call the number in this phone. I'll be home later. I love you." I pressed a kiss to her forehead and left.

CHAPTER
Twenty-One

THE CAB RIDE seemed to last forever. Hilton Head was about an hour and a half away, and I knew this ride would cost a fortune, but it was worth every penny. I had forced myself to stay away from Tucker and it was all for nothing.

It broke my heart to think of what I had put Tucker through because I thought it was the right thing to do. I was an idiot. All I ever worried about was everyone else. I never put myself first, and I was tired. It was my turn.

As the cab pulled up to the hotel, I nearly jumped out the door before we stopped.

Tucker stood just a few feet from the cab in low-slung, dark wash jeans and a deep gray T-shirt that hugged the expanse of his chest. I handed my money to the cabdriver and flew out the door. Tucker held out his arms for me and I ran into them, jumping and locking my legs around his waist. It felt so good to touch him again. He squeezed me tightly as he kissed my hair over and over. The stubble from his unshaven face tickled my cheeks.

"I'm sorry, Tucker. I am so sorry." I kissed his neck.

"Shh . . . It's okay. You're here now, sweetheart." He stroked my hair as I slowly slid my legs down his body and stood on my tiptoes.

He pulled back from me with hands on either side of my face. The pads of his thumbs wiped away my happy tears. I leaned my face into his hand, kissing his palm.

"I missed you so much," I whispered.

He laughed and a smile spread across his face, deepening his dimples. He pulled my face closer and placed a kiss to my forehead.

"Come on." His fingers laced in mine and we walked inside the lobby of the hotel to the elevator. He slid his card and wrapped his arms around me from behind. I sank my body into his and closed my eyes and inhaled the smell of coconut. I felt safe.

The elevator dinged and the doors opened much too quickly. I didn't want to move. I opened my eyes to see that we were already at his room. The walls were painted a chocolate brown accented by light blue fixtures and paintings. A small kitchen had tan, speckled countertops and a stainless-steel fridge tucked away in the left corner. A small brown couch was against the right wall, and straight ahead was the doorway to the bedroom.

"Wow," I said with shock as I took a step forward to leave the elevator.

"I upgraded when I found out you were coming. Do you like it?"

"It's incredible. You didn't have to do this." I shook my head and he smiled, running his hands over his hair.

He reached out and tucked my hair behind my ear and winked at me. "I would do anything for you, Cass." My knees went weak with his words. He took one step, closing the gap between us, and his hands circled around my back. "I'm so glad you're here."

"Me, too."

His lips brushed over mine, and as his eyes continued to search mine, he softly pressed against me. My fingers slid over his hard chest and up his neck to pull him closer. He coaxed my mouth open with his tongue, which I happily accepted.

The elevator doors shot open and a man cleared his throat, making me jump and pull away from Tucker.

He laughed and turned to the man. "Just leave it by the bed."

The man pushed his cart full of food into the room as I gave Tucker a quizzical look.

"Hungry?"

My stomach growled as the smell of the food filled the air. I had been so wrapped up in Tucker, I didn't even realize I hadn't eaten yet today. "Very."

He placed his hand on the small of my back and led me to the giant bed. The room had a small table, but I wasn't going to complain about being alone with Tucker in a bedroom.

Tucker tipped the man, who thanked him and left the room. Tucker pulled the silver domes off the plates of food, revealing a smorgasbord of things to eat. My eyes roamed over the chicken leg that was so big I wondered where they found an animal that large. The steak looked mouthwateringly juicy. Another platter was stacked high with sandwiches cut into triangles and arranged among stacks of exotic fruits chopped into tiny pieces. I reached over and lifted one of the forks, shocked by its heaviness. The handle had intricate flowers carved into it. I'd never seen anything like it before.

"I didn't know what you liked so I ordered everything that looked good." His lips quirked into a devilish grin.

"Looks amazing." I leaned over to inhale the scent of the steak, but my stomach revolted and I felt that I was going to be sick.

"Oh, God!" I jumped off the bed and made my way to the first door I could find. Luckily it was the master bathroom. I bolted for the toilet and clung to either side of the seat as my stomach twisted and I gagged, heaving the contents.

"Are you all right?" Tucker was behind me, gathering my hair as I continued to heave, though I hadn't even eaten today. Tucker reached over me and pushed the handle. "Are you still sick?" He got up and filled a cup from the counter with water. I shook my head no and took the glass, taking small sips.

He ran his hand over my hair a few times, his brows drawn together.

"It's nothing. It comes and goes."

"Have you been to a doctor?"

I rolled my eyes at the question. Of course I hadn't been to a doctor. Who could afford the outrageous bills or missing a day of work?

"It's just stress."

"If I'd known you were still sick, I wouldn't have asked you to come."

My heart sank at his words just as my stomach turned again, sending me lurching for the commode. "Oh, God." I rested my head against the cold porcelain.

"Maybe I should call Dorris."

"No." I pushed myself up, immediately feeling light-headed. Tucker wrapped his arm around my waist to keep me steady. "She already doesn't like me very much."

"She likes you, she is just . . . overprotective." He laughed and I rolled my eyes.

"It's good that she protects you." I was glad he had someone looking out for him.

"Who protects you, Cass?"

"I do." He turned me around to face him, placing his palms on either side of my face.

"Well, now I do." He tucked my hair behind my ear. His beautiful face was wrought with concern. I nodded slowly and he pulled me closer, kissing me on the forehead. "Lie down." He led me to the king-size bed and helped lower me down as if I might break. He slid his body in behind mine, pulling my back against his chest. His lips placed light kisses on my shoulder. "I wish I could take away all of your pain."

"You do." I smiled, thinking about the last time Tucker and I were in a hotel room alone together. I pushed my backside into him and he let out a laugh. "I've never felt the way I do with you with anyone else. No one has ever cared about what I wanted, how I felt . . ." I let my words trail off, unsure how to reveal to him that making love to him felt like the first time for me.

I focused on the lamp on the bedside table. It looked as if it had been smashed to shards on purpose and glued back together. That was how I had felt, as if my life had been shattered into a million pieces and Tucker was the glue that was holding me together when I wanted to fall apart.

He buried his face in my neck. I stared blankly at the lamp and counted the pieces of broken glass. When he pulled his body back from mine, I immediately felt empty because of the distance between us.

"I'll be right back. I just need a minute." He stood and turned to leave the bedroom but stopped short of the door. "Are you going to be okay without me?"

I nodded and he left quickly. I pushed up from the bed and made my way to the sink to freshen myself up. My skin was pale and I looked about as bad as I felt. I grabbed the toothpaste and squeezed some on my finger to clean my teeth and finished with a miniature bottle of mouthwash. I turned the water on cold and splashed it on my face.

"Confess your sins and be washed clean by the love of Christ."

I stepped forward, my hand curled in my mother's. I glanced up at her and she squeezed my fingers reassuringly. She released me and stepped back as I stared at the preacher, who towered over me.

I cupped my hands and dipped them in the icy water. He smiled down at me and I was cast aside for the next in line. I didn't feel any different, but I hoped that whatever I had done to cause my father to leave us would now be forgiven so I could have him back with me. I just wanted to be happy again.

I heard the elevator ding and slowly left the bathroom looking for Tucker. He was holding a small bag and handing the attendant from earlier some cash. Tucker clapped his hand on the man's shoulder and thanked him before turning and locking eyes with me, lowering his gaze as he made his way back across the room.

He made it halfway before his phone began to ring. He tossed the bag on the bed and picked up the receiver. "Hello?"

I sat down on the edge of the bed and looked over the food cart for something that wouldn't make me sick.

Tucker turned his back to me and his tone turned quieter. "No. I'll be right down. Thanks." He hung up the phone.

I grabbed a handful of grapes and popped one in my mouth.

Tucker ran his hands through his hair and was squeezing his eyes closed.

"Everything all right?"

"It will be." He pulled my head toward him and kissed me quickly on the top of the head.

"Hurry back." I smiled weakly and popped another grape in my mouth. Tucker left the bedroom, and a few seconds later I heard the familiar ding of the elevator.

I reached into the bag that Tucker had left on the bed and pulled out a bottle of Pepto-Bismol. I unscrewed the cap and drank down a third of the bottle, praying it would not come back up.

I reached behind me for the small bag and pulled it onto my lap. I opened it and found three boxes all labeled pregnancy test. I dropped the bag on the floor in front of me, and the contents spilled out. My hand immediately shot to my mouth. I couldn't be.

It wasn't possible.

Even as I thought it, I knew that wasn't true. I was never good at remembering to take the Pill, and Jackson and I almost never touched each other anymore, so it had slipped my mind.

My head was starting to spin. I slid off the edge of the bed and sank onto my knees. I picked up one of the packages and read it over through teary eyes. My stomach twisted into knots. I gathered up the boxes and headed into the bathroom. There was no point in being scared of the tests. Either I was or I wasn't. I needed to know as soon as possible.

I tore open the first box and read over the instructions quickly. They were fairly simple. I go to the bathroom and wait a few minutes for the results. I tore open all of the boxes and lined the tests up on the counter. I grabbed one of the disposable cups from the sink and forced myself to be brave.

The minutes ticked by like hours. I paced the floor, my eyes glued to the alarm clock beside the bed. After the allotted time had passed, I raced back into the bathroom. I took a deep, cleansing breath as my eyes danced over the sticks. The first one had a plus sign, the second had two lines, and the third read *pregnant*.

The world began to spin around me and I gripped the edge of the sink and squeezed my eyes closed. This couldn't be happening. How could I be pregnant? From just one night of passion with Tucker? Was that even possible? It couldn't be true . . . it couldn't be happening . . . I stared at the little white sticks, willing those lines to disappear, willing that plus sign to turn into a negative. But I knew it wouldn't happen. A part of me must have known this whole time, known there was a reason for my continued clinging to Tucker. Because now a part of him was in me.

I couldn't raise a baby by myself. And then there was Jax. . . . Oh, God! I couldn't think straight. Tucker would be long gone in nine months and I couldn't raise a baby in that trailer.

I staggered back into the bedroom and collapsed onto the bed, bringing my knees to my chest as I thought about the mess I had gotten myself into.

I squeezed my eyes shut and imagined my new home that I always dreamed of. I struggled to imagine Tucker by my side. I struggled to see him anywhere in my future. I forced myself to take deep breaths as I envisioned him by my side, his hand on my ever-expanding midsection. I could see him being there for me, caring for me. I could also see Jackson. See him destroying everything in my life that made me smile. I shook myself from the horrible vision.

My eyes flicked to the clock. Where was Tucker? I needed him more than ever. I got up from the bed and made my way to the elevator. I had to find him. I pushed the button for the lobby as I wrung my hands together. This elevator trip seemed to last a lifetime.

As the doors finally opened, I scanned the expansive lobby for Tucker. I spotted him from the back by the check-in desk. As I made my way toward him, I realized he wasn't alone. He was with a young woman. They seemed to be in an intense conversation, but their voices were too quiet for me to understand. I slowed down a few steps from them when the brunette who had been chatting with him locked eyes with me. I immediately recognized her face from the magazine Dorris had left in the diner. The brunette slid her hands up his neck and pulled his face down to hers, kissing him passionately. Suddenly I couldn't breathe. I felt as if someone had punched me in the stomach, knocked the wind out of me.

"Tucker." I hated the way my voice shook as I spoke. He pushed back against the girl and twisted his head around to see me. I bolted back to the elevator. I pushed the button repeatedly. I couldn't believe how stupid I'd been to think that I was as special to Tucker as he'd become to me. Of course not. I'd needed to believe that something better was out there for me. I'd believed in a fantasy that clearly wasn't real, had never been real.

The doors finally flew open and I hit a random floor number as Tucker raced toward me. The doors closed between us and I began my descent into my own personal hell.

The doors opened and I walked out onto the third floor on shaky legs. I needed to get away from here. I needed to run away. I staggered down the hall as the elevator opened again and Tucker raced up behind me.

"Cass! Cass! Don't do this. I wouldn't hurt you." He reached my side and placed his hand on the small of my back.

"Too late," I sobbed, and pulled away from his touch.

He stepped in front of me and wrapped his arms around me. "Please let me explain."

"Explain? I think I know what I saw. No excuse will ever make that go away. Oh my God. Was it her voice I heard on the phone that day? Jesus, it all makes sense now. Was this all just a game to you? Am I really *that stupid*?" I shoved his body back from mine as hard as I could.

"No! Sweetheart, I didn't lie to you."

"I'm not your fucking sweetheart! You know, I thought it was impossible to hurt worse than when Jax hit me, but I was wrong. None of that compares to the pain in my heart right now. I *trusted* you!" The elevator door behind me reopened and I bolted for it, hitting the button repeatedly. The doors began to close as I stared back into Tucker's tear-filled eyes. I sank to the floor of the elevator and wrapped my hands around my knees.

I hadn't known that I could ever hurt this much. I would take whatever punishment Jax had for me any day over this feeling.

The doors opened and I pushed to my feet, staggering out into the lobby full of people oblivious of my inner turmoil. I made my way through the throngs.

"He will never love you like he loves me, Trash," the voice of a female whispered in my ear from behind.

I froze in my tracks.

"Sweetheart!" Tucker's voice called from behind us.

"Right here, baby," the brown-headed bitch replied. I was tired of running from my problems, from people getting joy out of sucking the happiness out of me. It was time to fight for myself for once, figuratively and . . .

I spun around with my fist cocked back. It connected with her cheek and sent her head whipping back, brown hair flying into my face. Her hand shot up to grab her face in shock as her mouth fell open. I grabbed my fist in my other hand as pain throbbed through it.

"Security!" a man yelled from behind the reception desk.

"He was talking to *me*," I spat angrily.

Tucker's lips curved into a cocky smile as he made his way in front of me. I pushed by him back toward the elevator. He followed, not bothering to even glance at the woman I'd smacked.

He stood by my side, reaching out to hit the button for his room. "That was my ex. That was Cadence."

"I don't care." I folded my arms over my chest and tried to ignore the new wave of nausea that had overtaken me.

"Judging by the way you sucker-punched her, I'd say you care a lot, and I owe you an explanation." I didn't respond so he went on, "Cadence went to rehab, but I wouldn't take her back. I couldn't. Every few months she shows up and tries to change my mind. Sometimes I fall back into her trap. Everything goes well for a few weeks before she relapses. Living this kind of lifestyle isn't for everyone. I'm sorry . . . I'm sorry you had to see that."

I turned to look up at his face. "Did you? Did you change your mind?"

He cupped my face with both of his hands. "Never. You are all I want, Cass. I feel like I have been waiting my whole life for you, and I will wait longer if that's what you need, but I am not going anywhere."

I stared into his eyes, desperately confused and overwhelmed. I needed to get off this roller coaster I'd been on since the day I'd met Tucker and land on solid ground. Could I trust him? Suddenly, another realization dawned on me. "She's the one selling your story to the magazines."

"So you do read them?" He smirked.

"No. I've only read the one Dorris left in the diner for me."

His eyes narrowed and I knew I'd said more than I should have. "When did Dorris come to the diner?"

"Don't worry about it, Tucker. I think she was just worried for you. She was just trying to scare me off."

He clenched his jaw and didn't respond. I knew I had just caused a new rift between him and his adoptive mother.

The doors opened into his room and I stepped out in front of him, waiting for him to follow.

He did, grabbing my elbow and turning me, pulling me to him. "She has no say in what happens between us, I promise you."

I pressed my face against his chest and listened to his heart beating rapidly under my cheek. His chin rested on top of my head. I wasn't sure he would still feel the same way once he saw the results of the pregnancy tests, but I was ready to find out. If he wanted me gone, it was better to know now.

CHAPTER

Twenty-Two

I TOOK THE TEST." I stepped back and turned toward the bedroom. I felt as if I were walking to my death sentence.

"I didn't want you to go through that alone. I'm sorry." He slowly guided me to the bedroom and waited by the bathroom door.

I slipped out from under his arm and took a deep breath. This was it. I grabbed a test and held it out to him. "I'm pregnant."

He looked down at the test and back to me twice before he scooped me up in his arms and lifted me from the ground into a hug.

"Are you mad at me?"

"No, sweetheart, I'm not mad. How could I be? But . . . I am scared."

"I'm scared, too." I buried my face in his neck and inhaled his scent.

"It doesn't matter if . . ." He was lost for words. "It doesn't matter to me if it's not mine. It will be *mine*. This is *our* baby, Cass. You don't need to worry." He slowly lowered me until my toes touched the ground. My heart swelled. I couldn't imagine the amount of responsibility this man was willing to take on for me.

"It's been a long time, Tucker. This baby could be no one else's."

His lips found mine hard. His hands slid down my spine, coming to rest at the top of my shorts. I bowed my body toward him, unable to get close enough. I traced his upper lip with my tongue and he groaned into my mouth as he turned us toward the bed. I felt the mattress against my legs and slid myself back onto it without pulling my mouth from Tucker's. He crawled over me, kissing me hungrily as his body came to rest between my thighs.

My hands felt for the edge of his shirt, pulling it up so I could run my nails up his back. He pushed his hips into mine, and I moaned against his tongue. The phone beside us began to ring. Tucker ignored it, slipping his hand under my tank top and cupping my breast. I arched into his hand. The phone continued to ring.

"Fuck," Tucker growled as he pulled his mouth from mine and rested his head against my cheek as we caught our breath. "I have to get that."

I nodded even though I was disappointed.

He reached over our heads and grabbed the receiver. "Yeah?"

The length of him still pressed firmly against me. He sighed loudly and climbed off my body to sit on the edge of the bed, his free hand running through his hair. I rolled to my side and laid my head on my arm as I stared at his muscular back.

"Fine. Come up." He slammed the phone down and turned back to face me. He ran his finger along my jaw. "That was Dorris. She's on her way up." I could tell by his tone he was not happy.

I pushed myself up and crawled onto his lap. I knew this was going to be bad. The woman hated me as it was. She was going to go ballistic when she found out about the pregnancy.

The elevator opened and in walked Dorris. She spotted Tucker and me on the bed and didn't look surprised. "Why did you change your room, and what the hell was with that circus act in the lobby? Do you have any idea the hoops I'm going to have to jump through to fix this?" Her eyes shot to me and went immediately back to Tucker.

"Needed more space." He shrugged.

"Tucker, are you going to make it to the concert tonight?"

He eyes flicked back to me. "Of course." His arms tightened around me. "Afterward, I have to take Cass back home."

My heart sank. I wasn't ready to leave him.

I started to pull away from him, but his grip tightened and he placed a quick kiss to my forehead. "We have to get a few of her things."

My heart leapt back into my throat. Get my things? Was he going to take me with him? I couldn't just leave my mother and tour the country. Not with a baby. Not after what had happened to his last girlfriend. I thought of the brunette down in the lobby with her hands all over him and felt as if I were going to be sick again.

"Get her things?" Dorris looked down at the floor in front of her and narrowed her eyes.

I pulled from Tucker's arms just as she bent down and picked up the small white stick in her hand. Her eyes grew wide as saucers as she read *pregnant* on the front of the test.

"Take care of this, Tucker." Her teeth were grinding as she spoke.

He replied, "I'm not going to—"

Dorris waved her hand. "Take care of *this*. Get rid of it." She looked me up and down as if she were disgusted. I slid off his lap and sat next to him. "You've worked too hard. The band has worked too hard for you to ruin it over some . . . some fling." She turned and stormed out into the living room.

"Get rid of it? Do you even hear what you're saying?" He pushed from the bed and stood in front of her.

"You don't need to deal with this." She placed her hand on his arm.

He shrugged her away. "Like my parents didn't deal with me?

You want me to just throw away my kid? I guess I can just pick one up later down the road like you did."

"That's not fair, Tucker. Like it or not, I am your mother, and I only have your best interests in mind." She threw her hands in the air and stormed off toward the elevator.

"I know what I'm doing," Tucker called after her.

She didn't respond. The elevator doors opened and she stepped inside, glaring at Tucker as the doors slid closed.

He squeezed me against his chest and rocked me slowly. "I'm not going to abandon you. I won't. I don't give a damn what she thinks."

I nodded, but I knew that it wasn't true. Tucker had a future, and I would never forgive myself if he lost it because of me. I placed my hand down to my stomach. It was too late for all of that. I had already destroyed his future. His hand slid over mine.

"I promise," he said.

I let him hold me for a few more minutes before sliding off his lap. "You have a concert to get ready for." I smiled down at him as he leaned down and placed a kiss on my stomach.

"Let's go take our baby to its first concert." He stood up and made his way to the bathroom to get himself ready.

I sank back down on the mattress and let my head fall into my hands, overwhelmed.

Tucker came out of the bathroom with his toothbrush in his mouth and leaned against the doorframe. "It's going to be okay." He cocked his head to the side.

"I know," I sighed.

He flashed me a big smile and slipped back into the bathroom to finish up.

"Tucker?"

He leaned back so I could see him through the bathroom doorway.

"What did you mean about going to get some of my stuff? Are you taking me on tour with you?" I was nervous.

He gave me an odd look and spit into the sink before answering. "That wouldn't really be a good idea for a baby." He turned on the water and rinsed out his mouth. My heart sank again. Could he not just tell me everything he was thinking? The water shut back off and Tucker came out of the bathroom and knelt down in front of me. He lifted my chin with his fingers so I would look him in the eye.

"I don't want our baby growing up on a tour bus. I want us to have a home. I want to make a home for us. You and me. Together."

I practically flew into his arms and wrapped my own around his neck. I'd never felt so cared for, so . . . loved. Could this really be happening? It was overwhelming after the day I'd had.

"Now let's go. I need to put on a kick-ass show."

I gave him a quick kiss on the tip of his nose. "Let's go, rock star."

Tucker pulled me from the bed and wrapped his arm around my waist as we walked to the elevator. The day couldn't have gone any better considering all of the things that had happened, but I was still worried about Tucker. I couldn't be responsible for destroying his dreams and his relationship with Dorris. There was also the nagging question of whether we would ever have taken a big step like this if I weren't pregnant. Was I forcing him into this? Was he committing to me out of a sense of chivalry, or did he really want to make a life with me?

We stepped inside the elevator to leave. I wrapped my arms around Tucker's waist from the side and squeezed him closer to me. I was terrified of what the rest of the night would bring, but I pushed it to the back of my mind. I was going to watch Tucker perform and I couldn't wait.

We slipped out of the back entrance of the lobby and hopped on Tucker's motorcycle.

"I guess we'll need something more practical soon," he said over his shoulder. I hugged him tightly as his bike roared to life and we shot out onto the main highway on the island.

I closed my eyes and pressed my face into Tucker's back. I didn't want to forget this moment. I felt hopeful and wanted to hang on to that feeling for as long as possible. I thought over all of the time I had spent with Tucker. I'd taken a lot of chances to be with him, and now he was taking a big chance on me. The idea of starting a family terrified me. I hadn't had a good home life since my dad left, so I had never wanted a family of my own. I didn't think I could ever create a happy home for a child given that I could barely provide one for myself.

The bike slowed and veered to the left, pulling onto a small back road that was lined by trees and large beach houses. We wove down a few more streets and through a small park with tennis courts and a large, hidden soccer field.

Tucker pulled up next to a small building and backed his bike into a parking spot before shutting off the engine.

"Where are we?" I pulled off my helmet and shook my hair.

"You'll see."

I slipped my leg over the bike and stretched as I held out my helmet for Tucker to store.

"Come on." He held out his hand and smiled. I laced my fingers with his, and he pulled me across the small road and onto a blacktop walkway surrounded by trees.

"This is beautiful!" I pointed to a small pond on our left.

"It gets better." Tucker's thumb traced small circles on the back of my hand as we made our way through a clearing into another small parking lot. The path resumed, but this time it was sand.

"We're at the beach?" I shielded my eyes with my hand and tried to look ahead, but I couldn't see any water. Tucker nodded and I squealed. We walked a little farther before the giant, glittering body of water came into view.

Along the water, I also saw a large mass of people crowded around a black stage that was erected in front of the ocean. Dorris stood at the base of the path waiting for us. She shot me a glare and quickly ushered us to the rest of the band, who were hanging out behind the stage with the crew and a few other bands.

"Hey, bro." Chris slapped Tucker's hand and pulled him in to bump shoulders with him. He nodded his head toward me with a grin. "'Sup, Cass?"

I smiled and tucked my hair behind my ears, but didn't even know where to begin to answer his question.

A man took the stage and began to hype up the crowd. They cheered and hollered so deafeningly loudly that it was impossible for me to hear my own thoughts. That wasn't necessarily a bad thing.

Apparently, Damaged was the first band to take the stage tonight. Tucker pulled me into his chest and gave me a quick kiss before nodding to Dorris. She looped her arm in mine and guided me to the front of the crowd before the stage so we could watch the show. As soon as we arrived, I quickly pulled my arm free from hers.

The man was still onstage talking, and Dorris leaned in closer to me so I could hear her. "Tucker is a good man and he would do anything he had to if he thought it was right, but this band has been his dream and I will not see him throw that away." Her eyes stayed focused on the stage ahead as she spoke.

"Then we're on the same page," I assured her as Damaged stepped onto the stage.

The people around us went nuts, effectively ending our tense conversation.

I cheered along with everyone else as Tucker stepped into view. He smiled as he saw me and winked, making my heart melt into a puddle at my feet. The Twisted Twins began to play their guitars, and the crowd's enthusiasm only intensified. They started by playing "Loved." My heart melted at the sound of Tucker's voice.

His eyes locked on mine as he sang of driving miles and miles and winding up at my door. My hand went to my stomach and I swayed with the crowd as he sang to me. I snuck a glance at Dorris, who was smiling proudly at the band. She was right to be worried about Tucker's future. I was, too. I didn't want to take this from him. It was what he was born to do. Still, the idea of spending my life with Tucker was too much to resist. Even if he was on the road for months at a time, we could make it work, right? People did it all the time.

The song ended and the band flowed seamlessly into the next as he sang about trying harder and being scared. I could definitely relate to the lyrics, and they brought tears to my eyes. This song was much more intense, and he sang most of it with his eyes pressed closed.

Our entire world was crashing down around us and Tucker was able to make me feel safe and loved for the first time I could remember in my life. The day he'd stepped into the diner changed my life and set off a chain of events that would ultimately change the course of our lives forever, good or bad. I didn't know what brought him to me, if it was fate or karma, but I was grateful to have him in my life, even if it was all crumbling around us.

The sun was fading fast behind us and sparkled off the water behind the stage. It was magical. The women around me sang along to the beautiful lyrics and I even joined in.

Tucker transitioned into a new song that I hadn't heard yet, about secrets. I blushed as his eyes locked on mine as he sang, "I want you so bad." I loved every minute of it. I never wanted it to end, but as soon as this song finished, it was time for the next band.

I followed Dorris to the back of the stage, where Tucker was taking a long swig from a water bottle. His eyes lit up when he saw me. His arm hooked around my neck and he pressed his damp lips to my forehead.

"Hey, guys," Dorris called to the bandmates, who were already scouting the crowd for women. They gathered around Tucker and me as they waited to hear what she had to say. "Go ahead, Tucker. Share your news with the band. It's their future you're toying with as well."

Tucker's arm tightened around me. "I'm sorry," he whispered in my ear before kissing me on the cheek. "Cass and I are going to have a baby."

Everyone's eyes moved between Tucker and me, and at first no one spoke. I held my breath as I waited for them to say something, anything.

"Jesus Christ." Chris stepped forward, running his hand over his face in shock before pulling Tucker into his embrace. Terry followed suit, patting Tucker on the back and whispering something to him. You could see the looks of concern in their eyes, but mostly they were struggling to look happy for Tucker.

"Eric?" Tucker was looking at his drummer, waiting for a response as we held our breath.

Eric's eyes cut to me before he turned to the stage and punched a large trunk that was propped against the back of it.

"Don't do this, man."

"Don't do this? Do what, Tucker? Fuck up our entire future while only thinking of ourselves? Is that what *I'm* doin', man?"

"This wasn't planned. It just happened."

"Yeah, well, it can unhappen." Eric was fuming and a small crowd was starting to take notice.

Tucker stepped forward, shoved against Eric's chest, and pointed his finger at him. "Don't ever fucking talk about my child like that again!"

"Think about what you're saying." Terry stepped between them.

"He's only saying what you're all thinking," Dorris said, folding her arms over her chest.

"That's enough!" Tucker yelled at her before taking a deep breath. "Dorris, I love you like a mother. I could really use a mother right now. You know this band has always been my dream, and none of that has changed." He ran his hand through his hair. "You're like my family." His eyes scanned the band. "Cass is family now, too." He met each of their gazes. "Don't make me choose." The warning did not go unnoticed. "Because I'll choose her."

Eric stepped forward, his eyes challenging Tucker, who refused to look away. He wasn't bluffing, he was going to throw it all on the line for me and this baby. Eric sighed and looked up at the sky for a moment before pulling Tucker into a one-armed hug. The other members followed suit.

I was incredibly relieved. I didn't want to be the cause of any problems with Tucker's band, although clearly there would be a much longer conversation when I wasn't around.

The next band took the stage and it was impossible to talk any further. Tucker leaned in to Terry and talked directly into his ear and he nodded, giving Tucker one last hug before he pulled me back toward the sandy path we'd walked in on.

CHAPTER

Twenty-Three

"WHERE ARE WE going?" I shot Tucker a quizzical look.

"To get your things." He grinned and gave my hip a squeeze. I swallowed against the lump in my throat as reality came crashing down around me. I was going to have to face Jax. "It will be fine, don't worry. This is only the beginning."

I gave Tucker a weak smile. He was right. After tonight, we could be together and I wouldn't have to worry about anything but our future and our family. I took a deep breath and tried to push the worry out of my head as we traveled back the narrow path.

When we reached his bike, he pulled me into his arms and held me tightly while he whispered in my ear, "I know you're scared. I'm scared, too. We can get through this together." He pressed his lips to my neck before pulling back to look me in the eye. I nodded and grabbed my helmet from the back of the bike.

"How can you be so certain this will all work out?" I was terrified and I couldn't understand his calm demeanor.

He shrugged and looked off in the distance. "It has to. I couldn't live with myself if it didn't. I won't make the same mistakes my parents made." He pressed his hand to my belly and his mood lightened.

I ran my fingers over his cheek and along his jaw as it flexed under my fingers. I still couldn't understand how he'd made it through so much in his life and turned out so amazing. "Let's go begin our new life." I slipped my helmet over my head.

Tucker brushed my hair back from my face and buckled the clasp beneath my chin. He gave me a quick kiss on the lips and put on his helmet as well.

The drive back to the trailer park always seemed to go faster than the trip to leave. I knew Jax would most likely be passed out cold and I had little to worry about, but I was fearful nonetheless. Storms were approaching, and thunder cracked as lightning streaked across the sky. It seemed fitting for the day we had had. Today everything would change, either for good or bad, but I was ready for it.

As we pulled into the parking lot of the diner, Tucker parked near the trailer-park fence and I slowly forced myself to get off the bike. There was an eerie silence. Everyone was inside preparing for Mother Nature to unleash her fury.

"Wait for me in Aggie's. I just need to grab a few things and talk to my mom." I pulled off my helmet and handed it to Tucker.

"I don't think it's a good idea for you to go alone." He stepped off the bike. I watched him place our helmets over the handlebars. I sighed, not wanting to have this argument. If Jax was awake, things would quickly escalate with Tucker there.

"It will be fine. I promise. I will be in and out in five minutes. He doesn't even know about us." I leaned in and pressed my lips against Tucker's cheek, lingering for a few extra seconds. "I'll be okay. I've done this since I met you."

"Five minutes or I'm coming to find you, sweetheart." He was serious and there was no point in trying to convince him otherwise. I nodded and made my way through the fence. I glanced over my shoulder to see Tucker staring at me before taking a few steps back and heading for the door of the diner.

This was it. My life was changing, and in the instant it took to blink, it would all be different. I took a deep breath and pulled open the door to the trailer.

The living room was empty and the only sound came from the television. I let out a sigh of relief at the anticlimactic ending to my struggles. All of the lights were off, but as the lightning struck, I could see perfectly down the narrow hallway. I sidestepped around the bucket and gripped the doorknob to my bedroom. I pushed it open just as lightning flashed again, followed by a loud crack of thunder. Jackson sat on my bed. It was the only thing not over-turned and torn apart in my room. My dresser lay on its side, the drawers falling out and the contents spilled onto the floor. My closet doors were ripped off their tracks and lay on the opposite side of the room. My beautiful dresses lay in rags, strewn across the debris of what used to be my entire world. It looked as if a tornado had selectively touched down in my room. That tornado was staring straight at me.

"Where the fuck have you been?" His voice was low and men-acing. His eyes slowly rose to meet mine.

I tried to speak, but my throat swelled shut in fear. Jackson stood and stepped close enough that I could smell the liquor on his breath. I closed my eyes and summoned all of my strength to face him one last time.

"Before you fucking lie, I went to the diner and I also had a few words with your worthless mother." He eyed me with disgust. "I know you lied about where you were the other night, you fucking whore."

My eyes shot open as all of my secrets poured out. I flinched at the words. They'd never hurt me before. I realized after the last few days I had actually begun to doubt they were true.

"You've been lying a lot lately." He smiled, and it sent a chill down my spine.

"Fuck you," I choked out.

The first blow landed on the side of my face. I couldn't tell if lightning flashed or if my vision was suffering. A hot blast of pain knocked me sideways, and I hit the wall behind me. I grabbed my face, hoping to protect myself from the next hit. It was no use. The next blow was from his closed fist into my stomach. I fell backward and curled into a ball, gasping for air. I couldn't breathe. I struggled to suck in a breath as his foot came down hard on my hip.

"How could you do this to me?" he screamed, hovering over me with reddened eyes.

I reached for him, begging for his help as I finally managed to inhale.

He knocked my hand away in disgust. "This is all your fault! I didn't want it to come to this." He ran his hands through his hair angrily.

"Jax, please don't do this. Please, I'm sorry."

He looked at me with pain in his eyes and shook his head. "It's too late." He was calm, and that scared me more than his shouting.

He bent over me, fisting my shirt in his hands, and pulled my body from the ground as he leaned in closer. "All of this is your fault." He dropped my body back down and swung with a closed fist. His hand connected with my temple, and the world spun on its axis as my body absorbed the blow. "I loved you," he sobbed.

I cried, wailing as the pain took over. I gave up in that moment, just wanting it all to end. If I didn't make it out of that trailer, I wanted it all to end quickly.

"Say something!" he yelled as anger took over. I covered my face with my arms to shield myself.

"Get it over with," I moaned as I stared up at him.

He laughed and shook his head. "Your mother didn't even give up this easily."

Panic washed over me as the will to fight intensified. *What have I done?*

I scrambled out of the room on my hands and knees toward my mother's room. Jackson was behind me as I pushed open her door. He grabbed my hair and jerked my head back hard. My mother's bloody and beaten body came into view. She lay sprawled across the floor, her eyes fixed on nothing, unseeing.

"Oh, God! Jackson!" I screamed. His fingers released me and I scrambled to my mother's side, pushing her onto her back.

"Mom!" I clawed at her shirt, desperate to wake her. I placed my cheek over her face, hoping to hear her breathing, but my head was spinning from the pain that Jax had inflicted upon me. I placed my mouth over my mother's and pinched her nose shut. I tried to breathe life back into her as I began to hyperventilate. "Mama!" I clung to her lifeless body, praying away my life for hers. "You can't," I sobbed as my fingers uncurled from the blood-soaked fabric of her shirt. "You can't leave me, Mom! Oh, God! What have you done?" My fingers were stained with my mother's blood, and I rubbed them over my own clothes, desperate to remove any trace of it.

"You thought I was gonna just let you walk away, Cass?" His foot drew back and he kicked me hard in the back. My spine jerked straight and I fell to the floor at my mother's feet. I screamed in agony as I tried to curl into a ball and protect myself. It wasn't the first time Jackson had hit me, but this time I had infuriated him and unleashed the monster that had lain just below the surface inside him all these years. I didn't know how far he would go, or if he would make good on his promise to end my misery for me. I had to protect my baby at any cost. I tried to push to my hands and knees again, scanning the floor for my phone. Jackson just laughed at my sobbing.

"Looking for this?" He tossed the phone onto the floor. I scrambled for it and flipped it open, praying I could stop my fingers from shaking long enough to dial Tucker's number.

"Who is he, Cass? That fucking prick from the diner? I'll fucking kill him." Another kick. This one hitting me in the back of my thighs, sending the phone sliding across the floor into a sticky pool of blood.

"No one," I screamed as I tried desperately to protect myself.

His blows stopped, but I didn't dare try to look to see what he was doing. I had made that mistake before. You don't ever leave your face open. Last time, I'd walked around with a bruised and swollen cheek for three weeks.

His hand twisted in my hair as he pulled me to my feet. The pain from my back shot through my body as I tried to steady myself. How long had I been here? My mind raced as I tried to count the minutes. It felt like an eternity. Tucker should be coming to look for me soon. I wasn't sure it would be soon enough. Crippling pain radiated from my stomach and into my aching chest.

His face pressed against my cheek as he whispered in my ear, "You want to act like a whore? I will treat you like a whore."

I wanted to vomit. I stumbled and tripped over my feet as he dragged me back to my room. My head was swimming in pain and my eyes were blurred by my tears.

"No! No!" My hands flew up to his as I clawed at him, trying to free myself. He laughed as he shoved me into the room. I kicked and bucked, desperate to get free.

He finally let go of my hair and I fell against the edge of my bed onto the floor. I quickly got to my feet and dashed for my dresser, grabbing in my arms my father's bear that lay against the wall. I needed to leave, go anywhere but here.

Jackson cocked his head to the side and smiled. "That bear won't protect you . . . just like your father didn't protect you from the guys your whore of a mother brought in here."

My blood was boiling now. I narrowed my eyes at him as I squeezed the bear to my chest. I just had to get past him. If I could get out the door, I could outrun him.

"That was another secret you were hiding from me." His eyes glanced to the bear and he took a step closer. Jackson let out another sadistic laugh as he quickly closed the gap between us. His arms wrapped around my waist as he lifted me and threw me on the bed. I landed hard on my sore back, his body crashing on top of mine.

I beat against his chest with my fists, trying to pull my knees up between us. "I hate you!" I clenched my teeth as I struggled to fight him off. His hands found my wrists and he pinned my hands above my head with one hand. His smacked me hard across the face, and my mouth filled with the metallic taste of blood.

"Good." He slipped his hand between us and hiked up my shirt.

"Help!" I screamed.

Jackson stilled for a second, listening before smiling down at me. "No one is going to help you, Cass."

I pulled one of my hands free and struck him as hard as I could across the face. My palm burned from the harsh contact. Every ounce of rage and pain I had was in that hit. Jackson slowly looked back to me, a small trickle of blood oozing from his lower lip. His free hand shot up to my throat, gripping it painfully tight. I kicked and tried to fight against him, desperate for air. His eyes locked onto mine as he ground his hips into mine. His other hand tugged at my shorts, the material digging into my flesh as he yanked.

"Worthless fucking whore," he snarled as his grip tightened again.

I could feel my face cooling from the lack of blood flow. I wasn't scared to die, to end the pain, but I couldn't leave this world looking into Jackson's eyes.

A loud banging came from the front of the house. Tucker had come. He had come to save me. Jackson's eyes fixed on mine for a minute and I prayed he wouldn't kill me before I could see Tucker.

"Looks like the fun is over." Jackson kissed me on the cheek and lifted his weight off my body. I desperately tried to catch my breath as he stumbled out of my room. I could hear the front door open, banging off the wall outside.

"Where the fuck is Cass?" I heard Tucker yell.

I wanted to run to him but my body was too weak and the pain too great.

"Why the fuck do you care?" Jackson snarled.

His words were immediately followed by a loud crack. I prayed that it was Jackson taking the blows, but I couldn't be sure.

"Because I love her, you piece of shit."

Jackson laughed, and there was another loud bang off the side of the trailer.

"She's all yours, what's left of her. I hope you don't mind if I took her for one last ride," Jackson spat back.

I crawled my way down the hall, ignoring the agonizing pain that shot through my stomach and what seemed like every nerve ending in my body. My hands and knees sloshed in the water as I knocked over the bucket that caught the rainwater.

"Confess your sins and be washed clean by the love of Christ."

I pulled the front door open in time to see Tucker cock back his fist and land a hard blow to Jackson's nose. Blood spurted from his nose, coating his shirt, and spraying onto Tucker. I was shocked that there was so much.

Jackson swung wildly but was unable to land a blow. Tucker stepped forward and grabbed Jackson by the collar of his shirt and brought his knee into Jax's stomach. He made a deep, guttural groan as the wind was knocked out of him.

"Not so easy fighting someone your own size, is it?" Tucker taunted him.

"Fuck you!" Jax panted.

"This is for all of the times you hurt her. For all of the times I wasn't here to protect her from you." Tucker brought his elbow down into Jackson's back, forcing him to his knees. He struggled to get back to his feet, and Tucker stepped back to let him. It was like watching a cat toy with a mouse. Not a side I ever expected to see from Tucker.

Jackson managed to make it to his feet, but he swayed as he struggled to keep his balance.

"I will fucking kill you!" Tucker was seething, and I knew he meant what he said. His arm came back again and Jackson didn't even put his hands up to block him.

"Stop," I screamed. There had been enough death and enough sadness for one day. I couldn't witness any more.

Tucker spun around. His eyes grew large when he saw me on the floor, battered and bruised.

"Oh, God! Cass!" He rushed to me and picked me up in his arms like a baby.

As soon as I was safe against his chest, I began to sob uncontrollably.

"It's okay. You're safe now." He ran his hands over my hair soothingly as he squeezed me painfully tight. My whole body ached.

"My mother . . ." I pulled back from him to look in his eyes. He pushed my face back into the crook of his neck.

"Shh . . ." He carried me across the room and sat me gently on the couch to look me over. "I'll go find her."

"No!" I clawed at his shirt, desperate to keep him by my side. "Don't go back there."

"It's okay, Cass. I won't leave you."

More waves of pain shot through my body. His hand splayed across my belly, and I glanced down to my thighs and saw that they were now tinged red with blood. His gaze followed mine.

The pain and sadness in his eyes were enough to kill me. I should never have come back alone. I should have never lied and kept secrets from Jax. Now my baby and my mother had paid the price. I realized Jackson's leaving me alive was the ultimate punishment. I would live with the guilt of their deaths for the rest of my life. Any pain I suffered I deserved and would endure.

I couldn't look Tucker in the eyes for the rest of my life knowing what I had put him through. I made my mind up then and there that I had to save him from me.

CHAPTER

Twenty-Four

TUCKER NEVER LEFT my side. I faded in and out of consciousness until the muffled sounds of sirens filled my ears. Tucker carried me out to the ambulance and placed me on the gurney.

Cops swarmed in from every direction but I could hardly keep my eyes open.

"Be on the lookout for a white male, early twenties, named Jackson Fisher. Suspect may be armed and is extremely dangerous."

Tucker squeezed my hand as his face hovered over mine. "It's going to be okay, sweetheart. It's okay now. I love you. I love you so much."

I tried to respond but my throat felt bruised and sore. I could feel the hands of others on me, checking my injuries. I let sleep take over as they worked to mend all but my broken heart.

"Sweet girl, why are you pouting?" My mother finished putting the bobby pins into my hair.

"Daddy is gonna miss my birthday. You promised he would be here!"

"You know he wants to be with you, baby. He just couldn't make it." My mother got up and hurried down the hallway to her room. I heard a few things shuffle around before she returned.

"What's that?"

"Well, go on. Open it." I took the box from her hand and pulled off the newspaper.

"It's a teddy bear! Is it from Daddy?"

"Sure it is, baby."

I jumped up and wrapped my arms around her neck, squeezing her as tightly as possible.

"Where am I?" I rubbed at my throat.

"Welcome back." A cheery nurse smiled down at me and patted me on the shoulder.

The circumstances that landed me in this bed all came crashing down on me like a tsunami.

"Tucker."

"The doctor is going to look you over quickly and then I'll send in your guests, okay?"

I nodded as a man in a long, white coat entered.

"There she is!" He pulled out a small light and shined it into my eyes.

"I'm fine." I pushed his hand away. My head was throbbing.

"You're very lucky."

Lucky was the last thing I would call myself.

"No broken bones. Lots of bumps and bruises, but nothing that won't heal over time." He smiled, but it didn't reach his eyes.

"My baby."

"I'm sorry. You were only a few weeks along and the fetus could not withstand the trauma. The good news is you're still young and there is nothing stopping you from having a family in the future."

I shook my head no as tears welled in my eyes.

"I'm truly sorry for your loss."

I couldn't look at him. I felt his weight lift from the edge of the bed as he spoke quietly to the nurse.

"Ms. Daniels? Is it okay if I send in your fiancé?"

My heart began to race as the machine next to me beeped

faster. I prayed she meant Tucker and that Jackson was not here to finish me off. He couldn't hurt me any worse than he already had.

"Calm down, sweetheart."

"Don't call me that." I narrowed my eyes at her.

"You've been through a great deal. I can tell Mr. White you don't wish to have any visitors."

"No. He can come in." I struggled to sit up. The nurse nodded once and left the room. I tried my best to run my fingers through my hair. It was no use. It was a knotted mess. My mother wouldn't even be able to fix it. My heart ached as I thought of her.

"Cass . . ." Tucker stood in the doorway with my teddy bear in his hands. "I thought you would want this." He stepped closer as his eyes took in my ragged state. I held my hand out to him and he handed the bear to me.

"Thank you. It was from my mother."

He sat down on the edge of the bed and drew his brows together. "I thought it was from your father."

"I thought so, too." I picked at the tattered fur on one of the paws.

"Sweetheart, the baby—"

"I know." I didn't take my eyes off the bear. I couldn't stand to see the sadness in Tucker's eyes. The pain that Jax had inflicted upon me was minuscule in comparison to the pain I had caused Tucker.

"There's something else." He reached for my hand, entwining our fingers. His thumb rubbed over the back of my hand as he struggled to tell me what he needed to say.

I braced for him to tell me he didn't want to be with me anymore. I wouldn't blame him; in fact I knew it would be best for me to get as far away from him as possible before the damage I caused him was irreversible.

"Jackson is here."

I gripped Tucker's hand for dear life. I felt as if I were drowning. "Why? Why is he here? Oh, God, please keep him away from me."

Tucker wrapped his arms around me, cocooning me in his safety. "Shh . . . He can't hurt you anymore. The police are with him. He overdosed last night. They found him about a half mile from your house."

"So he just gets away with it? With everything he did?"

Tucker kissed the top of my head as he rocked us back and forth. "He's bleeding internally from our fight. Three cracked ribs, a broken nose, and a fractured jaw."

"Oh, God. Are you in trouble? Are they going to come after you? Tucker, I'm so sorry for all of this!"

"No. It wasn't your fault. Not mine either. It was self-defense. He can't hurt you anymore. That's all that matters."

I clung to Tucker as if he were the oxygen that I breathed.

"No one will ever hurt you again. I promise." Tears began to fall down his cheeks as he pulled me tight against him.

I was released the next morning from the hospital. Tucker rented a car so I wouldn't have to sit on the back of his motorcycle. He took me to the drugstore to fill my prescription. The woman at the counter looked horrified when she saw my bruised and swollen face. She glared at Tucker, but he didn't say a word. He didn't care what anyone thought. For once, my guy only cared about one thing: me.

We stayed locked away in a hotel room where no one could find us, only leaving for my mother's funeral. We had her buried in Eddington Cemetery, just a mile from the trailer park. Aggie and Larry showed up to support me and pay their respects to her. The preacher who ran the NA meetings we'd attended said kind words about her, never once bringing up her struggles and addictions. I left the teddy bear she had given me when I was a child in front of the plaque that marked her grave.

I never attended Jax's funeral, but I knew that one day I would need to visit his grave. Whether to condemn him or forgive him, I didn't know . . . but one day I'd need to make peace with everything Jax had given me . . . and taken from me.

"You don't need to go there, Cass. It's only going to make things harder on you." Tucker sank down on the hotel bed and scrubbed his hands over his face.

"Harder? I don't sleep, I can't eat, I hate myself for what you've had to go through. I don't see how it could get any worse."

"Please don't put *yourself* through anything more. Give your body and heart time to heal." He rubbed the pad of his thumb over my bruised cheekbone, causing me to flinch.

I stepped back from between his legs and stormed off into the bathroom, locking the door behind me.

He was at the door in seconds. "Come on, sweetheart. I'm just trying to make you feel better."

I didn't respond. I had no idea what to say.

"Fine. Do what you want." He kicked the door gently, but it still caused me to jump. "You're not the only one who's hurting here, Cass."

"I know." I clenched my jaw.

"He *killed* our baby. He doesn't deserve your sympathy. He deserves to rot in hell."

I sank down to the floor and hung my head in my hands. I had no sympathy for Jax. Not anymore, but I deserved to have my say, to feel the way I felt. And I deserved to tell him how I felt. The door to the hotel room slammed and I knew that it would be hours before Tucker returned. I pulled open the bathroom door and shut off the lights before crawling into bed and crying myself to sleep.

Tucker missed countless concerts and his band had to cancel the rest of the tour. He didn't care, but I knew that I was killing his dreams the longer he stayed with me. I knew they had to hate me by now, but Tucker assured me that they only wanted what was best for the two of us. I didn't believe him. I didn't believe in fairy tales anymore. How could any relationship survive what we had been through?

Jax had killed me in that trailer. I no longer lived, no longer smiled. I could feel nothing but sadness and pain.

I forced myself to get out of bed every morning and get ready for the day even though I had nothing to wake up for. I hadn't been back to the trailer park since that night. I couldn't work again until my bruises healed. The doctor gave me medication to cope with the pain. I refused to take it. I had grown accustomed to pain and it would be too easy to slip down the path of addiction, which had ultimately ended in the deaths of three people. I deserved to suffer through everything that was dealt my way.

Tucker spent his days writing songs and silently dealing with all of his own pain. I encouraged him to meet with his band. He needed to get back to what he loved doing. He told me he didn't want to ever leave me alone again, but I knew he missed his old life, and I was sure he resented me for all I put him through. I knew he regretted stepping foot into Aggie's Diner that day. I had to make it right for him.

While he was taking a shower one morning, I called Dorris and let her know where we were. The band was waiting for Tucker by the time he came out of the bathroom.

"What the fuck is this?"

"I knew you weren't ever going to call them."

"So you went behind my back?"

"I'm not doing this *to* you. I'm doing this *for* you."

"Funny. I thought I should have a say in what I want out of my life."

"Tuck, we know your hurtin', man, but we need you, too. You can't just give up on your entire life." Terry stepped forward, taking the heat off me momentarily. I was grateful.

"I'm not giving up on shit, Terry. In case you didn't notice, I didn't ask for any of this."

"Did we?" Eric crossed his arms over his chest.

"This isn't fair." Tucker paced the floor like a caged animal.

"It's not. None of this is fair. Are you going to let him win? He's destroyed everything you worked your entire life for and you're just letting it happen," Chris interjected.

"Fine. I'll try. That's the best I can do. I'm not making any promises." Tucker ran his hand over his unshaven face.

He was angry, but he didn't say a word to me. In fact, he pretty much gave up on talking to me altogether. I lashed out at him, with no one else to direct my anger toward. Neither of us knew how to deal with such a great loss. It was impossible to describe loving someone you had never even met. The band told Tucker they would wait as long as he needed for him to get past all he'd been through. If they waited for him to be ready, they would be waiting a lifetime.

A week later, after several secret phone calls to Dorris, the band had set up their first gig in over a month. They would be playing a small set at the Lucas Theatre in Savannah. It would kick off the second leg of their tour. I spent the morning looking for apartments in the local paper as he prepared. He was nervous.

"I have to go. The guys want to rehearse the new song before the concert tonight."

I smiled as he kissed me on the forehead. "Are you sure you're up for this tonight?"

"You didn't leave me with much of a choice, Cass." I looked into his eyes and he grinned. "Thank you for that."

"You refused to jump. I pushed you. Break a leg." I winked at him and he laughed, running his hand through his hair.

He kissed me again and looked down at the paper. "I pulled out cash from the ATM. You can check out some of these places, and if you find one you like, put down a deposit. The concert starts at six. Don't be late." He pulled out a stack of money from his wallet and laid it on the bed next to me.

"I love you."

"I love you, too." He grinned as he pulled me into his arms and hugged me tight. I squeezed him back, not wanting to let him go, but I knew I had to. I had to let him go so he could go on to be the rock star he was destined to be.

"Good-bye, Tucker."

"See you later, Cass." He left the room and I finally let the tears fall. Once again, it was time to let him move forward with his life.

I grabbed my purse and flew around the room, gathering my belongings. I had four hours before he would know I was gone. Four hours before I broke his heart. I had no other choice.

I made my way down to the sidewalk in the bright afternoon sun. I had to work fast. I hurried down a few blocks and made my way across Bay Street toward the river. I slipped past the Chart restaurant to Scarlett's.

"I saw your ad in the paper for help," I told the woman at the register. She smiled brightly as she handed her customer change.

"Do you have any experience in retail?"

"I've worked as a waitress, but I've always loved your shop." I thought back to when Tucker bought me my first dress from here. I hoped he would forgive me for what I was doing.

"Well, I just need someone who can run a register and help customers find their sizes. You think you can handle that?"

"Absolutely."

"Great. Be here at seven in the morning and I'll show you the ropes."

"Thank you so much," I squealed. I hurried out of the shop to execute part two of my plan. I needed to find an affordable apartment not too far away. The paper was advertising low-income housing just a few blocks from Bay Street, and I knew with the cash Tucker had given me, I would be able to pay the deposit and the first month's rent, with plenty left over for food until my first paycheck rolled in.

I knew Tucker would be crushed when he didn't see me at his concert, but I also knew I owed him this. One day he would thank me for letting him go. And if I wanted to get my life back together, I needed to be my own white knight for once.

I found my way to the apartment buildings. They weren't much to look at, but anything was better than the trailer park. I would never go back there. I met the manager, and after giving him my mother's name to make sure Tucker couldn't track me down, I rented my very first apartment. I figured this was my story and I could rewrite it, starting with a new name for my new life, just like Tucker had.

"Here ya go, Anne." The manager held out a set of keys.

"Thank you." I spun around to look at my new place as he left. It was about as big as a box, but if I stood on my toes, I could see some of the river from my living-room window. The furniture was old and musty, but it would do until I could save for something a little newer.

I curled up on the corner of the ugly hunter-green couch and pulled my knees to my chest as I waited for the next hour and a half to tick by. There would be no turning back now. I let my tears fall freely as the minutes inched on until it was six o'clock.

I knew I was doing what was best for Tucker, but it still hurt like hell. I didn't regret the time I had spent with him. I had finally felt loved and was able to love someone else, and that was truly amazing. Tucker had helped me realize that I was worth something, that I deserved something better out of life, and I would never be able to repay him for that. But I could act on it.

I hoped he would forgive me one day for putting him through all of this, and I hoped he didn't regret the time we'd had together.

CHAPTER

Twenty-Five

THE WEEKS TICKED by and I began to fall into my place in life. I worked endless hours to make money for the bills and even a little extra. Now that I had only myself to support, I was able to save a bit, too. I refused to let myself sulk over what had happened to me. I knew if I worked hard enough, maybe one day Tucker and I would cross paths again. I planned on being worthy of someone as kind and caring as him when that time came.

I began attending the local NA meetings. I still struggled with my anger and pain from what drugs had done to the ones I loved. I learned a lot about myself. My bruises had healed, but the pain in my heart still lingered. I needed to learn to cope with it and forgive the ones who'd wronged me in my life.

I gathered my things as I looked at the clock that hung in the kitchen. It was almost time for the first band to play over in City Market. I grabbed my purse and made my way through the crowded streets to Café.

"Hey, Anne. There's a good band tonight." The hostess adjusted her flaming-red ponytail.

"I heard. I'm really excited."

"Hard tea?"

I nodded and sat on the bench just outside the restaurant. The air was warm and heavy today, even as the sun began to sink behind the buildings.

"Here, darlin'."

I held out a $10 bill to Jewels.

She waved it away. "You know it's on the house as long as you stay and keep me company."

"Where else would I go?" I shot her a smile as the band began to play behind me. I recognized the first few chords to "Loved" instantly. It was ingrained in my heart. I jumped up, nearly spilling my drink as my eyes searched out the band. The lead singer had long, shaggy hair and a full beard. It wasn't Tucker. I sat back down on the bench with a thud as my heart broke all over again.

"You all right, Anne? You look like you saw a ghost."

"I was hoping to." The lump forming in my throat nearly blocked my airway completely.

"Just breathe, sweetie."

"I'm fine. I'm sorry, Jewels. I'm just not feeling well. I think I should go back home and lie down."

"Yeah, all right. Want me to come by and check on you after I get off?"

I stood and drank down my tea as quickly as I could, hoping the liquor would dull the aching in my chest. "No. I'll be fine. I just need more time."

She drew her brows together but gave me a sympathetic smile and nodded.

"Maybe next weekend." My life was like Groundhog Day. Every weekend I forced myself to come to the Market. Most times I made it two or three songs before the memories became too hard to ignore.

Music used to be an escape for me, and I desperately craved that again.

I made my way back to my apartment, defeated once again. Becoming someone else was nearly impossible when your old memories refused to fade.

I grabbed a beer from the fridge and kicked off my sandals, settling in on my couch. The house was so quiet. Something I used to pray for when I came home from the diner. Now it was all-consuming. The silence was deafeningly loud. My next purchase would be a television, I decided, as I took a long pull from my beer. I picked at the label as the minutes ticked by, turning into hours. Finally, exhaustion took over and I could no longer fight sleep. I curled up on the couch and let one day fade into the next.

I awoke to a pounding on the door. "Not today," I moaned, and pulled a throw pillow over my head.

"No rest for the wicked, Anne."

"Ugh." I threw the pillow at the door and pushed myself up from the couch. I ran my fingers through my hair before yanking open the front door.

"Well, aren't you Miss Sunshine. Here." Jewels held out a cup of coffee for me and stepped inside.

I groaned. "It's only noon and my day off."

"Yes, so you have time to make the meeting this afternoon." I had met Jewels at the NA meetings.

"I don't feel like going today." I took a sip of the coffee, burning my tongue.

"No one *feels* like going, but we have to. It works if you work it," she joked.

I rolled my eyes as I pulled open the freezer and grabbed an ice cube to drop in my coffee. "I'm not even an addict."

"Oh, you're addicted all right, and one of these days you'll tell me his name."

"You don't know what you're talking about." I walked by her to the bedroom so I could change my clothes.

"Darlin', I don't know much, but I know what a broken heart looks like."

I ignored her as I ran a brush over my hair.

"Fine. Let's skip the meeting then. Go do something fun."

"Fun?" I poked my head out the door.

She smiled and took another drink of her coffee. "Sure. Why not? I have the perfect place."

"Fine." How bad could it be? I walked out of my room and grabbed my purse.

"That's the spirit." She laughed and held the front door open for me.

We walked to the front of the building and scanned the street.

"Hey! Over here!" Jewels yelled to the man across the road on his bike taxi.

He pedaled across the street toward us and stopped at the curb. "Where to?"

"McDonough's." She turned back to me, smiling.

I climbed onto the bench seat behind the rider and Jewels squeezed in beside me.

"So what's at McDonough's?"

"Therapy." She smiled as we pulled out onto the street and made our way across town.

I was already regretting leaving the house, but I wasn't sure jumping out of a bike taxi in the middle of a busy road was a wise option.

We pulled up outside the restaurant a few minutes later. Jewels paid for our ride as I stared up at the green canopy that lined the building.

"Looks pricey."

She looped her arm in mine and pulled me through the door. "We aren't here to eat."

"What are we here for?"

"That." She pointed across the room. I followed the direction of her finger to a woman on a small stage preparing to sing karaoke.

"You want me to sing? I can barely listen to a song without breaking down, and you want me to *sing*?"

"You don't have to do it today. Just think about it."

"This is stupid."

"So is keeping everything bottled up inside you until one day you explode and go on some crazy murdering spree."

My jaw fell open.

"What?" She looked at me as if I had gone crazy.

"I need a drink."

"That's the spirit!" She pulled me over to a corner booth and held up her hand to the waiter.

He came and she ordered us a round of beers. She told him to keep them coming until we were onstage singing or passed out.

I grabbed my bottle and drank until my lungs burned for air.

"Come on, Anne. It's not that scary. No one here even knows who you are. If you make a fool out of yourself, you never have to see them again."

She was right about no one knowing who I was. I was still getting used to turning around when I heard the name Anne.

"So what was his name?"

"I can't."

"All right. Pick a song."

I took another drink from my beer and held up the bottle for the waiter. He nodded and quickly replaced my empty bottle with a full one.

"Thanks." I picked at the label, thinking of the time I sat across from Tucker in a booth.

"Fine. I'll go first." She cleared her throat. "Jason and I met two years ago. He was incredibly sexy. He was a tattoo artist, so of course he was covered in them." My eyes flicked to hers and she continued. "He was big into going out and barhopping all night long. I could barely keep up and get to work on time. We started doing coke, just to keep up with the crazy lifestyle."

I took a drink from my beer as the music from the karaoke singer faded into the background. "So what happened?"

"I caught him in the bathroom fucking my best friend. He was so high he actually smiled when he saw me."

"Jesus."

"Yeah." She took a drink of her beer. "But that's not the worst of it. I was so fucked-up I couldn't think straight. I went for the one thing I knew he loved. His truck. I smashed the windows and flattened the tires. The whole bit. I was like a bad country song."

"Did you get in trouble?"

"I spent three weeks in jail and will probably be working to pay off the damage for the truck for the rest of my damn life." She laughed. "But I'm clean and sober, so there is that." She took another drink of her beer. "Well, not quite sober."

Another singer took the stage and began to sing an eighties love balled.

"His name was Tucker."

Jewels sat back in her seat. "What happened?"

"Jax happened." The lump began to form in my throat again.

Jewels quickly sat forward, placing her hand on mine. "Let's save it for another day. I think we did good today, Anne. You've already sat through three *horrible* singers and not run off." She smiled.

"It's Cass. My name is Cass."

"You know, from my experience, when you try to hide from your demons, they find you anyway."

"Well, my demon is dead. He can't hurt me anymore." I set my bottle down on the table and stood up. "Let's go sing a damn song before I change my mind."

We kept it safe and stayed away from any bleeding-heart songs about love and, for Jewels's sake, country songs about getting revenge.

We decided on a drunken rendition of "Let's Talk About Sex." Unfortunately, halfway through I realized that on a good day I had no clue what the lyrics were. It didn't matter. The patrons cheered us on and sang along as we swayed to the beat and belted out the tune to the best of our ability.

For once I didn't run and do what was easier, and I actually enjoyed myself.

We stayed for a few more hours until the rowdy late-night crowd began to flow in from the streets.

"That was fun."

"Wait until next time, when I make you incorporate an interpretive dance into our routine." She laughed.

It felt good to laugh and joke our way through our fears and our secrets. Maybe what I'd needed all along was just someone to share my time with. I could definitely see living on my own getting a little bit easier.

We walked down the crowded street, weaving through the hordes of people back toward my apartment.

"Jewels, have you ever thought you wouldn't be able to get through it all?"

"Every day, but there is always a tomorrow. Karaoke starts at noon."

CHAPTER

Twenty-Six

I HADN'T BEEN BACK to a meeting since I started karaoke therapy with Jewels. She didn't press me for details of what had happened to me but listened when I felt the need to confide something. It was nice to have a friend in my life that I could count on. The only other people I had were Aggie and Larry, and without a car I could hardly ever see them. Not that I wanted to set foot near the trailer park. It was too painful. Larry told me they'd removed my trailer and none had been put back in its spot. That seemed fitting. As if a tornado had swooped in and removed that chapter of my life. I was glad I would never have to look at it again. It has been over two months since I left Tucker behind and started life on my own. I worked as much as possible to keep from getting lonely and having too much time to think. I'd saved up enough to buy myself a small television and actually have cable.

I saw last week on an entertainment gossip show that Tucker's band would be playing live at an awards show and they had signed with a major record label. I was so proud of him. It still hurt, but I'd done the right thing for him. His career was important to him.

The show also spoke of his being linked to an up-and-coming actress. He was quoted as saying, "I am very much in love." He wouldn't divulge any more details on the matter. I was happy for him and told myself that the tears that fell down my cheeks were from joy, not for what I had given up.

I was glad the band was able to stay together after all we'd put them through. I wouldn't be able to live with myself if I'd destroyed all of their dreams. I am still not able to listen to their music, but I know it is only a matter of time before I am able to hear him without thinking of our past. He is Tucker, the rock star, now, not my Tucker, and I need to get used to that.

I slipped on a white sundress with purple flowers that was identical to the one Tucker had bought me that Jax had destroyed. I pulled my heart locket up to my lips and kissed it before slipping on my sandals.

The air was cool as winter began to creep in. I made my way to the City Market to grab a coffee before my shift started at Scarlett's. Horse-drawn carriages lined the streets, preparing for their next tours. I rubbed a horse on the nose as I walked by them on my way to Vinnie Van Go-Go's. I loved to sit at one of their bistro tables and remember my time with Tucker. Yeah, I was doing a great job of moving on, I thought with a sigh.

"I hear this place is amazing." Tucker's voice sent a chill over my body as I turned to see if he was really there. The imaginary world I had built for myself without him crumbled around me instantly.

"Sometimes we don't know what we're missing until we find it." I echoed his words from our last visit here. I stood on shaky legs just feet from him. The pain of seeing him nearly doubled me over. God, how I'd missed him.

"I knew what I was missing the moment I lost you." His voice shook as he took a step closer to me. "I thought you went out to find us a place so we could start our new life together. I waited for hours. When I found your phone, I knew you had left me for good."

"I'm sorry, Tucker."

"Jesus, Cass. Do you know what I went through? I went back to that fucking hellhole looking for you. I went back to that trailer." He swallowed hard, trying not to break down.

"I didn't think you would look for me."

"You didn't think I would *look* for you? I spent all night outside of the diner waiting for you to show up. I had no idea where else you would go. Chris and Terry had to physically remove me. I *never* stopped looking for you."

My hand subconsciously covered my heart, trying to shield it from the pain.

"Why did you do it, Cass? Why did you leave me like that?"

"I was ruining your life. You had a dream and you were going to give it up for me. I couldn't let you do that. I had hurt you enough already." My voice began to shake.

"Hurt me? You nearly killed me when you took off. I was so worried."

"You have nothing to worry about. Jax is long gone."

"If I know you at all, you have been killing yourself with the guilt of everything that had happened."

"How did your find me?" I asked, as I'd known this moment would eventually come.

Tucker smiled. "Larry is very loyal to you. I've been calling him every day for the last six weeks. He convinced me you had moved to Ohio with some aunt. I searched the state, but you were nowhere. As soon as I had some downtime, I flew in and demanded the truth. I guess he liked that I was fighting for you. He finally admitted that you were living in the city under your mother's name."

I had talked to Larry at least once a week since I had left, and he had never mentioned to me that Tucker had contacted him.

"Tucker, I—"

He put his finger to my lips to stop me from talking. "The only thing I ever wanted out of my life was someone to share it with." His blue eyes searched mine.

"I've heard you found that." I shrugged and looked down at my toes. *This is what you wanted for him*, I reminded myself.

He took his fingers and tilted my chin up again gently. "Yes, Cass, I am very much in love."

My heart twisted in my chest. I deserved to hear his words. I deserved whatever he wanted to put me through. I'd left like a coward. I could at least have stayed and explained to him he would be better off, but instead, I ran away.

"I'm happy for you." My voice cracked as I blinked back my tears.

He smiled and ran the pad of his thumb along my jaw. "I love *you*, Cass, or Anne, who whoever the hell you want to be. I have never ever wanted anyone else. I told you—money, fame, fans . . . none of it really means anything. It doesn't make you happy. If you don't have someone to share that stuff with, you will still be lonely. I'm lonely without you, Cass. I need you in my life."

"I love you, too," I admitted on a shaky sob.

His arms flew around me and he lifted me off the ground as he squeezed me so hard I could barely breathe. "It won't always be rainbows and butterflies, but I promise you I will do everything in my power to make you happy, Cass. Just don't ever leave me again. Promise me," he whispered in my ear.

"I promise."

Look for

WHITE TRASH

Damaged

Book Two in the
White Trash Trilogy
Coming in Fall 2013 from Gallery Books